I0744368

Claimed by the Shifters

K. Loraine

USA Today Bestselling Authors

Meg Anne

Edited by Mo Sytsma of Comma Sutra Editorial

Cover Design by CReya-tive Book Design

Photographer: Wander Aguilar

Model: Camden

To JJ. You know what you did.

"You are the bane of my existence and the object of all my desires."

— ANTHONY BRIDGERTON

CLAIMED
BY THE
SHIFTERS

Authors' Note

Claimed by the Shifters contains mature and graphic content that is not suitable for all audiences. Such content includes dubious consent, degradation, impact and blood play, bondage, and more. **Reader discretion is advised.**

A detailed list of content and trigger warnings is available on our website.

ONE

The worst thing I ever did was fall in love with my wife.

What a useless emotion. But how could I have avoided it? She died, and still I yearned. Still craved her scent and ached for her touch. That wasn't me. I didn't need someone to make my twisted heart bloody sing.

Until Roslyn let me have her blood.

She *changed* something within me. Woke a long dormant beast, and now I'd never be free of it—of her. Like a dragon who'd found the most beautiful jewel, I wanted to keep her protected and never let another threaten my treasure. And she was *mine*.

Even if she allowed others to touch her. It wouldn't erase my claim. I got there first. I had her before any of them.

"G-Gavin . . ." Roslyn's eyes were wide, the stain of arousal leaching from her cheeks.

"Is this any way for a duchess to behave, Mrs. Donoghue?" I strode deeper into the bar, forcing myself to stay cool and collected. It was a herculean task with the way that Mercer arsehole was holding on to my wife.

"I'm not a duchess."

Oh, how little you understand, petal. "Oh, but you are. It seems someone had been slowly poisoning my father with colloidal silver. By the time we discovered it, there was nothing for it. He slipped away only a few weeks after *your* tragic demise."

"Wait, this fucker is your husband?" Remington snarled as he held her closer.

"No."

"Yes." I spoke over her, loud and strong.

"Well, which is it? Because it looks a lot like she doesn't want you, buddy." He turned her around to face him, one palm cupping her jaw. "Is this who you were running from, baby girl? Just say the word, and I'll get rid of him for you."

"You could bloody well try."

"You've seen what I can do, Dracula. Don't think I can't take you."

I cocked a brow. "Yes, but you haven't seen what *I* can do."

"What are you talking about? You two know each other?" Roslyn tore herself from his grasp. "You . . . you knew about Gavin?"

"Yes, please. Explain to my wife how we know each other, Remington."

I can't wait to see how you're going to get out of this one, Mercer.

"What's he talking about, Remi?" I loved the accusation in her tone. The uncertainty. That little spark of fear.

The wolf's jaw clenched, his eyes flashing with anger before glancing down at Roslyn.

"Oh my God. Is he your"—she looked at me then back at him—"were you two . . ." She had to lower her voice before she could manage, "*together*?"

"Fuck no! God, nothing like that. I would never lower myself to fucking a vampire."

"First of all, I would be the one doing the fucking, so you meant to say you wouldn't lower yourself to being *fucked* by a vampire. Secondly, you would be so lucky to find yourself under my whip, Mercer. And you know I'd make you beg for it until you were weeping. Don't act coy. I've seen the way your face lights up when you watch me perform at *Iniquity*." I had no interest in the wolf, but I couldn't help goading him after that insult. Let my wife chew on that little morsel.

The way Roslyn's breath hitched had me wondering if her reaction was because of his harsh words or the image mine had conjured. I hoped for the latter.

"Why are you here, Gavin?" she asked, her sweet voice stronger than I'd ever heard it.

"You know exactly why, darling. I'm here to reclaim my wayward wife. The one who left me a shattered man when she . . . died."

She sucked in a breath. "Don't toy with me. You weren't shattered. It was an arrangement, nothing more."

All playfulness left me. "You know that's not true."

"Do I? In some circles, an unconsummated union is grounds for annulment. You and I certainly never joined as a mated pair. You were too busy with Daniel."

Remington's brow quirked at that, but I ignored him, my attention wholly focused on my Roslyn.

The vein beside my eye twitched. "I already explained that to you."

"You did not."

"I told you it was over. That's all you need to know."

She crossed her arms, defiance stamped on her features. "That's nowhere near good enough. But even if it were, it doesn't change the facts. We were married to salvage a political alliance between our families. It wasn't a love match. Stop pretending otherwise."

Anger burned up my chest. "It could have been! You left before you gave it a chance. You made me think you were dead."

"Fuck, Rosie, that's messed up."

"Whose side are you on?"

I glanced at Remington, nodding. "Right?"

He growled, glaring at me. "I'm not talking to you, fuckface."

"I did what I had to. I didn't think you'd miss me anyway." Roslyn raised a defiant chin. Oh, the punishments I was going to dole out flashed through my mind. When I got her home . . .

"You are mine." I said it slowly and simply, stating the fact as though it wasn't up for debate.

"Not anymore," Remington said, his chest puffing out and eyes going an eerie blue.

"Enough of this," I snarled. "I don't need your permission to collect what's mine." I blurred over to where they stood, taking Roslyn by the wrist.

"Gavin, no," she protested, trying to jerk out of my grasp, but her hybrid strength was no match for the pure vampiric blood running through my veins.

Remington grasped me by the shirt, attempting to push me back. I bared my fangs at him. "Unhand me, dog."

"She told you to let her go. I suggest you do it unless you want to lose your arm."

"I'm not leaving without her."

"Well, you're sure as hell not leaving *with* her."

It looked like I was going to have to do this the old-fashioned way. A fight to the death, my favorite. Releasing her, I nodded at my wife. "Don't go far, petal. I just have to deal with this stray before we can be on our way."

"Gavin, don't. I love him."

The wolf's face blanked in shock, and I used that momentary distraction to strike, my attack fueled by my rage at her words. She wasn't allowed to love him. She was supposed to love me. If I was cursed with the damned affliction, she sure as hell should be too.

I had him by the throat, his eyes wide and bulging, face already turning a mottled purple as he struggled for air.

"Love hurts, Petal. You should know that by now."

Bloody hell, she had tears in her eyes. It was as beautiful as I remembered.

The thought was cut off by an explosion of pain between my legs that sent me doubling over. "You fucker," I rasped, hands curling over my throbbing balls. "That was a dirty move."

Remington wheezed for breath. "Excuse me . . . for not . . . playing fair when you're . . . trying to kill me. Shall I . . . slap your face . . . with a glove next time?"

"You'd have to be a man of class to be worthy of a proper duel."

He pulled out his phone, holding my gaze with a smug satisfaction I wanted to pummel out of him. "Hey, Siri . . . add white leather gloves to my shopping list."

"Okay, sexy beast. White leather gloves added to your list."

"Seriously, Remi?"

"Not the time, baby girl. I'm in my element."

"Is your plan to annoy me to death?" I groaned, finally able to stand upright. I was going to kill this cocky wolf.

The arse simply smirked and took up a fighting stance.

"Enough posturing. Roslyn, pack your things. Once I dispatch this runt, we are going home."

Remington growled. "Who you calling a runt, Mr. Darcy?" He lunged at me, surprising me with his speed and knocking us both back into a barstool. The spindly piece of furniture shattered under the force of our combined weight, and we tumbled onto the floor in a tangle of thrashing limbs.

"You can call me the Duke of Tears." I rolled us so I was on top of him, pinning him with one arm across his chest as I used my other hand to tug his head to the side, baring his throat. "Because you'll be crying for me soon enough."

The door swung open, revealing a tall figure in a hooded sweatshirt. I recognized his scent instantly, Asher. The cursed hacker who'd nearly burned me to a cinder with his hands. His eyes widened in recognition.

There was a blur of motion in the periphery, my only warning before I was knocked backward, an immense pressure reverberating in my chest.

"I thought that would work. Why didn't it work?" Remington asked, glancing down at the broken-off piece of wood in his hand.

"You tried to stake me!"

"I know! I did stake you. It was supposed to be foolproof. Stupid cheap furniture," he muttered, tossing the broken stool leg to the ground with the rest of the rubble.

It took a second for my mind to catch up on this sudden change of events. I patted my chest, half expecting to find a hole, finding instead a familiar solid weight resting over my heart. Reaching into my jacket, I pulled out the tungsten cigarette case. Not a scratch on it.

"Mother*fucker*, you *would* have a stake shield."

Roslyn gasped from behind the bar where she'd taken shelter from the fight. "Where did you get that?"

CHAPTER
TWO

ROSIE

Nausea clutched my stomach as Remi staking Gavin replayed in my mind. He'd done it. He'd killed my husband, and I wasn't the least bit relieved. I was horrified.

How could I be horrified when the man I'd faked death to run away from was going after one of the men I loved? I should be grateful, or at the very least, numb. But I wasn't. Not remotely. My heart ached as if I'd just lost something vital.

What a forking disaster this day had turned out to be. Ben was in jail. Remi and Gavin were at each other's throats, literally, and I . . . I hadn't done a bloody thing to stop them. Gavin was dead, and Remi would now be in the Donoghues' crosshairs.

It wasn't until I saw their lips moving that I realized they were both alive and relatively unharmed.

How could Gavin be alive? I saw the stake. I saw the pain in his face and the resignation to his fate in his eyes.

My estranged husband pulled a familiar cigarette case from his breast pocket. I immediately recognized the etching on its surface; I'd had it commissioned myself. The intertwining thorns and roses across the calligraphy D representing the merger of our two houses. It had been a wedding gift for my groom, back when I thought perhaps ours would be a marriage in more than name.

But I'd never given it to him.

I sucked in a breath, the oxygen burning my too-tight throat. "Where did you get that?" Rushing to him, I plucked the case from between his fingers and inspected it.

He was still mostly sprawled across the floor, his elbow supporting his weight as he stared up at me. "It was one of the only things that survived the fire."

"What fire?"

Asher, standing in the doorway, cleared his throat. "I thought you knew. Isn't that how you faked your death?"

My focus trained on him, I clutched the cool metal to my chest. "What bloody fire?" The tremor in my voice couldn't be disguised.

"There was a devastating blaze at the manor. It's very nearly in ruins. I was told your mother was gravely wounded. If not for your father's"—Gavin's gaze cut to Remi, who was now seated beside him, rumpled and still breathing heavily—"*intervention,* she wouldn't have survived."

"I . . . no . . ." All I could do was splutter nonsense. My mother. My home. "And my brothers?"

"Are fine. The only one of import who didn't make it was *you.* It wasn't until they cleared the rubble that your corpse was discovered. Ashes and a necklace were all that identified you."

"How?" It was the only word I could manage.

"The fae were presumed to be responsible."

I shook my head. "The fae? Or the Donoghues? Did your family think they'd finally be able to ruin us?"

"Roslyn, no. They might be devious, but they'd never blatantly attack. Not after I realized you—"

"Asher, you knew about this?"

His guilty expression answered my question before he opened his mouth. "I thought . . . I'm sorry, Rosie. I figured you wouldn't want to talk about it. If I'd known this was how it was, I would have mentioned it to you."

I turned away from him, his betrayal too raw, even if it was unintentional. He's the only one who knew the full truth of my identity. My only connection to the past, and he'd kept something this big from me.

At some point during this exchange, Remi got to his feet, but I was in a spiral of guilt and panic I couldn't escape. My mother was hurt, my family homeless, and I was here, blissfully unaware of the true consequences of my actions.

"Come on, baby girl. You need a minute. I can sense it." Remi's warm palm pressed to the small of my back.

I shrugged away from him. "No. I'm fine."

"You're not. Let me take care of my mate."

"Remi—"

"Please?"

Gavin curled his hand around my wrist, holding me in place as he climbed to his feet. Somehow he managed to make the movement graceful despite the splinters that rained from his clothing. "You mean *my* mate."

I jerked as if I'd been electrocuted. "Your what?"

His eyes darted to mine, and there was an unexpected hint of vulnerability. "You heard me."

I shook my head, a hysterical laugh bubbling up because it was true. I felt it. That pull between us was just as strong as the one I felt for the twins. That didn't mean I had to admit to it, though. "This is too much. I need to get out of here."

"I'll take you home," Remi said at the same time Asher offered, "You should come back to my place."

"The hell she is. Roslyn belongs with me."

"No one asked you, Count Chocula," Asher snapped.

Remi let out an appreciative snicker, but I was still amidst my spiral. What I wanted more than anything was to call Noah and cry on my big brother's shoulder. But I couldn't, and that gutted me.

"Call me that again, and you'll lose that sharp tongue of yours, human." Gavin reached up and straightened his tie. Who wore a three-piece suit to a fight in the Alaskan wild? Gavin Anthony Donoghue, vampire Duke of Canterbury, that's who.

"You sure about that? Remember what happened last time?"

My eyes widened. "Last time? You knew he was here? Asher, what else haven't you told me?"

Gavin smirked. "Plenty, I'm sure."

Asher stepped closer, reaching for me, but I shrank back into Remi's arms. "Rosie, come on. I told Remi."

No. Not him too.

Remi balked. "Wait, hold on. You told me there was a vampire, not that it was her fucking husband."

"Former husband," I corrected.

"Current husband. Forever fucking husband." Gavin's words were a whip's lash in the room.

"We'll see about that," Remi muttered darkly. "'Til death do you part, right? Seems an easy enough solution."

"Not for you. You tried and failed."

"How was I supposed to know you'd have a fucking

breastplate hidden in your pocket? Who ever heard of such a stupid thing?"

"It's a cigarette case."

"That's worse. And fucking pretentious. The rest of us use a baggie or keep it in a drawer."

"Uncivilized dog. As if I'd deign to keep a gift from my bride anywhere but close to my heart."

I knew he didn't intend for that to make me swoon, but my belly swooped a little anyway.

"Fucking gag me," Asher groaned. "Did you read that in the romance novel you fell out of, Heathcliff? Where's your puffy shirt?"

"The name is Gavin, thank you. Or Lord Donoghue to you."

"Whatever you say, Dracula."

"Christ," Gavin muttered. "How have you not killed these arseholes by now, Roslyn? Seriously, the company you keep leaves much to be desired. It's a good thing I'm here to spare you any more of their drivel."

"You won't be for much longer," Remi muttered, holding me tighter.

"Gavin, you need to leave," I said, staring into his startlingly intense brown eyes.

"I beg your pardon?"

"I said you need to leave. The people of this town will kill you once they realize you're here."

He snorted. "They can try."

"Oh, please stay," Asher begged. "I'd love to see you strung up in the public square. You'd feel right at home with a public execution, right? I mean, isn't that what you people do?"

"What do you mean 'you people'? Are you referring to vampires?"

"No, musty old castle people. Counts. Like the purple guy on Sesame Street. One dead asshole, ah-ah-ah."

I did *not* giggle. But it was bloody hard.

Gavin let out a long-suffering sigh and turned away from Asher, pinning me once more with his gaze. "If you want me to go, then come with me, Roslyn."

"No."

"Then I stay. I will not leave here without what is mine."

"You really are a stubborn sonofabitch, aren't you?" Remi grumbled.

"You don't know the half of it."

"It's your funeral," Remi said. "Come on, Rosie. Let's go." He took my hand in his, pulling me toward the back exit. "You coming?" he called over his shoulder.

Surprise flickered on Asher's face. "Is that okay with you?" he asked me.

I debated saying no, but my heart didn't want to. I might be upset by his omissions, but Ben needed us. All of us. "Of course." The relief bleeding through his eyes told me I'd made the right call.

"Where's my invitation?" Gavin drawled.

Remi gripped my hand tighter. "In hell. Waiting for you."

"I'm not going anywhere, Roslyn. You'll come to your senses, and I'll be back for you. This isn't over."

"That's what I'm afraid of," I muttered as my husband turned on his heel and strode confidently out the door.

THREE

REMI

"Where are you taking us?" Rosie asked as we walked away from the bar, veering off the path that would lead us to where I parked.

"To see my brother."

I'd thought the news would bring a flicker of relief to her worried eyes, or maybe even some semblance of a smile. If anything, it only amped up the tension rolling off her. Her posture was as tight as it had been that first time I saw her. Wary. Uncertain. Hesitant.

"Rosie," I said, pulling her up short. "You know he didn't do the things they're accusing him of, right?"

"What? Of course he didn't." She blinked up at me, looking stunned I'd even mention it.

"Then what has you so wound up?"

"Oh, I don't know, pick your poison. Did you miss the fact that my husband just strolled into town? The same one I gave up everything to escape? Not to mention the part where I just found out my entire family, the very people I left to protect, were nearly lost to a bloody house fire. Oh, and that husband tried to take out one of my new boyfriends in his boorish attempt to win me back mere minutes after the other was arrested for murder?"

"Mate," I corrected immediately, maybe a little too harshly. "I'm not your fucking boyfriend." Boyfriends were replaceable. Temporary. Mates were anything but. Right now, after that bullshit back in the bar, the distinction mattered. Especially when a *husband* was now involved. Husband trumped boyfriend, but nothing trumped mate.

"Not the point, Remi. Chill the fuck out. You don't have to bite her head off. She's obviously rattled. Jesus." Asher took her hand and tugged her out of my hold. "Come on, princess. Let's go talk to Ben. Remi's an asshole, but he's right. It'll make you feel better to see him."

How did I even respond to that? Was I an asshole?

I huffed and dragged my hands through my hair, needing something to take my focus off my mate and her resistance to admitting how important our connection was. She said she loved me. I'd heard it plain as day. But there was still a barrier keeping us apart. Was it Gavin? Maybe. I was a jealous prick. Surprisingly, though, seeing Asher walking with her hand-in-hand only made me wish I was there with them.

As if he plucked the thought from my head, he looked over his shoulder at me, holding out his other hand. "Well?" he demanded.

It wasn't exactly a declaration of love, but that outstretched hand felt like the start of something. Something more meaningful than the frantic hate-fucking we usually engaged in.

I glanced to Rosie, who was staring at me expectantly as well. She gave me a little nod, and the tension in my sternum loosened enough I could finally take a full breath.

Taking Asher's hand in mine, I had to fight the wave of emotion this show of unity set crashing through me.

"I just want it on the record. I draw the line at skipping down the road."

"What about singing?" Asher joked. "Is Ben the wizard?"

"No singing. We aren't in a fucking musical."

"You're being such a moody fuck."

"I bet you like it. It's probably a nice change from you being the grumpy asshole in our . . ." *What the fuck were we now?* "Situation-ship."

Asher chuckled. "I see the appeal."

"So do I," Rosie offered. Some of her tension seemed to have slipped away, her voice lighter and a soft smile playing on her lips.

Asher's teasing made sense. He was putting on this little performance for her. That tracked. I couldn't see him willingly making a fool of himself for anyone else, but he'd had a soft spot for her from day one. I was willing to bet there wasn't much he *wouldn't* do for her.

"Will they let us see him?" Rosie asked as we approached the sheriff's office. The light was on, and I could see Dallas's silhouette, cowboy hat and all, through the small window.

"They can try and stop me. I'm going to make sure he's okay." The growl in my voice betrayed how close to the surface my wolf got when my pack was threatened.

"Rein it in, beast boy. I don't think we want both Mercers in the cell." Asher squeezed my hand. "We'll get him out."

I blew out a breath. The hacker made an excellent point. "Are you coming in with us?" I asked, suddenly realizing what Asher's presence—his *undisguised* presence—meant.

There was no way for him to keep a low profile if he waltzed straight into the station.

"Uh . . . shit."

"You should wait out here," Rosie said gently, resting her hand on his chest. "Keep an eye out and do your usual sexy spy stuff."

His lips twitched. "Good call."

Part of me wilted as he released my hand. I didn't like losing that connection to him. Rosie pressed a soft kiss to his cheek before backing away, but Asher wasn't done with her. He snatched her wrist and yanked her to him, a little puff of air escaping her as she collided with his chest. Then he stared down at her, his expression soft and tender, more tender than I had ever seen.

"I'm sorry."

"For what?" she asked.

"Everything. I wouldn't have kept any of this from you if I'd known."

"Already forgiven."

He tucked a lock of hair behind her ear, then gripped her nape in a hot as fuck move I wanted him to use on me later. "Now give me a real kiss."

She lifted up on her toes and laid one on him. They melted together, and heat curled in my stomach as my body woke up. I knew this moment was for them, but fuck if I didn't want to be part of it.

Before I could do something stupid, like thread my fingers through their hair and go in for a Girls Gone Wild style three-way kiss right there in front of the sheriff's office, they pulled away from each other.

I let out a little cough, clearing both my throat and my head. "We should . . . you know . . . before someone sees him." I was a mess. These two jumbled up everything inside me. I couldn't remember feeling this way about anyone before, and to suddenly have feelings for both of them at once . . . I clearly wasn't equipped to handle it.

Imagine how Rosie must feel. She's got four of you. Maybe I could ask her for pointers later. Offer to paint her nails or braid her hair and then ask for some boy advice. I couldn't help but chuckle at the mental image.

Rosie blushed, then feathered one last kiss on Asher's lips before she joined me at the door.

"I want mine when we get home, baby girl."

Surprising me, she rose on tiptoe and kissed me right then, her lips tasting of Asher. The combination was heady and intoxicating. It was officially my favorite flavor.

Rosie might be my mate, but Asher was mine too. Not in the same way, but in one that felt every bit as vital.

Christ, when did things get so complicated?

The day you were born, Remi. Your life has always been complicated.

"Ready?" I asked, reaching for the door handle.

"Yes. I need to see him. You're right."

Pulling open the door, the first thing we were greeted with was a smirking sheriff.

"Here to turn yourselves in for aiding and abetting?"

"Thought I might try my hand at a jailbreak."

His smirk fell away. "I'd highly suggest you don't." He moved his hand to cradle the revolver at his hip.

"Unless that's silver or a fucking tranq dart, it won't stop me."

"You wanna test me, boy?"

Rosie put herself in front of me, her much smaller frame not doing anything to protect me, but I loved that she did it anyway. "What evidence do you have to keep Ben here? So far all I have heard is circumstantial."

"We've got probable cause, little lady. His alibi doesn't check out."

"He was with me."

"You can't account for his whereabouts while you were sleepin'."

"You're reaching, Sheriff."

Fuck, she was hot when she got lawyery on me. "Yeah. You're reaching."

Great job, Remi. You're really adding to the conversation.

"Let us see him," I demanded, sounding far more certain this time.

There you go. Show him who's boss, buddy.

Ben's voice echoed down the hall. "I d-don't want v-visitors."

"Too fucking bad."

"You heard the prisoner. He doesn't want to see you. 'Sides, visiting hours are over anyway."

I rolled my eyes. "Since when do we have visiting hours, Dallas? Come the fuck on, my brother is right there." I gestured to the single cell behind him where I could make out my twin's grouchy profile.

"T-tell my brother t-to fuck off."

Dallas smirked. "Ben says to fuck off."

I stared at the sheriff. Seriously? Did the lion think I needed that repeated, like I wasn't standing all of twenty feet away? Fine. Two could play this game.

"Yeah, well, tell *my* brother, too-the-fuck-bad. His mate wants to make sure he's okay."

"He's just fi—"

"I'm f-fine, sugar. G-go home w-with Remi. He'll t-t-take care of y-you."

"Ben, you don't belong in here," Rosie's voice was pleading, and the sound of her pain made my chest ache.

Didn't he know what he was doing to her by refusing to see her?

"You don't need to punish yourself like this. You didn't hurt anyone. You were with me last night. Please—"

Dallas stepped in front of her as she tried to head down the hall to Ben's cell. "That's enough. You heard the boy. Go on home."

I pulled her away from him, not trusting this over-stuffed peacock with a badge to keep his hands off her. "Come on, baby girl. We'll come back. Ben's not guilty. Dallas just wants to close the case so bad he doesn't care if he's wrong."

The sheriff sneered at me. "I'm the law in this town. Leave the investigating to me."

"Maybe if you'd do your job—"

"Remi!" Ben's voice cut through our posturing. "S-stop it. Y-you need t-to look out for her. Y-you can't do that i-if you're sh-sharing a cell w-with me."

"Why not? We share everything else," I quipped, but I'd already stepped back and taken Rosie's hand in mine. He was right. She was our priority, especially with that fucking vampire on the loose. Man, was Ben going to lose his shit when he learned about Gavin's ties to Rosie. Best to get through this first before giving him anything else to stew over. Although . . . maybe telling him when he was locked up and unable to do anything about it was the smarter play.

I opened the door and paused just before I left, offering him one parting shot. "Oh, and just so you know, brother, her husband is here, and he wants her back."

"H-her what?" he roared.

"And he's a vampire!"

"Did you really have to tell him like that?" Rosie asked as I ducked out the door, towing her behind me.

"Remington, get b-back here!"

"Too late. Visiting hours are over!"

Asher was waiting for us, his eyes wide as he caught the tail end of our shouted conversation. "What the fuck did you do now, Mercer?"

"What any man in my position would do. Threw the grenade and ran like hell. But at least now the dumbass is motivated to get out."

"Bad boy, Remi." Asher's low murmur in my ear had me shivering, and Rosie sucked in a sharp but interested breath.

"You can spank me later."

"I just might."

"Boys, we still have a vampire to deal with and a murder investigation to conduct. Save the spankings for when we can all play."

"Does my mate want to watch?" I asked, nuzzling her.

"I do like to watch." Something about the flush stealing up her cheeks told me she liked to do a whole lot more than watch. "But only when I can properly enjoy the experience. We have more important matters to sort out first."

"Then we should get home. Get you out of the middle of town where the Count of Monte Cristo can't find you." Asher began walking back to the bar. "Or where he at least doesn't have the upper hand."

I glanced at him. "Mine or yours?"

"Yours, it's closer."

"All right, sleepover at the Mercer Mansion it is."

"Oh, goody. Can we do makeovers?" Rosie asked, a laugh in her question.

"Remember what happened last time you gave yourself

a makeover?" Asher asked, laughing at some shared memory.

She punched him in the arm. "We promised never to mention that."

"What about the sexy dungeon?"

Sexy dungeon? We'd have to revisit that later. But for now, I had a mate to take care of. "We can do anything you want, baby girl."

FOUR

BEN

"Remington, get b-back here!" I brought my body as close to the cell bars as possible without touching the silver, vibrating with possessive fury.

Her husband?

Her fucking husband?

My twin had to be messing with me. Punishing me for not being willing to see him. Didn't he?

"Too late. Visiting hours are over!"

I slammed my hand on the bars, wincing at the burn. Asshole.

"Didn't take you for a cheater, Bentley. I'm surprised. Then again, you are a murderer, so what's a little adultery in the grand scheme of things?" Dallas leaned against the wall, his hands resting on the holster around his hips.

I glared at him, knowing better than to try to defend myself. Wasn't like he'd believe a word I said anyway.

"Aw, come on. Cat got your tongue?"

I sneered, the stupid saying getting under my fur and rubbing me every kind of wrong way. Kids had been saying variations of the same for as long as I could remember.

"Then again, I guess sharing a woman's nothing new for you, is it? What are a few vows, so long as the pussy's good, am I right?"

"D-don't talk about h-her like th-that." Rosie wasn't a random hookup. She was my mate. And there was no way she was married—and to a vampire, of all things. Remi was just fucking with me.

"You know, if you'd give me more than one-word answers about what happened, I could help you out of this mess you're in."

The hell he could. He'd try to twist my words into a confession. The truth was, I didn't know where I'd been, not since the fight with Alexi. The two of us had shifted, let our beasts free, and everything had been a blur. All I knew was that I'd gotten away alive. I woke up naked and shivering, miles away from the churchyard where we'd met. No sign of the bear aside from deep scratches on my skin and his blood in my mouth. But that was hours before the coroner said Alexi died.

"H-here's two w-words for you. N-not g-guilty."

Dallas rolled his eyes. "You're gonna have to do a lot better than that, son. Especially with the evidence stacking up against you."

Evidence?

Shit. What the hell happened last night? I didn't actually kill the fucker . . . did I? I might have. Seeing him come after my mate, I'd been fucking enraged. There's no telling how far my wolf and I had gone to protect her. And I couldn't find it in myself to feel guilty about it either.

"W-w-w–" Goddammit. I closed my eyes and took a long breath, forming the word in my head first. "What evidence?"

"Your blood on his body, for starters. Under his fingernails."

"W-we had a fight. Everyone s-saw it happen."

"And then you killed him."

"N-no."

"And then went to that girl's bed to fuck away the guilt."

"N-no. H-he was alive when I l-left." At least I hoped he was.

"So you got in bed with her, rolled around for a while, then went after him when she fell asleep."

"Th-that's not w-what h-h-happened."

Fuck's sake. Get it together, Ben.

I slept all night. I remembered waking at four in the morning, my wolf on edge, desperate to knot her again and this time give her my mating mark as I fucked her full.

"I w-was w-with her. All n-night. Until f-four in the f-fucking morning."

Dallas cocked a brow. "Now we're getting somewhere. What did you do when you woke up? Did you let your wolf take over?"

"I w-went for m-my m-morning run." It was the only way I could think of to blow off steam that didn't involve railing Rosie into the ground.

His grin turned patronizing. "So you *did* give your wolf control."

"I r-run every morning. You kn-know that."

"Doesn't matter what I know. Matters what I can prove. And you, out for a run before dawn, puts you at the scene of the crime right in the window of the possible time of death."

"H-how do you kn-know where I ran?"

His grin was huge, and I'd never wanted to punch anyone in the face more. "Paw prints."

There were dozens of shifters in this town. They could belong to anyone. "N-not mine."

"We'll see. We've got a cast made. We'll get you to shift and compare."

My wolf growled low in my throat, unhappy at the idea of anyone trying to make him do anything.

"Careful there, boy-o. I might could take that as a threat. And you're not stupid enough to threaten an officer of the law, now are you?"

"You d-don't have any r-real evidence that c-can't be explained."

"Don't I?"

"If y-you d-did, you wouldn't be t-talking to me."

His eyes narrowed. "Only a matter of time, son. Only a matter of time."

"L-let me out, D-Dallas."

"You know, I don't think I will. Get comfy, Mercer. And be prepared to shift for me like a good dog. If you won't, I'll get Scarlett to mix up one of her potions that'll do the trick, but it's not pleasant."

He shoved off the wall and began whistling as he walked away. Then he chuckled and called, "I don't know why it's more surprising that you'd let yourself be tangled up with a married woman than it is for you to be a murderer, but damn, boy. I really didn't expect that one."

The fucker was pushing my buttons. Trying to get me to do something that would further incriminate me. I wouldn't bite. My brother knew me well enough that if there was a threat to our mate, I'd be motivated to get myself out of this. That had to be the reason he said something. A vampire? Rosie wouldn't marry a dirty vampire.

And if she had, she wouldn't be with me now. He'd have locked her up and thrown away the key. That's what vampires did.

Besides, she'd already bared her soul and told me her darkest secrets. Why mention her deal with the demon, but not a husband? It didn't make sense.

I sat on the uncomfortable bed chained to the wall, the mattress barely an inch thick and smelling of sweat and alcohol from all the drunks who spent the night here. My thoughts were racing as the word husband flashed over and over.

Rosie didn't have a husband.

She fucking didn't.

Did she?

"D-dammit, Remi."

FIVE

There was just something . . . soothing about being in Remi's house. It smelled like him and now, like Rosie. Remi's distinct scent of cedar, sunshine, and fresh, clean air mixed with Rosie's delicious sugar cookie and citrus created a heady combination that made me think of a picnic outside on a warm summer day. Fucking idyllic.

"What are you doing?" Remi asked, smirking at me.

"What do you mean? I'm standing in your house. I literally just walked inside."

Rosie giggled. "Your eyes are closed, and you keep taking these big deep breaths."

Embarrassment blazed a path up my neck, and I pushed past both of them. "Shut up."

"Your comeback game is weak, Asher."

"Oh yeah? If you want my cum back, maybe you should scrape it off your tongue."

Rosie turned a bright shade of pink, and Remi's mouth fell open before they both burst into laughter.

"Don't threaten me with a good time."

"Is it hot in here? Did someone leave the fireplace going?" Rosie asked, fanning her face.

There was something really fucking weird about openly flirting with two people who were also flirting with each other. Sometimes, it almost felt like they were ganging up on me, and yet our relationships were still very much separate from one another. Rosie and I were just getting started, and Remi and I . . . were figuring it out, I guessed.

I scratched the back of my neck, feeling off balance. Who was I kidding? Everything about this was new, and strange, and . . .

The word you're looking for is exciting. You haven't been a stiff breeze away from an erection like this since you were a teenager.

"Someone mentioned a sleepover," Remi said, his eyebrows waggling.

"You. You mentioned the sleepover." I chuckled under my breath and finally let my shoulders relax as I shrugged out of my hoodie and slipped my shoes off. "I'll make the popcorn. Remi, pour some drinks." Then I leveled my stare at Rosie. "Go get in your pajamas, princess." I slapped her ass lightly, making her jump as she scurried away.

The wicked gleam in her eyes as she glanced at me over her shoulder told me she enjoyed the command. Good to know.

Remi and I both walked into the kitchen. "Popcorn's in the cabinet by the microwave," he said, gesturing with his chin while pulling open the fridge and grabbing what he wanted. He laughed softly as I did the same. "Can't say I ever imagined us doing something so domestic together."

"Making popcorn is domestic?"

"You. In the kitchen with me. Doing non-sexy stuff. That's domestic."

I raised a brow, pausing as I poured kernels into the popper. "Did you want to do sexy stuff?"

The way his breath hitched told me he liked the idea. "Not yet. I just . . . this is different. Not a bad different. But it's really not something you ever acted like you wanted. I never pictured us as old men puttering around the kitchen together."

I huffed out a laugh, because the mental image was fucking hilarious. "I'm more of the sit at my desk and eat whatever's open kind of guy." I couldn't remember the last time I used something other than the microwave.

Silence stretched, but it wasn't uncomfortable. Just different.

"Is this awkward for you?" Remi eventually asked.

"Being in your house?"

"That, and . . . I don't know. Dating someone?"

"Is that what we're doing?" I asked, turning around and leaning against the counter as I looked at him. He was hot as fuck, but that wasn't news. Remington Mercer had smolder down pat.

"Well, we're both with the same girl. And it's not like we don't have a good time together . . ." His cheeks darkened, and he looked away.

"Aw, Remi. Are you blushing? Do you like me? Is that what you're trying to say?"

"Of course I fucking like you. You think I'd let you in my ass if I didn't?"

Shock sucker punched me in the throat. How the hell had I missed that? Not sure what to say, I went with my usual off-handed joke. "Here I was just thinking you were horny."

"If that's all it was, I wouldn't have gotten so pissed every time you turned into a fucking ghost."

Guilt flared uncomfortably in my stomach. After Sam, I didn't let myself consider anything past physical release. She broke me and betrayed me. Not only that, but relationships weren't on my radar because they *couldn't* be. That meant I put up an impenetrable wall, but in addition to Rosie breaking it down, Remi had been chipping away at it each time we were together. I was the asshole who left him on the outside so I could protect myself and stay hidden. From everything.

"That was never about *you*. You know I—"

"Yeah, yeah. I get it. You're a recluse. A hermit. Double-O-fucking-seven. It's just . . . it sucks when you're into someone more than they're into you."

He still wasn't meeting my gaze, but there was no missing the hurt in his voice. I don't think I'd ever felt like a bigger ass than I did in that moment.

"I'm sorry I made you feel like that."

Shrugging away from me, he pulled the cork out of a bottle of wine and poured three large glasses. "Forget I said anything."

Here's your chance, Asher. If you want to see what this really is, you need to step up before he closes the door on it for good.

I moved in close, putting my hand on his shoulder and turning him back to face me. "What if I don't want to?"

His brow crinkled in obvious confusion. "What do you want, then?"

"Her . . ." I had to swallow past the lump in my throat before I could continue. "And you."

One step closer brought us chest to chest, my lips inches from his. We didn't do this tender shit. But both of us needed it. My gaze dropped to his mouth. That wicked smirk was nowhere to be found as his breath fanned out.

Spearing my fingers through his hair, I tugged his head down, claiming him with a possessive kiss.

He had me moaning as soon as the brush of his stubble hit my skin, and when he parted his lips and let me slide my tongue inside, I knew we'd crossed from fuck buddies to something a lot more meaningful. And while it scared me to death, not being with him scared me more.

Since this wasn't about sex, for once, I pulled away far sooner than I was ready to.

"So," Remi said, eyes fluttering open, throat bobbing. "Dating, then."

I laughed and shoved at his chest. "Yeah. I guess we are."

"Do I get to call you my boyfriend? Are we a throuple now?"

I shook my head. "I don't fucking know. Can we take five minutes and just see where it goes before we have to label it and start picking out china patterns?"

Remi grinned, happy looking good on him. "Sure. Whatever you need . . . hubby."

"I fucking hate you."

"No, you don't."

"No," I agreed easily, something loose and warm in my chest. "I don't."

The soft sound of feet on the hardwood floor drew my gaze from the man I'd just opened part of myself up to. On instinct, I backed away a fraction.

Rosie stood near the kitchen table, a smile on her face, eyes expectant. "Am I interrupting? Don't stop on account of me."

"We . . ." I didn't know what to say.

Remi did, though. He wrapped an arm around my

shoulders and dropped a loud kiss on my cheek. "We're boyfriends."

Rosie clapped her hands together. "Finally!"

"Finally? Have you been waiting for this or something?" I asked, amused and relieved that she was so obviously here for this new development. I didn't have a reason to think otherwise, but it was nice to know for sure.

She nodded eagerly. "I was shipping the two of you so hard. I was worried you were going to think choosing me meant you couldn't choose each other. And then we wouldn't get to do all the things I'd been fantasizing about. Not every woman is lucky enough to have mates who are also boyfriends, you know. We need to take advantage of it. For science. Or womankind . . . or something."

She called me her mate. I wondered if it was just a slip of the tongue or if there was more meaning to it. Even though I was a human. Even though she couldn't possibly be claimed by me in the same way.

"Can we go back to these *things* you mentioned?" Remi asked, closing in on her from one side while I did the same on the other.

"What kinds of things are you fantasizing about, princess?"

She blushed, her eyes bright with arousal as she sucked in a breath. "Sexy things . . ."

"Sexy *dungeon* things?" I asked, my voice barely above a whisper.

"Uh-huh."

"I'm gonna need you two to explain the sexy dungeon to me."

I couldn't stop the rush of need even if I wanted to. Remi and Rosie at my disposal. Yes, please. I didn't actually have a sexy dungeon, or any dungeon, just a basement. I should probably do something about that.

"Later. I promise." I feathered a kiss over Rosie's cheek. "Are we doing this sleepover shit or what? Popcorn's ready. Remi poured the wine."

"It's not too late for me to grab Twister," Remi offered.

Rosie laughed, and the sound of her joy after such a shitastic evening made me happy in a way I didn't know was possible. "Maybe we start with a movie," she said. "I could go for a cuddle on the sofa."

"I make a damn good blanket, and your cinematic education *is* sadly lacking," Remi said, tipping her chin up and stealing a kiss. "Let's go. Indiana Jones awaits."

"Oh, a Daddy with a whip, my favorite," I joked, my smile slipping when Rosie let out a soft moan.

"Mine too."

"That explains so much," Remi breathed.

Hell yes, it did. And it was fucking hot. "Well, that certainly wasn't in your file."

SIX

ROSIE

"There we are, all done and fabulous." I put the bottle of black glittery nail polish on the coffee table and blew on Remi's fingernails. Asher had fallen asleep before the first movie ended, leaving Remi and me to our own devices. He'd been the one to offer me a manicure, and I couldn't resist returning the favor.

He inspected the job I did and then lifted my hand, his lips curling in their signature smirk. "I did better. Not a single smudge."

"I didn't realize it was a competition."

"Baby, it's always a competition."

"And what was the prize I didn't know I was aiming for?" God in heaven, the way his lips twitched as his gaze went molten did things to my insides. The smudged black liner and hint of smoky gray shadow on his eyelids only emphasized the pure blue of his irises. And his hair was sexily rumpled, as if someone had been raking their fingers through it as they rolled around in bed together. Blimey, I wished that someone had been me.

Remington Mercer was bloody beautiful. Model worthy.

I could so easily picture him on the cover of a sexy men's magazine . . . or romance novel.

He sat back on the floor, white shirt unbuttoned to the waistband of his tight black jeans with holes in the knees. The way the denim enhanced his toned thighs . . . shivers ran through me. What was it Moira called Sunday? A thirsty trap? No. That wasn't right. A thirsty . . . b-i-t-c-h.

"Did you need a napkin?" His voice broke through my lust-addled thoughts.

"What?"

He grinned. "You're drooling."

Embarrassment flooded my face as I reached up and swiped across my lips. "No, I am not."

The pad of his thumb swept over my bottom lip. "Yes, you were, baby girl. But it's all right. Look as long as you want. As long as you don't just look with your eyes."

"How else am I meant to look, if not with my eyes?"

His fingers trailed down my throat, over my shoulder, and then along the length of my arm until he reached my wrist.

"Your hands . . ."

He turned my palm up and skated each line of my fingers, just a featherlight touch that somehow sent tingles radiating through my whole body.

"Your lips . . ."

God help me, my gaze found his perfect mouth, and my breath hitched as he rolled his lower lip between his teeth.

"Your tongue . . . mmm, yes. Definitely your tongue."

Shifting my position so I was kneeling, I shuffled closer, leaning in until my nose was filled with the warm scent of him.

"Like this?" I asked, licking a path up the side of his

neck, following the cord of muscle to the sensitive hollow behind his ear.

"Oooh, God, fuck yes." The way he groaned the words had arousal flooding between my legs. He took a deep inhale and whispered, "Do it again."

I straddled him, sliding my fingers through his hair, our breaths mingling as we locked gazes. Then I dipped my face so I could trace another path along the opposite side of his neck. I didn't stop with only using my tongue. I bit him softly, drawing another long moan from him.

"Jesus, baby girl. You're killing me. I can smell the desire rolling off you."

Rocking my hips, I pressed my most private parts against the hard ridge of his. "I can feel yours."

His palms went to my thighs, holding me in place. "Don't tease me. I've wanted you for too long."

"I'm not." I rubbed along him again, the friction building a delicious buzzing pleasure between my thighs.

"Prove it," he demanded, grasping my face with both hands and pulling me down until our lips crashed together. He kissed me like he did everything else. Completely. Perfectly. With an attention to detail that left me breathless.

Remington kissed me like he was laying siege. To me. To my heart. He wanted me to know I belonged to him. As if there was ever any doubt.

He tugged on my hair, pulling back just enough that he could meet my gaze, our chests rising and falling in time as we fought to collect our breaths.

The raw vulnerability in his eyes startled me before he whispered, "You said something earlier . . . did you mean it?"

It took my mind a second to catch onto his meaning,

but there was only one thing he could be referring to. I'd said I loved him. At the time, I hadn't really thought about it; I just sort of blurted it. But now that it was out there, I could hardly deny the truth of it.

I cupped his cheek. "Of course I did."

"But . . . we've barely gotten to spend any time together." He looked so stunned. "And I'm . . . a lot."

I giggled. "Remi . . . darling. You are so easy to love."

He sucked in a breath. "I am?" It sounded like he was afraid to believe me, but desperately wanted to.

"Trust me, loving you is not a chore. It feels like the most natural thing in the world to me. Far easier than anything else I've done recently."

My heart quivered at the slight tremble of his bottom lip, the sheen in his eyes, the way his breath hitched.

He pressed our foreheads together, holding me tight. "You're the first person who ever said that to me."

"That it's easy?"

He shook his head. "That you love me. I was starting to think it was impossible. That there was something wrong with me that kept people from feeling that . . . for me."

"Oh, Remi." I kissed him gently, holding him as if he was something fragile I cherished and wanted to keep safe. Because he was. And I did. "Don't you know what that means?"

He shook his head, holding my gaze.

"It just means that you've been waiting for this."

"To find my mate. For us all to be together."

"Exactly. You were never unloveable. We just had to find our way to each other." Pressing my palm to his chest, right over his heart, I kissed him.

Holding me to him, Remi deepened our kiss, the embrace turning from tender to hungry and passionate. I was ready. I wanted him. A flicker of unease shot through me. Was I putting him in danger by giving in to what I wanted—no, what I needed? Because fork me, I needed him. There was still the possibility that Pan played a part in Ben's captivity. But . . . I hadn't felt the demon all day. Not even the faintest twitch.

"Pan?" I tentatively called in my thoughts.

Nothing.

I could only assume that when I'd broken our deal, I'd rid myself of him and his hold on me. I'd told the demon he'd never willingly have my body again. There was nothing keeping me from giving myself to Remi.

"Rosie?"

"Hmm?"

"You okay? You just sort of went stiff on me all of a sudden."

I kissed him, trying to erase that look of uncertainty clouding his beautiful eyes. "I'm here. Sorry."

"We don't have to take this any farther if . . . if you're not ready. I know I joke about being left out, but I'd never want you to think you have to do anything you don't want to do just because of my ego."

Was there anything he could have said in that moment that would've been sweeter? He might not think it, but he was a good man. A worthy man.

"I want you, Remi."

His breath caught. "Are you sure?"

"More than anything."

He grinned. "Shall we take this to the bedroom . . ." He glanced over my shoulder to where Asher lay sleeping on the couch, his soft snores somehow endearing him even more to me. He looked so sweet. Far less troubled and grumpy than he usually did. One might even say boyish.

"I don't mind being quiet."

"But what if he wakes up?" he asked, but he was already working his hands up my pajama shorts.

"Asher likes to watch," I whispered.

"Fuuuuck, baby girl. You're naughtier than I gave you credit for."

"I'm full of surprises."

"I intend to discover all of them."

"Oh?"

"Mmhmm. Starting with the treasure between your legs."

"Are you a pirate now?"

"Arr, matey. Prepare thy booty. I intend to plunder you thoroughly." The words were a playful, sexy growl that somehow had me swooning instead of laughing. Only Remi could make pirate talk into an act of foreplay.

"Will I have to walk the plank?"

"Ride it. Definitely."

I backed up just enough to pull my thin tank over my head, baring my naked breasts to him. The flare of hunger in his eyes had me wriggling atop him, rolling my core against his erection again.

He reached out and flicked the ring piercing my nipple, making me gasp as the bud tightened. "What's this?"

"I guess I have a little pirate in me too."

"Not yet," he said with a grin. "But you're about to."

"Remi," I groaned, but he pulled me to him, catching the piercing between his teeth and tugging. It sent a wave of desire careening through me, and I couldn't help but squirm on his lap. "I need you inside me."

"Shhh. We're supposed to be quiet, remember? You're moaning and calling my name already." His scolding wasn't even close to serious as he shifted us until I was on the floor, spread out across the blanket we'd laid down. "I'm going to eat you until your thighs are clamped around my ears and my lips are glistening with your slick. If you need to scream, you can suck on my fingers instead."

Anticipation built inside me as I lifted my hips so he could remove the last stitches of clothing I wore. The look on his face was a mixture of control and reckless need, both warring for the win.

"Open up, baby. Let me see that treasure you're hiding."

I did as he told me, little tremors already working their way through me. Fitting his shoulders between my thighs, he parted me with two fingers, then chuckled softly under his breath. His gaze traveled up my naked body until he locked eyes with me. If I'd been wearing knickers, the smirk that curled his lips would have destroyed them.

"Ah, x marks the spot."

SEVEN

Jesus fucking Christ, she was dripping. Fucking soaked and glistening for me. I loved the way her soft thighs already gripped my ears, the little hitches of her breaths as I brought my face closer to the sweetness of her cunt.

I couldn't resist toying with her. Drawing the moment out and savoring every second of it. I blew two intersecting lines across her clit, chuckling when she bucked up and moaned my name.

"Remi . . ."

"That's right, baby girl."

"Don't play with me."

I laughed as I pressed a kiss to the top of her pussy. "That's what I do."

But I gave her what she needed. Honestly, it was what I needed too. I ran my tongue along her slit, making her whine as she slipped her fingers into my hair and I sank mine inside her.

Already going for the head control. Good. Take what you want, Rosie. It's yours.

She lifted her hips to meet my mouth, grinding herself on me, chasing the release I could tell was building just by the tension in her slick walls. Those undeniable flutters grew in intensity as I curled my fingers and pressed on that special hidden spot inside her.

A flood of arousal coated me as she rode my face and took what she wanted. Then I sucked hard on her swollen clit, and she shattered. The sound of her coming on my tongue was the most gratifying noise I'd ever heard. I'd done that to her. Satisfied my mate. Provided what she needed.

My wolf let out a happy rumble, and the vibrations set off a little aftershock of pleasure as she clamped down hard on the fingers still buried inside her.

"Remi, God," she panted. "Give a girl a second."

I was throbbing in my jeans. Fuck, why was I still dressed?

A rough hand gripped me by the hair, tugging my head back and nearly making me spill in my jeans as Asher's intense stare found mine.

"Give me a taste."

I moved to pull my fingers from her. But he claimed her slick from my lips, his tongue delving inside my mouth and taking everything he wanted. Rosie fluttered around me and held me in place with her hand, shackling my wrist as Asher stole the taste of her from me.

"Fucking delicious," he breathed, pulling away from me.

He stared down at me, all dominance and sex. God, the chokehold he had on me was impossible to deny. Rosie was my mate, but Asher was mine too. I knew it now more than ever.

"What are you waiting for?" I taunted.

He arched a brow. "Not a damn thing."

I removed my fingers from Rosie, lifting them to my lips so I could get more of her inside me, but he caught me by the wrist and shook his head.

"Mine," he murmured. Then he sucked me clean, stealing her once more.

In a blur, I removed my clothes, wishing to God I'd chosen looser jeans as I struggled to gracefully take the tight denim off. They looked fucking hot, but this was a situation for easy access, and they didn't provide it.

It didn't help that Asher and Rosie both stared at me, their eyes hooded and filled with desire. For me.

Fuck, my hands were shaking. I'd never been so turned on in my whole damn life. I'd been in group situations before, but never with anyone I cared about. Never when my heart was involved. It took things to a whole new level.

Asher pulled his shirt over his head and undid the button at the top of his jeans with far more grace than I managed. Everything about the way he moved was a seduction, but also a command. I swear to God, if he told me to get on my knees and suck him until I gagged, I would. Hell, I wanted to.

"What do you want, princess?" Asher asked, his focus on the beauty at his feet.

"I . . . I want you both to feel good." Her cheeks were a pretty pink, eyes bright, lips swollen from biting them as I made her come.

"Fuck," Asher groaned. "This is like my perfect fantasy come to life, you know that? The two of you at my disposal."

"Then make it come true," she breathed.

"Christ." He removed the rest of his clothes, the three of

us suspended in pure anticipation until he growled. "I want you to fuck her. Slowly."

"What are you going to do?" I asked, my voice a rasp I barely recognized as Asher fisted his impressive length and gave himself a long stroke.

His lips curled up in a way that had both Rosie and me panting.

"Fuck you."

"Oh God." Rosie's moan had my already aching cock jerking.

"You like that idea, baby girl? You want him to take me while I take you for the first time?"

"Yes."

The flood of arousal dripping between her legs only confirmed it. She was as turned on by the idea as I was.

"She fucking loves it." I spread her open so Asher could look. "See what we do to her?"

"Give her what she wants, Remi. Fill her up."

All my usual quips vanished, and I was helpless to do anything but obey. I returned to my position between her thighs, taking myself in my hand and running the tip of my weeping cock through her slickness.

"Protection?" Fuck, I hadn't thought about knocking her until right now.

She shook her head. "I can't get pregnant."

She didn't have to tell me twice. I couldn't give her anything. We didn't carry STIs in the supernatural world.

Notching myself at her entrance, I watched as I slowly sank inside her perfect pussy. Fuck, she was warm and welcoming. "Jesus, baby, you grip me so tight."

Asher lazily stroked himself as Rosie and I adjusted to me being inside her. His little rumbles of pleasure echoed as tingles down my spine. I was so fucking attuned to him that each sweep of his hand along his thick shaft felt like it was happening to my own. I could barely stand to move. Between the way she gripped me and my reaction to what he was doing to himself, I was already seconds away from coming.

"You said you were going to fuck me," I said through clenched teeth, trying not to beg. "How can you do that from over there?"

Asher cocked one brow, then bent down to his discarded jeans and retrieved a condom and a packet of lube from his pocket.

"You carry lube?"

Shrugging, he opened it with his teeth and poured it into his hand. "I'm always prepared."

I huffed out a laugh, the slight compression of my abs making me rock deeper inside Rosie. She moaned beneath me, raking her nails down my back.

Asher put one hand between my shoulder blades and shoved me until I was on all fours, body hovering over Rosie, lips inches from hers.

"Spread him open for me, princess. Help me make him ours."

Her lips parted, but she was quick to nod, her gentle hands smoothing the rest of the way down my back so she could grip my ass. Fingers digging in, she spread my cheeks apart as wide as she could manage.

From the corner of my eye, I could see Asher run the palm of his hand along her arm. "Perfect. Just like that. God, I can't tell you the number of times I dreamed about having you both exactly like this." His voice was a rough whisper along my nape, and the need in his words had goosebumps breaking out across my skin.

I was shaking with the need to move. To come. I was so

primed it wasn't going to take much. Then his lubed fingers were at my sensitive pucker, pressing slowly inside, preparing me for his cock, but I wasn't sure I'd make it that far.

Rosie shuddered and writhed, and all I could do was beg her with my eyes not to move. If I spoke, I'd moan. If I moaned, I'd give in and thrust. If I thrust . . .

Asher pressed in deeper, and the pressure had me gliding forward the barest inch.

"Please," Rosie begged.

"I can't."

"Don't you dare come," Asher growled. "Not until I tell you to."

Fuck, I was dying.

He pulled his fingers from me, and I instantly missed the feel of him. Out of the corner of my eye, I saw him reach for the foil packet next to us.

"No," I moaned, my voice a ragged thing. "I don't want anything between us. Never again."

His low growl of approval would have had me wondering if he was a wolf if I didn't know better. But I didn't have any more time to think about that. Not when his freshly lubricated dick was pressed against me, and he held my hips still as he whispered, "Let's show her how much you love taking my cock, Remi. When I move, you move."

Rosie squirmed beneath me, her chest flushed with pent-up need. I leaned down and stole her lips in a kiss. "Brace yourself, baby girl. He's not gentle. I might not be either."

"Good. I like when it hurts."

"Je-sus," Asher groaned.

"Fuuuuck," I said at the same time.

Then he was sinking slowly into me, the stretch and burn almost too much. I rocked forward involuntarily, and Rosie whimpered in pleasure.

"The look on your face is . . . Oh, Remi. Don't stop."

"You heard our girl," I panted, my body on fire. I was hot and cold all at once, every nerve ending in my body feeling awake and firing with pleasure. "Don't stop."

"I couldn't if I wanted to," Asher rasped. As he pulled back, I copied the movement, feeling a bit like I was chasing him. Then he slammed back in, the motion hitting my prostate and lighting up my whole body. My hips jerked and sent me bottoming out in Rosie. The combined sensations were mind melting.

"Nobody fucking move," I gritted out. "I'm going to come if we don't stop."

"Good. Show her what I can do to you." Asher pulled out and slammed home again.

Rosie's fingers flexed on my ass. "Do it. I want you to fill me up like you promised."

"God, how am I going to survive the two of you?"

"You won't," Asher said, a smile in his voice, "but you'll die happy."

His teeth found my shoulder as Rosie leaned up and kissed the other side. When she tightened around me and whispered my name as she climaxed, I was lost. Then I came, and Asher grunted, stilling inside me as he found his release. My orgasm was a nearly painful rush, and a sob broke free as, for the first time, I truly felt like I was home.

They were mine. I'd never let them go.

CHAPTER

EIGHT

ROSIE

It was the heat that woke me. We were all tangled together, arms draped over torsos, legs over thighs, fingers intertwined. There was a moment when I wasn't sure whose limbs belonged to whom. I grinned. I was in the middle of a sexy sandwich, and I really bloody liked it. But it was the way Asher and Remi held each other as they nestled me between them that made my heart flutter.

I'd lost count of how many times the three of us fell apart with each other. By the end, we'd been little more than sweaty panting messes, but I'd loved every second. Especially the way they worshipped each other.

I could see how some women might get jealous of the attention they paid one another, but I wasn't. Not remotely. The way they touched each other only amped up what I felt when they touched me. I never wanted it to end. Except, of course, for right now. I had human needs to see to. Morning breath chief among them.

Sitting up slowly, I disentangled myself from the two men and grinned as Remi sighed and scooted closer to

Asher to fill the space I'd left behind. Shifters love a cuddle, especially Ben and Remi.

My chest tightened at the thought of my missing Mercer. I needed him home with all of us, sharing this.

Padding down the hall, I bypassed the bathroom I normally used and went into Ben's room. I needed to be around his things, to smell echoes of him in the air, to feel close to him in any way I could.

Taking care of my needs, I stared at my bedraggled and thoroughly forked appearance in the mirror. My hair was a wild tangle, eyes mascara-smudged from the tears Remi pulled from me as he'd made me reach my peak over and over.

"Rosie, babes, you're a fright."

I was also sticky . . . everywhere. Sex was far messier than anyone ever talked about. Adding extra participants only made that little fact even more true. No one prepared you for . . . fluids. I chuckled under my breath. God *must* be a man. A woman would have found a far better solution. A without fluids option, if you will.

"Right, time for a shower."

Seeing as I was already nude, all I had to do was turn on the water and wait for the spray to heat. A flash of Ben stepping out of the stall the night we'd been together had my heart aching.

It had barely been more than twenty-four hours since we'd been together last, but it felt like weeks. I missed him. I'd been denied the pleasure of waking up beside him, that simple intimacy stolen from me because of a restless wolf and an overzealous sheriff.

I would not cry. Crying helped no one.

The cascade of hot water beat down on my shoulders as I fought the waves of sadness and panic that threatened to overtake me. I closed my eyes against the tears, unwilling to let the emotions cripple me.

A flutter of cool air rushed over me as the curtain was pulled back. Asher's low groan had my heartbeat spiking. "Please tell me we're going to play drop the soap," he said, joining me without waiting for an invitation.

When I didn't laugh, he tipped my chin up and stared at me. "Hey, what's wrong?"

I leaned my forehead against his chiseled chest and sighed. "It's stupid. I just can't stop thinking . . ."

"You miss him."

"Yes. What if we don't get him back?"

"We will. You know there's no way I'd let him rot away in there. Remi either. We'll get it figured out. But right now there's nothing we can do. Legally, Dallas can keep him for up to forty-eight hours."

"What happens after that?"

"Either he has to let him go, or he has to formally charge him. At that point, he'd be taken to the federal detention center in Anchorage to await trial. Well, he would if it wasn't a supernatural situation."

"I doubt he'd be prosecuted by humans. They'll throw him to the shifter council."

My breaths came in sharp gasps as my words hit. I didn't know what shifter politics were like, but if they were anything like vampires, their Council was just as ruthless. He'd be lost. I didn't think we had forty-eight hours.

Asher's large palms cupped my face. "Breathe, Rosie. Look at me. It's not going to come to that."

My brows pulled together, but everything softened in me when he pressed a gentle kiss between them.

"How do you know?" I asked, my voice barely loud enough to be heard over the water.

"Because I'm really fucking good at what I do."

My breath stuttered out, and I closed my eyes, relaxing as his words penetrated my fear. He was right. Asher dealt with stuff like this all the time. Made people disappear. Changed their life stories on a dime. Invented new ones. Oversaw complex prisoner extraction missions. Okay, the last I wasn't sure about, but it sounded like something he could do. He was my black-hatted knight for a reason.

"Turn around," Asher murmured, the scent of Ben's soap filling the air as I did what he told me.

"What are you doing?"

"Helping you wash your ass. You're filthy." There was a teasing lilt to his words, and I knew he was trying to help me feel better.

"Just my arse?"

"It's one of my favorite body parts."

I snickered. "I never would have pegged you for an arse man."

"Then you obviously haven't been paying attention. But that begs the question, would you peg me?"

"What's that? Is it one of Remi's pirate things?"

He let out a low groan. "That's a conversation for another day."

His slick palms ran across my skin, tender and gentle, as he washed my back and shoulders, then my arms, hands, and fingers. He didn't leave an inch of me unwashed, paying special attention to my breasts and the cleft between my thighs. Every slip of his fingers was as much a tease as it was a comfort. It wasn't long before I was rocking into the touch, especially once he began sliding his digits inside of me.

"I have to be thorough," he rasped. "So Remi and I can get you dirty again later."

And then he pressed a finger against the tight ring of my arse, teasing me.

"Asher," I moaned, pushing back against him, needing more. "I love how you touch me."

"And I love how you feel beneath my hands."

That finger sank inside, sending sparks of pleasure through me at the intrusion, reminding me of Pan and his magical tail.

"Maybe next time, I'll take your ass the way I took Remi's. Would you like that, princess?"

"God, yes."

He pulled the showerhead down and ran the water over my body, carefully rinsing the soap. When he aimed the spray between my legs, I gasped as the vibration of the pulsing water hit my clit. He'd adjusted the setting, and I was ever so thankful for it. How had I never experimented with *this* before?

"Uh oh," Asher laughed as my hips sought out more of the delicious pressure. "Looks like somebody might be taking a lot more showers in her future. I think I created a monster."

"*Ma petite monstre.*" Pan's seductive voice echoed through my mind. I knew it was just a memory, but the sound of it while Asher held the spray *just so* tipped me over the edge.

"Asher, more."

The water disappeared, and I whined in response until he dropped to his knees behind me and ran his hands up my thighs.

"Spread open for me, princess. I got you all clean for a reason."

I thought he meant my legs, so I tried to adjust my stance, but he stopped me.

"Like this," he corrected, taking each of my cheeks in his hands and pulling them as far apart as they would go.

Then his warm tongue was . . . there. He licked a path up my seam, not stopping until his tongue was where his fingers had been. No longer licking, but probing. The sensation made me cry out. It was so foreign. So naughty and unexpected, I came again instantly. My hand shot out to press against the tile and keep me upright.

"Like shooting fish in a barrel," he murmured. "Let's see how many more I can get out of you."

He stood and spun me to face him, his eyes blazing with desire. I hadn't taken my time and appreciated his gorgeous body earlier. I'd been too wrapped up in my spiral of worry. But now? He was a god. His dirty blond hair, darkened by the water, hung in his face, the tendrils curling at the ends. The dark spikes of his lashes only made his eyes glow brighter, their light blue currently a stormy gray. He held my gaze, leaning forward and running his nose along mine.

"I loved sharing you with Remi. But I can't lie, I want you all to myself too. You're irresistible, do you know that? I don't think I'll ever get enough of you."

"Technically, you haven't had me yet," I teased.

"We're about to rectify that right the fuck now."

He grasped my hips and lifted me up, fully supporting my weight as he pressed me against the wall, his erection already at my entrance.

"I don't have a condom," he said, his muscles trembling as he worked to control himself. "I've been tested. And . . . Remi's the only one I've been with in a long time."

I threaded my fingers through his hair. "I may seem human, but I'm still part *fae* . . . there's no risk of infection or pregnancy. I'm okay without the condom if you are."

Staring into his eyes, I waited as the statement washed over him. "Asher. I trust you."

Not breaking eye contact, he slowly rocked forward, sheathing himself all the way inside me in one long thrust. "Don't you dare close your eyes, Rosie. I want to watch you as I take you." He pulled slowly back out, his gaze dropping and his teeth catching his lip as he stared at the place he'd entered me. "Fuuuck, princess. Do you have any idea how much I love the sight of you stretched around my cock? I've pictured this so many fucking times."

"When you watched me on your cameras?" I asked with a slight gasp as he worked himself back in.

"Who else was I supposed to picture you fucking?" He wasn't mildly repentant as he looked back up and held my stare. "But I've wanted you for a lot longer."

"Have you?"

"Fuck, yes. Since the moment I saw your pretty picture when I was researching your family. I fucked my fist to the fantasy of you the very first night. And a lot of the ones after."

"Asher . . ."

"I never actually believed you could be mine. I still don't, if I'm being honest."

"I'm yours. You're inside me right now."

"God, I know it. And you feel fucking amazing."

"As good as the fantasy?"

"Better. So much better."

His length swelled inside me, growing thicker as he and I moved together. I wanted this. Him spilling inside me, filling me with everything he had, making me his in every way. Just like Remi. Just like Ben. And in a dark part of my mind, just like Pan.

With every rocking thrust, his pelvis hit that sensitive

bundle of nerves, lighting me up from the inside out. He didn't look away again, not once, not hiding anything he was feeling from me as he made me his.

It was intense in a way even the filthiest sex couldn't be. Intimate. Magical.

"I'm close, princess. Are you going to come for me?" The way his words were barely more than a desperate rasp had me grinding on him.

"I'm . . . I need . . ."

"Tell me." He thrust deeper, shuddering.

"Pain. I need pain."

A flash of heat in his eyes was my only warning before he dipped his head and bit down on my shoulder hard enough to send me straight over the edge. He followed behind, pulsing long and deep inside me as I milked him for every last drop he had.

"Oh, Asher . . . God." It felt like stars were exploding behind my eyes, beneath my skin. I felt full and whole and . . . loved.

He hadn't said the words, but the truth was still there, shimmering between us. Asher had just *loved* me with every inch of his perfect body.

Breathing heavily, he glanced back at me, his lazy smile one of a man who'd just sated his lover and was immensely proud. As well he should have been. I was mostly boneless at this point. Held together by sheer force of will and Asher.

He slid one hand down my arm, tracing my wrist with gentle fingertips, brushing across the mark Pan had etched into me. A curious tendril of pleasure unfurled at the contact, and I let out a soft mewl. Was it Pan? Or the remnants of the climaxes Asher had just given me?

"Did you forget about me, ma petite monstre?"

I'd given her twenty-four hours to come to her senses, but my petal's time was up. This would not stand. She was my wife. Bound by blood and ritual.

I had a perfect view of the back door to the Mercers' bar. Someone should have been here by now, but the place was quiet. What if they'd run and taken her with them while I'd been hiding away from the daylight? I had a brief moment of terror at the fleeting thought.

She wouldn't escape me again. There was nowhere on this earth she could hide from me.

A flash of red on the other end of the alley caught my eye. My gaze sharpened, focus shifting in that direction. I didn't recognize the woman walking toward the bar, but her shirt bore its logo, and she twirled keys around on her finger. Perfect. She would do nicely.

My fangs descended as hunger threatened to overtake me. I hadn't fed yet tonight. The Mercers would more than likely recognize my calling card if I left their barmaid's corpse at the door.

But if I killed her now, I couldn't reap the benefits of

having an inside connection to Roslyn. Perhaps I'd just have a little taste to tide me over. This wench's use to me was not limited to the life-giving elixir in her veins. No need to get greedy and spoil this opportunity.

As if the universe were handing me a gift, she dropped her keys before she could unlock the door.

"Balls," she muttered under her breath.

I dropped silently down from the rooftop, landing on my feet behind her before she'd recovered her keys.

She spun, eyes wide, and I immediately caught her in my stare. "Look at me, little one. You're mine to command now."

There was nothing, not a flicker of fight in her as her focus went hazy and her plump red lips slackened.

"Very good. Now, tell me your name, poppet."

"Darla."

"Darla," I repeated, testing it out. Not one I would've chosen, and if she'd become my submissive, I would likely have changed it. But this would do.

"Who are you? You smell nice." Her voice held a dream-like quality, reminiscent of patrons at *Iniquity* who'd partaken in Lilith's aphrodisiac potions.

"You may call me Master. I own you now, do you understand?"

"Yes, Master."

"I have a very important job for you. Are you paying attention?"

She nodded eagerly, her eyes locked on mine as I held her in my thrall.

"Your coworker, the female . . ." I let my words trail off as I waited for her to supply the information I needed. Roslyn wasn't here under her real name, but I also wasn't privy to her pseudonym. Yet.

"Nadia?"

"Yes, very good. She has something very special to me, and I need you to get it back."

"Wh-what is it?"

"That's a secret."

"Okay."

"In order to recover what belongs to me, I am going to need you to collect information. I need you to report back on any and all conversations you have with her. I want to know where she's going, who she's with, what flavor bubblegum she chews, etcetera."

"Does that mean I get to see you again?"

I stroked her cheek gently, fighting the urge to shove her away. "Yes, poppet. And when you do, you'll let me into your mind so I can see everything you've learned."

"Will it hurt?"

"No. Not unless you want it to."

She shivered. "I don't think I'd like that."

Roslyn would.

My cock gave a happy twitch at the thought. My wife truly was made for me. I couldn't wait to break her in properly.

"What do you want me to talk to her about?"

"Why she's here. What she's hiding from. Her hopes. Her dreams. What she's doing with those . . . dogs."

"The Mercers?"

"Yes," I snarled, their surname alone enough to make my skin crawl. I hated that they had access to what was rightfully mine. They'd befouled her with their stench. It was only a matter of time before they sullied her skin with their marks.

"Learn everything you can about her husband."

Darla gave a slight shiver, brows pulling together. "Nadia doesn't have a husband."

"Yes, she does."

"Ben is going to have puppies when he finds out."

I smirked at that. Good. Let him. It was only the beginning of the agony I would rain down upon him.

"Is there anything else?"

"No, poppet. That will be more than enough. I will find you when I'm ready for your report."

She turned to the door, but I stopped her with one word. "Wait."

"Yes, Master?"

"I do require one more thing from you."

"Anything."

Brushing her hair away from her neck, I trained my gaze on the pulsing vein in her throat. "Close your eyes, poppet. And whatever you do, don't scream."

TEN

PAN

"Is this the spirit of Amelia Earhart? Did you die in the Bermuda Triangle?" The stupid teenager's voice cracked on his last question, the sound echoing through the connection we shared via my demonic spirit board.

Using my tail, I lifted the tumbler of brimstone whiskey to my lips as I slid the planchette across the wood, letting it land on the 'Yes.'

"Will Selena Gomez fall in love with me?"

Rolling my eyes, I nudged the wooden marker around the board, spelling out: Keep Dreaming.

I couldn't hear the other participants, but I could feel his embarrassment through our connection. So, he was desperate. That was good. I could get him to summon me, then maybe I'd have another soul to add to my collection.

Mother would be so proud.

I snorted, waiting for the next round of pathetic inquiries to come through. The link between the boy and I broke, and another took its place, making me grumble.

"Will Brad die a virgin?" a young girl asked, a teasing giggle in her voice.

My eyes nearly rolled back in my head as I sent a pulse of power through the piece joining us and made her yelp. Then I shoved the spirit board away from me and stood, pacing the length of my swimming pool. Yes, demons have swimming pools. How else do we keep fit? It's not all vigorous fucking and crunches.

The bottom of my robe fluttered around my calves, making the aubergines printed on the claret-colored silk dance. My briefs were part of the matching set, the massive eggplant down the front sporting a cheeky smirk. Say what you will about the succubus, but Lilith Duval gave the best All Souls gifts.

As I padded toward the diving board, Roslyn's voice tickled my mental barriers. I'd put her on timeout after her very naughty behavior, though she'd been relentless in her attempts to contact me since. I knew what she was after. She wanted to know if I was involved in the unfortunate turn of events surrounding the wolf.

Good. That played right into my hand.

I wanted her desperate.

Begging for my help.

Crying at my feet for something only I could give her.

I know what you're thinking. No. Not *that*. Although, I would happily give her that until she was gagging on me. The briefs don't lie. No false advertisement here.

In a word, I was hung.

But I digress.

A bargain.

Her voice pressed against my mind once more, this time less of a tickle and more of a slap. Not the fun kind.

"All right, all right, keep your shirt on." I downed my

whiskey and poured myself another before dropping the robe and slipping into the pool. If she wanted to come see me, she'd get the thirstiest thirst trap she'd ever encountered.

Would you turn down a dripping wet demon, rippling muscles, barely restrained erection threatening to poke right out of his Speedo, if he sauntered up to you fresh out of a pool? I think not.

She'd never be able to resist.

Running my hands through my hair, I took special care to make sure my horns were visible. She'd fancied those last time. Quite a lot, if I remember right. Or maybe that was me. It was all a bit of a blur; I'd come so hard I'd been nearly cross-eyed, and then she pulled the rug out from under me before I'd even finished enjoying my afterglow.

Who did that?

And they call *me* the demon.

So I left her knocking on the proverbial door as I did a lap in the pool. I'd let her in when I was damn well ready.

"Pan, please?" her voice skated over my skin, the sound clear in my head and sending tingles straight to my cock. "I need to see you."

"Oh, yes you do, *ma petite monstre.*"

Her shock pulsed through me, followed by a wave of relief. Oh, but I was so going to make her work for this. She thought all was forgiven because I deigned to acknowledge her? Please. She hadn't yet begun to learn the meaning of the word beg.

But she was about to.

I opened the portal between our worlds, and she fell straight into the water in front of me, all flailing limbs and a sharp gasp of surprise.

I leaned against the edge, arms stretched out, tail

bringing my whiskey to my lips as she coughed and spluttered.

"What the forking hell was that for?"

I raised a brow.

"Was that really necessary? What if I couldn't swim?"

"Then I guess you would have died."

"You would have let me perish?" She sounded genuinely hurt, which made me irrationally defensive. I was only having a bit of fun.

"I'm not allowed to touch you anymore, remember? I wouldn't want to go and do something you didn't *consent* to."

Brows drawing together, she splashed me, the chlorinated water hitting me square in the face and getting in my glass.

"Now you've done it. That is eleven-hundred-year-old brimstone whiskey, *mon coeur*. I shall have to teach you a lesson."

"I should have known asking for your help was a mistake."

"All tits, no brain. What a pity."

"Pardon me?"

I waved a hand, elaborating, "Apparently, you aren't very smart. You should have figured that out after the first time."

"I was desperate."

"Yes, love. I know."

"And you . . . enjoyed it."

I groaned at the thought. "Yes . . . I know."

And then you took it away from me because you want some foul dogs instead.

"You needn't be so smug."

"Sweetheart, I'm a demon. Stop viewing me through

the filter of your pathetic human morality. It doesn't apply to me. Stop expecting me to act the hero. I'm not one, and I never will be."

I raised the glass to my lips again and took a sip, grimacing instantly because I'd forgotten the drink was spoiled. Disgusted, I tipped it into the water and stared at her.

"Ruined. Just like you."

She glared at me, still standing in the pool, rivulets of water running down her face and chest. It was all manner of distracting. I was tempted to shove her back under just so I wouldn't have to look at her and accidentally reveal my hand. She couldn't know I wanted her.

"Oh? And who's the one who ruined me?"

I opened my mouth, more than ready to fire off an answer, when she half swam, half stomped over to me so she could poke me in the chest.

"That would be *you*."

"No, darling. I did no such thing. You were perfectly unspoiled until you let him take what was expressly mine. Now you reek of shifter cum and tragedy."

She blushed, her eyes dipping. "Why does it matter to you? It's not like you care about me."

"Because you were mine, and I don't like others playing with my things."

"I am not a thing you . . . you . . . knobhead."

I played at being hurt by her ridiculous insult. "Oh, I'm wounded. I don't think I'll ever recover from such a scathing comment. My poor demon heart can't take it."

Then, tired of playing this game. I stalked forward, grabbed her by the throat, and spun us so she was pushed against the pool wall. I pressed my hard form along her soft one, looking down my nose until our foreheads touched.

"Why. Are. You. Here?"

"You know why."

"Do you actually believe I'd waste breath on a question I already know the answer to? I've told you before, I am a very busy demon. I haven't got all day. So spit it out, or I'll give you something to swallow."

"You know, that's very nearly copyright infringement."

I shrugged. "How do you know they wrote it themselves? Many a deal has been struck for an Academy Award."

"Tell me you weren't part of this," she demanded, changing the subject. "Tell me you aren't the reason Ben is in jail for murder."

"No."

"What do you mean, no?"

"I mean I will not give you what you want. You broke our deal. I do not do anything for free. You want something from me, *ma petite*, you pay for the privilege."

"So you're a dirty trollop, then?"

"Takes one to know one."

"Let me get this straight. You want to help me in exchange for a favor? Of the sexual persuasion?"

"Do I *want* to help you? Not particularly. Will I help you? Yes. That *is* how this works. You give me what I want, I give you what you want. Tit"—I flicked the breast still pierced with my ring—"for tat."

She gasped and let her mask slip, a little shiver of longing rolling through her body. "I won't let you inside me."

"I don't have to be inside you to make you come."

"That's what you want? To make me come?"

I grinned at her, but it was a feral thing. "No, darling, I want you to want to make me come."

She licked her lips. "That shouldn't take long."

My growl was rough with warning. "The number of ways I could absolutely destroy you without finding my own release . . ."

She raised a brow. "You aren't buying that rubbish you're spewing either, are y—"

Squeezing her throat hard enough she had to stop speaking, I stared deep into her eyes. "Name your terms, Roslyn Blackthorne."

ELEVEN

The pressure of Pan's fingers around my throat had my heart pounding, apprehension and arousal singing in my blood. How was it this monster had me wet and ready for him with one flick of his tail?

Asher had said he'd try to exonerate Ben, but trying wasn't enough. I needed more assurance. I needed a guarantee. I'd resolved to call Pan, to lay myself at his feet so I could get Ben out of jail. I knew what I was walking into. I prepared myself for this moment, but I hadn't expected to want it so badly.

I didn't think I'd ever understand my pull to this demon. Even before our deal was first struck, I'd been drawn to him. He'd appeared after my summons, and a spark ignited between us. It was no different now that our initial bargain had been severed. Was that just the nature of demons in general? Or was there something about Pan that called to me?

Unease cut through some of my arousal. It couldn't spell anything good for me if it was the latter. I already had a stable of men at my disposal. I didn't need another, let alone a forking demon. This was a business transaction. That was all. My eagerness had nothing to do with the . . . Pan, and everything to do with my libido.

"Let go of me so I can speak, Pan. I won't be able to give you anything if I'm unconscious." My voice was a breathy, strident thing from the combination of desire for him and a need for air.

"Debatable."

I glared at him, and he relented. Barely. He left his fingers curled around my neck but loosened his grasp enough that I could draw in a full breath. There was something possessive about the move. As if he was collaring me. Or ensuring I knew it wouldn't take more than one wrong word before he was choking me once more.

I licked my lips, hating that it made me recall the time he'd done the same while thrusting inside me. The lack of oxygen had made every other sensation more intense.

"I want Ben freed. No. Not just freed. Exonerated. Cleared of all charges."

Something a lot like jealousy flared in his gaze. "How do you know he's innocent? Perhaps your stuttering wolf did kill that bear. You'd be letting a murderer walk free."

"Murderers aren't all that uncommon in my world. My father has quite the body count. As do I." Flashes of the fae I'd taken out with well-shot arrows only months ago ran through my mind. "But even if Ben did end Alexi's life, the bear likely deserved it."

"Ah, then my name for you is even more fitting than I realized. Isn't it?"

"Yes. I'm just as much a monster as any of you."

He ran a blackened claw down my cheek. "No. You aren't. That's part of my charm. You crave the danger, knowing you put your life at risk every time you part those creamy thighs of yours. I could snap your neck with one flick of my wrist, and you know it. You *love* it."

"No." But my denial was weak at best. He was right. Blast him.

"I'd wager that if I slipped my fingers into your cunt, I'd find you wet and ready for me right bloody now."

I scoffed. "I'm in a pool. Of course I'm wet. That's nothing you caused."

Unfortunately, my attempted insult failed because he did exactly as he threatened, his claws shredding my knickers before receding. Blunt digits slid along my center, parting me and . . . yes, finding me slick with desire for him.

"You really are a filthy liar, aren't you, *mon ange*?"

I swallowed, unable to form words as he slowly pressed two fingers inside me.

"You missed me. The way I hurt you. The way I pleasure you. You want me to do it again. They can't give you what I can."

"N-no."

He removed his fingers and leaned in close, his lips a breath away from mine. "I don't believe you."

God help me, I moaned and arched my back. In that moment, I didn't believe me either.

"You have a way of making *no* sound an awful lot like *yes*."

"Do we have a deal or not?" I bit out, my heart racing. I wanted to get this over with so I could get away from this monster and back to the men who deserved my attention.

He rocked his hips into me, the solid steel length of his erection rubbing over my most sensitive places. "You give me your body, I give him his life back."

"I give you my body, you give him his life and protect me and my family."

His lips ghosted over mine, not quite touching, but a twisted part of me wanted them to. That mouth didn't find purchase with any part of me until he dipped to the underside of my jaw and finally dragged his blazing kiss over my skin. The scrape of fangs sent a shiver through me, and his breath feathered over my pulse point in a barely restrained moan. He wanted this. He wanted me desperately, even if he was trying to hide it.

"Done," he groaned.

"Wait."

The frustrated grunt he let out proved my point. "What now?"

"How long? How often? I'm not falling into one of your never-ending traps."

"Whenever I need you, *ma petite monstre*."

"No. Once every six months."

The derisive snort that escaped him as he rolled his hips into me was proof I'd reached too far. "Every. Fucking. Day."

"Absolutely not."

"Once a week," he snarled, impatience giving his voice a velvety rasp.

"Once a month."

"Deal."

I swallowed, not sure if I was being had, but relieved that at least I would know when to anticipate the call. It made me feel like I had some control over the matter.

His fangs sank into my neck, the rush akin to how I'd felt when Gavin had tasted me. I whimpered and writhed as he fed from me, and our bargain was sealed. The way he grunted in pleasure ensured I wasn't the only one getting something out of this. Then he broke the moment, backing away to stare at me, crimson smeared on his lips, his pupils blown as though he was high on something other than blood.

"Delicious. As always, darling."

Pan took me by the hips, twisting around and setting me, arse first, on the outside of the pool. Then he pushed up in a rush of muscles and water as he jumped out to stand beside me.

I was lightheaded, trembling with anticipation. Pan was never gentle, and that knowledge alone was enough to make me squirm.

"On your knees for me, my filthy. Little. Slut."

A bolt of arousal hit me between the thighs, tingles gathering as need rocked my body. The bastard was right. I did require what only he could provide.

Swiveling around, I moved into a kneeling position, the pool to my back, my eyes not quite level with Pan's impressive erection. Perhaps daunting might be a better word to describe it. But my mouth watered nonetheless as the crown peeked through the top of his briefs.

"Touch me, Pan," I whispered, gaze shifting to his tail, which flicked back and forth like a cat's as it stalked its prey.

His hands cupped my cheeks, tipping my head back until I was looking up at him. He held me there, gently restrained as he skimmed the tip of his tail along my damp skin. I shivered when it scraped down my spine. Moaned when it dipped between my legs. Cried out when he stopped.

"No," he said simply.

"No?"

"This isn't about your pleasure. It's about mine." He released me and stepped away, sliding the tight spandex down until it strained around his thighs.

I opened my mouth on instinct. Ready to give him what we'd agreed to. *Wanting* to give it to him. What did it say about me that I was so willing to do this in exchange for Ben's freedom? Was that just the excuse I was using in order to be here again? I didn't want to examine that too closely. Gavin had awoken something inside me, but Pan was my first. Perhaps I would always be drawn to him. Just as I was drawn to all of them.

He ran a palm over the thick, veiny shaft, a drop of precum falling to the cement between my knees. Still holding himself, he slapped my lips with the weeping tip just hard enough that my teeth cut gently into my flesh. Not enough to break it, just enough to sting.

I went to seal my lips around the dripping crown to give him what he so obviously needed. But he pulled just out of reach.

"What are you doing?" I moaned, the salty taste of his arousal bursting on my tongue.

"You want it too much."

"It's our deal. This is me holding up my end of the bargain."

"No. Our deal is that I get you however I want you. And I don't want you doing anything that makes you feel good."

He was still mad at me. What a pouty, spoilt child.

He began stroking himself, brows furrowed, gaze focused on me as his fist shuttled along his manhood. This wasn't slow and seductive. He was bringing himself off and denying me the pleasure of being the one to do it. Showing me exactly who was in control.

"I am going to spill myself all over you." His words were punctuated by harsh breaths as he continued chasing his release. "I'll mark you and then send you back home to explain why you smell of me, why you're wearing my bite mark on your throat."

"Pan," I groaned, perfectly able to picture it and knowing that was the true punishment. He wanted to shame me.

"I'm going to come all over that pretty little face. And those perfect tits. And that dripping cunt. You will *never* be rid of me. Do you understand, *ma petite monstre*? I own you." He reached for me and swiped a claw down my front, shredding what was left of my clothes until I was all but bared before him.

"Fuuuuck, tilt your head back. Grab your tits."

The sight of him on the brink was affecting. I was as wet as if each stroke of his hand was running along my folds. As eager for him to finish as he was. Doing as I was bid, I took my breasts in my hands and pressed them together, opening my mouth as wide as I could.

He grunted, his muscles flexing and tensing as his shaft pulsed, and he came. Hot jets of release striped across my face, neck, and chest, coating me in his essence. The evidence of his climax dripped down my body as his bark of pleasure echoed off the walls.

Gripping my chin in his hand, he tugged, forcing me to my feet. Holding my gaze, chests rising and falling in time, he smeared his seed across my body. Taking extra care to rub it in. His palm glided down my torso until he cupped my center and used two fingers to push some of it inside me.

He grinned and leaned forward.

I thought he was going to kiss me, but instead he purred, "See you next month," before spinning me around and spanking me hard on the arse as he shoved me through the portal he'd opened without my knowledge.

TWELVE

GAVIN

Standing on the outskirts of the stupid little pub these wolves owned, I waited for my thralled to make her appearance. It would be her first report since our little interlude in the alleyway, and I couldn't deny I was eager to hear what she had to say.

I flicked open my lighter and lit the opium cigarette at my lips, taking a slow inhale as the paper caught. The smoke filled my lungs, a slight burn, followed by the delicious buzz of the drug hitting my bloodstream. The high wouldn't last, but I appreciated the momentary reprieve from the world. Thank God I was born into this, a pureblood in every sense of the word. I couldn't imagine being a made vampire and having to rely on feeding from drunkards or junkies to get a fix. I could enjoy these pleasures, if only for a short while.

Darla—still a bloody annoying name—skipped toward me after parking her car behind the building. Her bubblegum pink lips were spread in a beaming smile as she stared at me like a lost puppy.

"Hello, Master. I'm so glad you're here. I've been looking for you."

"Does that mean you have what I requested?"

She pulled a spare set of keys out of her pocket and held it up like she'd found the bloody Magna Carta. "I do!"

I snatched them away from her, tucking them in my breast pocket for later use. "Good girl. Now, what have you found out? How is she? Does she miss her husband terribly? Is she withering without him?"

"You mean Ben? Of course, she misses him. She's trying to keep it together, but she seems devastated. I would be too if I had to go without his huge d—"

"That's enough."

"Are you jealous, Master? Wait, are *you* the husband?"

Oh no, she couldn't start wising up now. My thrall was strong, but her shifter blood was fighting against me in a way a human's couldn't.

Staring deep into her eyes, I pushed my will out and imposed it over hers, reinforcing our ties and effectively shutting up her internal voice. No one wanted a thinker. I needed a *doer*.

"I want you to listen closely, Darla."

"Yes, Master."

"You're doing a brilliant job. I need you to tell me when she will be working and what it will take to get the Mercer twins to let her go."

"You mean cut her shift?"

I rolled my eyes. "No. I mean *her*. What will it take for them to toss her aside like so much rubbish?"

She blinked a few times, swaying under the effect of my compulsion. "Well, she's . . . on shift tonight."

Brilliant.

"And the Mercers? How can we ruin their relationship?"

She snorted. "You can't. She's their mate. Everyone can see it. Smell it. Sure, they haven't marked her yet, but it's coming. Then it will be permanent."

"Unless I stop that from happening—with your help."

"How can I help?"

"I think I'll pop in for a pint, poppet. You'll serve me with no questions asked."

Her eyes widened. "Oh, I can't do that. They'll kill you. You're a vampire. They"—she wrinkled her nose, seeming confused—"*I* despise vampires. This whole town does, but *especially* the Mercers. One killed their parents."

This made no sense. If they hated vampires, why would they be willing to be anywhere near my Roslyn?

"Then why don't they hate Nadia?"

"She's not a vampire. Why would they?"

"Yes, she is."

She shook her head with a little laugh. "No, she's not. She's fae."

And the penny finally drops. She was fooling them all. Crafty minx. Why did that make me hard?

The Mercers didn't know about her bloodline. Maybe it was time I let them in on her little secret, offer her a shoulder to cry on when they sent her packing.

Oh, yes. I liked the sound of that.

THIRTEEN

The air in the bar sat stale and heavy as we began the process of reopening. There was a gloominess I'd never felt here, an oppressive sense of wrongness because Ben was missing from the atmosphere.

So were the patrons, for that matter. Even though the door was wide open, and the sign turned on, no one had braved setting foot inside. I'd wager buying a pint from a potential serial killer's establishment wasn't high on the list of townspeople's priorities.

"Come on, Pan. Hold up your end of the bloody bargain," I muttered under my breath as I wiped down the bartop.

"I think it's clean, baby girl. We haven't had a customer the entire time we've been open."

I tossed Remi an embarrassed smile. "You know what they say about idle hands . . ."

"I can help you with that. We could close up, take a little trip to the office?"

My cheeks heated as thoughts of what he could do to me on that desk materialized in the forefront of my mind.

But he had a business to run, a livelihood to ensure. I wouldn't be a distraction that could further damage my wolves' lives.

"How about after we serve our first customer we can start thinking about how we want to spend our break? Darla should be here soon to handle anyone who comes in."

He scrunched his nose. "Now you're starting to sound like Ben. All work. No play."

"It's been no work for days, Remi."

"I know, I know. Fuck. I just . . ." He leaned in and ran his nose along my neck, inhaling. "I want you all the damn time."

My eyes fluttered closed as my body lit from within. "It's the same for me. But we really shouldn't."

"Or . . . hear me out. We really should." His hand slid around my waist, and he pulled me into him, the thickness behind his fly digging into my back. "We could leave the office door open. I can use my super hearing and keep an ear out for customers."

When his hands dipped between my waistband, I nearly gave in. But then the sound of boots scraping over the floor caught my attention and sent my eyes flying back open.

Ben's tired but handsome face filled the doorway.

"You're back!" I shouted, running to him. I all but threw myself into his arms, wrapping my legs around his waist and holding onto him like a barnacle.

"M-miss me, sugar?"

A rush of pleasure flooded me as his low rumble caressed my senses. I'd missed his voice, his touch, his scent. Every single part of him. But until this moment, I hadn't realized how much.

"Yes. So much."

I hugged him tight, tears of relief pricking my eyes. It was worth it. My deal with Pan. This moment alone made the sacrifice worth any price.

Sacrifice? You hardly suffered besides a couple of bruised knees and unsatisfied need.

"How'd you get out? Dallas was pretty rock solidly against releasing you," Remi asked, striding across the floor as Ben put me on my feet.

"N-no clue. M-maybe he r-realized he didn't have anything c-concrete?"

Remi made a low humming sound as he considered it. I didn't get the sense he believed that was a very likely possibility. After the way the sheriff had treated us, I didn't either, even if Pan had somehow interfered with Dallas's will. Come to think of it, I wasn't sure how Pan had accomplished his task—nor did I care. Ben was free; that was all that mattered to me.

"I honestly d-don't fucking care. I j-just wanted to be home."

"Don't look a gift horse in the mouth and all that."

"I never understood that expression," Remi muttered. "Why would you look a horse in the mouth at all? They can bite your fingers off."

I giggled, feeling lighthearted for the first time in days. "It means don't find fault with something that's been gifted to you."

"Unless there are strings. There are always fucking strings."

I bit the inside of my cheek. That put a damper on my elation. I was the proverbial string in this equation. I wondered what Ben would say if—when—he found out. Remi and Asher too, for that matter. There was no way I could keep my running off once a month from my mates a secret. Nor did I want to. I was so bloody tired of secrets.

"About that . . ." I started, but trailed off as the shadows of three gargoyles darkened our doorway.

As one, they attempted to shove their way in, and as one, they all got stuck . . . again.

"Move your great bloomin' arse out of me way, you bloody blowhard," Harry grumbled, shoving at Tom as he tried to free himself.

"My arse is quite firm and a sight to behold. It's yours that needs some work."

Dick got out first, practically falling at our feet as he did. As soon as he saw Ben, his expression went from excited to crestfallen. "Oh, bloody hell, you already know."

"That Ben's home?" Remi asked, one brow raised in that sexy, piratey way he had. "Obviously."

"That there's been another murder," Tom announced, earning himself a searing look from Dick.

"I was gonna say that!"

"You snooze, you lose."

"For f-fuck's sake," Ben groaned. "I've o-only been out f-for an hour." I knew what he was getting at. He thought Dallas would try to pin it on him.

"Not to worry, lad. This happened last night. They found her on the rocks by the marina. Poor lamb." Tom was a fair bit too excited about this.

Dread curled in my gut. "Who?"

Please don't say Darla. Please don't say Darla.

"Ginny," Dick replied.

"A mouth like a hoover, and a heart as big as . . . an elk's." Tom's voice wavered.

Harry nodded and swiped at his eyes. "An arse like two pigs fighting under a blanket."

"And oh, the sweater puppies were unmatched." Dick sighed in fond remembrance. "Two great handfuls a man could happily suffocate in." He mimed motorboating as the others sighed tragically.

"Let us spare a moment of silence for the sweet lass," Tom said.

"To Ginny," they crowed. As one, they removed their caps—each more ridiculous than the last—and placed them over their hearts. Harry wore a fisherman's cap, Tom a plaid hunter's toque, and Dick a bowler hat straight from the 1920s.

"What exactly did Ginny do as a profession?" I whispered to Remi.

"She was a kindergarten teacher."

My eyes widened. That was not what I'd expected.

"Also a s-succubus," Ben whispered back.

That made more sense.

"Well then, that was quite a . . . colorful memorial. Shall we raise a glass to her?"

"Och, aye. She'd a loved that," Tom said, wiping away a stray tear.

I shared a soft smile with the twins, knowing it was more likely the gargoyles would love that. As soon as my back was to the room, my smile fell. This was my fault. I may not have killed Ginny with my bare hands, but it was my demon that signed her death warrant.

Maybe I *did* care how Ben got free. I never meant for an innocent woman to die.

"It's good to be back at The Tip," Tom said as I slid three shots of Jameson in front of them.

"I reckon Sheriff Walker is none too pleased to deliver the news to Mayor Dubois." Harry shuddered, then locked gazes with me. "That pussy of hers gives me the willies."

"Pussy?" I couldn't hide my shock.

Dick hiccupped. "Her cat. Lady Godiva Sassafras."

"Evil little bitch of a thing," Harry confirmed.

Tom leaned forward and picked up his shot in a toast. "Anyway, we're chuffed you're not a murderer, Ben."

"Never doubted you for a second," Dick said.

Elbowing him hard, Harry grumbled, "Yes, you did. What was all that nonsense you were spewing about how you saw a wolf with red eyes and foaming at the mouth? One that looked like Ben."

I pulled back his shot. "Pardon me?"

"It's true . . ." Dick said, shoulders lifting defensively. "At least, I thought I saw one. It was dark, and I might've had a few too many, so my vision wasn't what it usually is."

"So it could've been a fucking tree branch," Harry chastised. "Meanwhile, Ben's locked up for a murder he obviously didn't commit, and we can't get our nightly pints."

"Worst two days of my life," Dick said mournfully. "Never go away again, Ben. Promise me."

He quirked a brow. "I'll t-try my best."

"That's a good lad," Tom offered.

Ben slid his hand over the small of my back, his touch soothing me even as guilt gnawed at my heart.

"Justice for Ginny!" Dick crowed.

The other two followed and slammed their shots. I poured them seconds before they even had to ask.

The sound of footsteps had all of us craning our necks back toward the door.

Not now. Oh God, please, not now.

"Well, wife. Have you come to your senses yet?"

Harry's shocked gasp was the only thing that pulled me out of my fear-riddled state. "Oh, which one of you had secret husband on your bingo card? It certainly wasn't me."

Gavin strolled right up to the bar and took a seat, his handsome face a sharp contrast to the unease settling in my gut.

"G-Gavin. I thought you'd gone."

"Oh, silly petal, I'll never leave. Not without what's mine."

Ben's low growl vibrated straight to my bones, but then he turned his gaze to mine, and the hurt there stole my breath. "Sugar? You're m-married?"

I bit my lip, turning guilty eyes toward him. "Um . . . yes?"

FOURTEEN

Oh, the poor stuttering shifter was sad. I couldn't find it in my heart to feel for him. He'd had her. Ruined her. I hoped he never forgot my face after I took her back.

Darla chose that moment to saunter in, her complexion pale due to the blood she'd donated. She perked up when she saw me, smoothing her hands down her cropped shirt and offering me a smile as though I hadn't just fed from her in the alley. I glared at her, her smile faltering. Thankfully everyone else was too busy looking at Roslyn to notice.

"You're m-m-married to a v-v—"

Bentley closed his eyes and took a deep breath, clenching his jaw. It was all I could do not to laugh. Then he finally spit it out.

"Vampire?"

She winced. "Can we not do this in front of everyone? Please?"

"Oi, who you calling everyone? We're part of the family, ain't we?" one of the three men sitting at the bar said, attention rapt.

"My o-office. Now."

Roslyn's shoulders slumped forward, but she turned to make her way down the hall, the other Mercer close on her heels.

I reached out and took hold of her wrist. "You aren't going anywhere without me, petal."

Bentley glared at me, his focus lasering on her wrist. "F-fine."

"Get your goddamned claws off our mate, pal. Unless you want to lose a few fingers." Remington came right up to me, the heat of his body radiating off him as he got in my face. "I'm not fucking kidding."

His eyes blazed an electric blue, a wild, feral scent filling the air around us.

But I was not remotely intimidated by this child throwing a tantrum. I had suits older than him. Leaning forward, my nose nearly touching his, I whispered, "Make. Me."

The rumbled snarl that left him had the three men at the bar squirming, and Darla's eyes were wide from her place at the taps.

"Uh, boss, I think you guys really should listen to Nadia and take this to the office. Or . . . outside?"

Remington didn't move until Roslyn broke the hold I had on her and touched his cheek. "I'm all right, Remi. Come on. Let's sort this behind closed doors, yeah?"

Bentley snorted. "Y-you're m-m-married to a v-v-vampire. What's to s-sort?"

Oh, this was delicious. Perhaps I wouldn't even have to mention her secret or kill him to come between them. Simply existing was enough. But where was the fun in that?

"Of course she is."

"What do you mean, of course?" Remington asked.

Roslyn's eyes widened as her face paled. She pleaded with me silently to stop, but I pressed on. What kind of sadist would I be if I wasn't immune to begging? Besides, I was here to cause a little chaos.

"Why, she's the Blackthorne Princess. Didn't you know? She may be human, but she's vampire royalty. Twice over, if you count her being my duchess. Which I do."

The room went silent. Not even the sound of breaths being drawn graced the air. Until one of the customers let out a low, "Bloody hell, I didn't see that coming."

"Shut yer gob, Dick. Can't you see they're having a moment?"

Bentley's expression shut down completely as he grabbed her by the bicep and tugged her down the hall. I followed, hands in my trouser pockets, relaxed as could be. It was all unraveling so easily.

Remington's breath hit the back of my neck. I glanced over my shoulder. "Would you mind backing up a bit? You're befouling my air."

"I would, actually."

He was in dire need of being put in his place. Soon enough.

As soon as we were all through the office door, Remington shut it and threw the deadbolt. Roslyn stood in the center of the room, brow furrowed, bottom lip between her teeth.

No one seemed to know where to start.

She cleared her throat. "So, erm . . . I suppose I have some explaining to do."

"I th-thought you t-told me all y-your secrets."

"I told you the important parts."

I scowled at that. "Being married wasn't an important part?"

She glared at me, looking as though she'd happily shove me into sunlight if she could. "Not when I faked my own death to be rid of you."

Bentley seemed to relax at that.

Why did her words feel like such a slap in the face? "Rid of me? You'll never be rid of me. You're mine. My wife. My mate. My fucking duchess."

"Mate?" Remington breathed, sounding betrayed. "But you're our mate."

My gaze flicked to her neck, relieved to see she was still free of mating marks. "It doesn't appear so to me. Unless she's let you mark her elsewhere. But I know where wolves put their brand on their mates. It's here"—I reached out and slid the backs of my fingers over the spot on her neck where they'd bite her—"Or here."

She shivered, proving once again that she wasn't immune to my touch—or me.

"Not for lack of trying," Remington muttered.

Roslyn blushed.

"H-how did th-this happen?"

"The marriage?" Roslyn asked.

"All of it. H-how are you h-human but also v-v-vampire?"

The wolf really did struggle with that word. I almost wanted to make a drinking game out of it. I wondered if I could get Darla to bring me some scotch.

"I'm not a vampire. I never will be."

"Not true. I could turn you here and now."

Bentley was almost faster than my eyes could track as he rushed me, his meaty paw gripping my throat and shoving me against the bookshelf behind me. "Touch her and die." He didn't stammer then, and the force of his grasp had me thinking the poor creature really thought he'd done something there.

I pried his fingers off my throat one by one, making him clench his teeth when I nearly shattered one of his knuckles. "I will touch her all I please. She is my *wife*."

"Death seems like a pretty permanent solution to dissolving a marriage."

I bared my fangs at Remington. "She is not dead. Our marriage is intact."

"I know for a fact you didn't consummate it. That's grounds for annulment."

"Vampires do not get annulments."

"Rosie isn't a vampire."

"She's bound to me by Council law. The ritual mating ceremony sealed our joining." My palm gave a slight throb at the memory of the silver blade they'd rammed through it when we became one.

Grabbing her hand, I placed it over mine, the faintest line between the bones of her two middle fingers visible now that I'd called attention to it.

"I'm not going with you, Gavin. I have a life here. One I enjoy." Roslyn pulled her palm from mine and backed away. "You don't have any say over what I do. Or who I love."

Love?

My stomach twisted, and I was worried I might sick myself right there.

"I think the Council would be very interested to know that not only is Roslyn Donoghue alive, but she is also reneging on our families' arrangement. What do you think they'd do to your parents then, Roslyn? To you? Not to mention that charming brother of yours. What was his name? Westley? They'll burn them all."

Twin spots of pink blossomed on her cheeks. "You wouldn't."

"Try me."

"You'd really blackmail her into being with you?" Remington asked, disgust curling his upper lip.

"There is nothing I wouldn't do to keep her."

"Hostage, you mean? Because this isn't how you treat someone you love."

"Who said anything about love? She's my mate, that trumps all other claims and is far stronger a bond than some trivial emotion."

"Yeah, well, she also happens to be ours."

"I know a surefire way to take care of that."

We held each other's glares, but Roslyn had eyes only for Bentley.

"Ben . . . say something."

"I . . . I d-don't know who y-you are."

I felt it the moment her heart broke.

"You do. I'm your Rosie. I'm still yours."

He shook his head, eyes squeezed shut. "But y-you're not."

She bit down into her lower lip, eyes blurring with tears. "If you had any idea what I've done for you, you would never question me or my feelings."

He stared at her, anger morphing into fear. "Rosie, w-what have y-you done?"

"Oh, my naughty little bride. Please, do share with the class."

Roslyn cast a glance at Remington, worry in her eyes. "You should call Asher. He needs to be part of this conversation."

But the shifter shook his head. "He's already here. I smell him. Unlock the door in three . . . two . . . one."

Bentley did as his brother instructed, and standing in the doorway, hand poised to knock, was the hacker. Disheveled, breaths heaving, pathetically human.

"Oh brilliant, the last member of this merry band of misfits has arrived."

"Who are you calling a misfit, Count?" Asher came in and immediately took up his position at Remi's side.

The look the two of them exchanged was . . . affectionate? That was new. The last I'd heard, they hate fucked each other when one or both had an itch that needed scratching. Were they a thing now?

I stood behind the desk, unable to sit down because of the apprehension spiking my blood. We had to hash this out. I knew it, but I didn't like it. My mate was apparently part vampire and had a whole ass husband she didn't tell me about. What other secrets was she keeping?

Remi settled on the corner of the desk, arms crossed, as we all trained our gazes on Rosie and her *husband*.

"Does someone want to bring me up to speed?" Asher cocked one eyebrow as he assessed the situation.

"Aren't you already? You have cameras every-fucking-where."

"Not in here. Look, I know she's got a husband. I know

her whole story because I'm the one that helped her disappear."

"I knew I didn't like you," Gavin softly snarled, eyes narrowed on Asher's face.

The hacker ignored him. "What I don't know is why you're all locked in this office in a standoff."

"My *wife* was about to fill us all in on her misdeeds. Apparently she's been up to no good." Gavin reached for her hand, but she jerked it away.

Good girl.

"A-are we really d-doing this here?"

I didn't want to have this conversation in my bar. It felt bigger than something that was going to take a few minutes. The only other option was letting this asshole in my house, and I didn't much like the idea of that either. Bar it was.

Rosie looked like she was about to pass out. With the four of us all staring expectantly at her, that wasn't surprising. Part of me wanted to tug her into my arms and tell her it would be all right. The other part wanted her to explain because I had a sinking suspicion I knew exactly what she'd done, and I wasn't sure I could handle any more revelations right now.

"T-tell me you d-didn't contact the d-demon," I demanded when a few seconds had passed and she still hadn't said anything.

"Demon?" Gavin asked. "What bloody demon?"

I smirked. I liked seeing him surprised. "Th-the one she m-made a deal w-with to escape y-you."

Asher's face paled. "You made a deal with a fucking demon? When?"

"I . . . It was the night I sent you those texts."

"You *drunk dialed* a demon?"

"Yes?" She shrugged, looking so small surrounded by the four of us. The guilt hung heavy in that one word. Like she was answering both of our questions at once. Yes, she made a deal. Yes, she'd gone back to him.

My heart was racing. I didn't like the idea of her tying herself to a demon before, and I fucking hated it now because I knew without her saying it, she'd done it for me. She'd cut ties with him and had been so relieved to be able to give me that confession. The only reason she'd have gone back was that she'd been worried about losing me.

Fuck.

"But only the first time," she added.

As if that made any-fucking-thing better.

"There have been more times?" Asher was angrier than I'd ever seen him. His hands balled into fists, his chest rising and falling with rapid breaths.

"She's b-bound to him. Or sh-she was."

I glanced at my twin, feeling his outrage as if it was my own. He hadn't said a word, but his silence spoke volumes. He was livid.

"Why?" The question was barely more than a low growl. His eyes locked on her, jaw clenched tight.

"What he said," Asher added.

The vampire seemed content to let us drive the conversation for now, but he was radiating anger as well. We were just one big group of pissed off alpha males.

She fidgeted with the hem of her shirt. "I needed to hide my scent. It was the only way I could stay hidden and ensure my family was safe. So I summoned him, and we made a bargain. I ended things, but then Ben got taken, and we didn't have a way of getting him out. I just couldn't let him rot away in that cell—"

"I told you I was going to get him out," Asher interrupted, looking devastated that she hadn't believed in him enough to just wait.

"Getting him out and clearing his name are two different things."

"Wh-what did it c-cost you?"

"This time? My body. Once a month." She stared straight into my eyes as she spoke. No wavering, no guilt in her gaze. "And I'd do it again if it meant freeing you."

"'This time' means there was a price before. Demons don't do anything for free, princess. What did you give up when you made your first deal?" Asher crossed the short distance between them and tilted her chin up so she couldn't look away. "What did you give him?"

"My virginity . . ."

Gavin's sharp inhale was the only sound in the room as she trailed off.

"And," I prompted when she didn't seem inclined to say anything else.

"My blood."

"And."

"My womb."

The way she said it, as quickly and with as few words as possible, sent pain lancing my chest. She might pretend she hadn't lost anything, but now that she'd found us, things had changed.

Asher let out a low whistle. "That's a steep price."

"One that doesn't seem worth it now that the whole reason I'd called him is standing in front of me, ready to bring my family down."

Gavin sneered. "Didn't prevent you from going back for seconds. And I was already in town when that happened, so don't pretend that was your only excuse."

She tilted her chin up. "My goal was different the second time."

"Or you got a taste for his cock. We all know it's easy for a whore to spread her legs."

"Call her that one more time, and you won't have a tongue to wag when I'm through with you," Remi snapped, his voice cold and deadly.

Gavin shook his head and started for the door.

"Where are you going?" Rosie asked, eyes wide.

"To get you out of this bloody mess you've landed yourself in."

She watched him leave with a telling expression of longing. She wanted him too. Even if she was running from his family, Gavin Donoghue was important to her. I'd seen that same look in her eyes when she'd let her gaze trail after Remi.

Fuck.

First the hacker. Now a vampire *and* a demon. I had to get out of here and get my head on straight. I didn't know where to begin processing the day's revelations, but my wolf wasn't going to let me think clearly with her in the same room.

Asher blew out a heavy breath. "Fuck. This is . . . a lot, princess."

"What he's trying to say, baby girl, is we're pack. You don't get to make these kinds of decisions without us anymore. Your deal affects all of us. We should have at least been part of the conversation, especially if you're going to be sleeping with the guy."

"I didn't sleep with him this time."

Remi's lips twitched. "You know what I mean. We know sharing is caring, but we also want to know who we're sharing you with."

I knew who it was. A fucking demon who took advantage of her in a vulnerable state. Why couldn't she see that? Why did she think my freedom was more important than her safety?

My wolf was on edge, ready to tear something or someone to pieces. Christ. I had to get out of this room. I made for the door, knowing the routine of working behind the bar would keep me out of trouble while my mind sorted through my tangled thoughts. Not a snowball's chance in hell I'd let my wolf out for a solo run. I'd already been accused of murder once. I wasn't going through that again.

"You're leaving too?" she asked, voice pitched high with worry.

"I n-need some time to p-process all of th-this, sugar."

A small wrinkle built between her brows as she fought the urge to argue. "Ben, please don't shut me out."

"I'm n-not. But I can't l-look at you w-without thinking about y-you with h-him. I n-need time." I sent a pleading look to my brother. "T-take her h-home. I'll h-handle sh-shit h-h-here." God, I could hardly get the words out.

Remi nodded. "You got it." Then he slid his arm around Rosie's waist and gave her a comforting squeeze. "C'mon, baby girl. Let's give Benji some space."

SIXTEEN

GAVIN

"A bloody demon," I grumbled as I dragged a hand through my hair and paced the sanctuary of the desecrated church where I'd taken up residence.

I punched Lilith's contact in my phone and listened to the series of rings with a low snarl. My calls never went unanswered. I was a fucking duke; I didn't wait for anything.

When her recorded greeting kicked in for the second time, I nearly crushed the bloody device in my hand.

"You've reached the voicemail for your very own fairy sex mother. Unfortunately, I'm tied up . . . or rather, have someone tied up at the moment. Leave me a message, and I'll call you back—if you're a good little poppet."

My eye twitched. "Lilith, you conniving little bitch. Answer this message or so help me, you will know the taste of my wrath, and it will not be pleasant. Not even for you. I am not a patient man, and this will not stand." I stared at my phone before adding one final detail. "This is Gavin, by the way."

Slamming the slim device on the dust-covered altar, I

resumed my pacing, my agitation ratcheting up with every passing minute. I needed my wife extricated from this deal as soon as possible. Lilith was the only one who would know how to go about breaking it.

"Succubi, they can't be trusted. Useless creatures. No wonder there are so few left in existence. All they do is fuck and feed. People think vampires are bad, but these sorry excuses for demons are—"

My phone rang, and I made a mad dash down the aisle to answer.

"Lilith."

"Your royal dukeness. My deepest apologies. I seem to have summoned your—what was it you said? Wrath."

"Yes, well, all is forgiven now that we can finally discuss the matter for which I—"

"Lord, that's a mouthful. What is it you need, Gavin dearest? I'm quite busy, believe it or not."

"I need to break a demon's bargain."

A little noise of interest washed over the line. "Well, well, dukie-poo, that is quite a leap from what I was expecting."

Ignoring her offensive bastardization of my title, I pressed on. "I'm not the one who made the deal. I would never be so stupid as to lower myself to become beholden to a demon."

She made a tsking sound. "Careful, Duke. You wouldn't want to offend the very creature you're soliciting help from, would you?"

"You're barely a demon."

"Sweetheart, I am *the* demon."

"Can you help me or not?"

"This doesn't, by chance, have something to do with your erstwhile Roslyn, does it?"

"It does."

"Ah, that explains so much. Well . . . deals are complicated matters. Do you know what manner of demon she entered into a bargain with?"

"No."

"What do you know?"

"She made a deal."

There was a beat of silence that felt like suppressed laughter. I shifted as unfamiliar embarrassment crept up the back of my neck. People did not laugh at me.

"Yes, darling, I got that. What did she give up?"

I shared everything Roslyn had told us in the office; all the while, Lilith's hums grew more intrigued.

"Well?" I asked, impatience coloring the word.

"Well, it would seem your little wife has gotten herself in quite the pickle."

"You're referring to a deal with a demon as a *pickle*?"

"I'm sorry, should I have called it a gherkin? It seems like a rather big pickle if you ask me. Much larger than a gherkin."

"Lilith . . ."

"I can practically taste your frustration from here."

I sighed, ready to demand she open a portal and bring me to *Iniquity*. If anyone could, it would be her.

"Oh, all right, let me think. I'd wager you could kill the demon. That would break the agreement. It would also undo any protection he was providing, so doing so would put your precious petal at risk, but that's the quickest way to nullify a bargain."

"Perfect. How do I find him?"

"Have Rosie summon him, I suppose. But demons aren't as easy to kill as you might think. The price he extracted sounds like he's been around for a while. Could even be a first tier."

"First tier?"

"The strongest of us. All but immortal."

"Of course he bloody would be."

"From what you've said, it sounds like she's quite enjoying her time with him, Gavin. She might not want to be freed from his clutches."

I gritted my teeth at that. She couldn't remain chained to a filthy demon for her entire life. I wouldn't allow it.

"Too damn bad."

"Hmm . . . perhaps there are other ways around it. Where did you say you were?"

"A nothing town in Alaska called Aurora Springs. Why?"

"Weellll . . . demons leave a special mark only visible to others of their kind. A brand of sorts to warn off any from trespassing on their territory. If I see it, I'd know exactly who your wife is dealing with."

"Could you undo it?"

"Me? But of course, poppet. I am the original demon. There's none stronger than me. My mark would overwrite all others."

"What price would you demand for this *service*?"

She hummed. "Now that is the question, isn't it? I suppose it depends on whose *wrath* I'd be facing. My brethren can be such pests. I'd have to make it worth my time, and I have some loose ends to deal with before I can jet off, but we can discuss the particulars when I arrive."

"When you . . . Lilith—"

"Ciao, darling. See you soon."

"Li—" but the call was over before I could finish warning her off. Another demon was not what this town needed. Or did they? Perhaps she could distract them from me, and I could feed in peace.

My fangs throbbed in my gums at the thought of feeding. Darla would come if I called. She'd let me take from her. But I had to be careful with her. If she ended up dead and drained, she'd be of no use to me.

No. Tonight, I'd hunt the wild game of this nowhere town. And then I'd continue unraveling my bride from the mess she'd made of our life.

SEVENTEEN

Rosie radiated discomfort as she busied herself folding the laundry bin of towels I'd left on the couch this morning.

She'd barely spoken a word since we'd gotten home, not that I blamed her. After the bombshells that were dropped, I wasn't exactly feeling like Shakespeare myself. It didn't help that my wolf was pacing restlessly inside me.

I wouldn't be that guy, though. The one who heaped more on her. God knew we all made choices we wished we could take back sooner or later. I just worried this demon deal would end up getting her killed—for real.

No. Remi, don't think about shit like that. You're only inviting it to happen. Manifesting . . . or whatever the hell those new age people called it.

"You, uh, wanna talk about it?" I asked when she punched a cushion she fluffed a little harder than necessary.

"And hurt you more than I have already? No, thank you."

"It only hurts because it was a secret." She opened her

mouth, but I spoke over her, already knowing what she was going to say. "I know *why* it had to be a secret. Trust me, I get it. But if this is going to work between us all, we need to know who *we* are. Who do you want? Which of us are yours?" I sat next to her and slipped my hand into hers. "You can have anything. I'll give you every single thing you want, but I need to know who else gets to give it to you too."

Her expression went soft, her eyes misting with tears. "Remi . . ." She threw her arms around my neck and held me tight. "I don't deserve you."

"That's debatable. Fate seems to think otherwise."

She laughed softly in my arms, and it felt damn good to hold her . . . so I did just that, not pushing for an answer, though I was desperate for it.

Something in me eased as her scent washed over me, my wolf nuzzling her neck just as much as I was. I pressed my lips to the soft skin there, overwhelmed with the need to make my mate happy and help her see she could be herself around me.

"I'm sorry, Remi. I ruined everything."

"You haven't. I promise."

"I can't choose."

"You don't have to."

"No, you don't get it. I went to Pan because I was desperate to save Ben. I would have done anything to help him. Same as I would for any of you. But I *wanted* to let Pan touch me. Even without the deal. What is wrong with me?"

"Nothing is wrong with you. You're polyamorous. So am I. So is Asher. But Ben isn't, and I'm willing to bet your vampire isn't either. It's harder for them to understand the pull because they aren't wired the same way as us. But that doesn't make it wrong. In fact, if you think about it, this is actually good news."

"How is any of this *good news*?"

"Everything is out in the open now, which means we can deal with it and move on. *Together*. We just need to know *who* we're moving on with."

She looked so lost. "But isn't it cheating?"

"Not as long as it's talked about and consensual among all partners."

"So we what, have a meeting when I find someone I feel drawn to and put it up for a vote?"

I laughed. "Maybe? I think it's more an open understanding that before things get serious with someone new, you talk to us about it so everyone gets to evaluate where they're at and if they're comfortable adding them into the mix. We're a pack. A family. We need to feel safe above everything else. Talking through this shit is how we feel safe and make this work." I nudged her with my shoulder. "I'm pretty sure you're the one who told me that."

Sitting back, she sighed, "You're right."

But she still looked so conflicted, and all I wanted to do was make this easier for her. Help her understand there was no reason for her to be at war with herself. She just needed to be honest about what she wanted. And that much, at least, I could help her with.

Hey, look at me. When did I turn into the mature twin?

"Do you want Gavin, baby girl?"

"Yes." Her voice was small and apologetic.

"So why did you run from him?"

"I didn't run from *him*. I ran from his mother and father and their plans for me and my blood. The life they had designed for me wasn't something I wanted to live."

"Your blood?"

"My mother has the blood of the sun. She passed it on to my brothers and me."

I had heard the stories of the Blackthorne vampires and their magic cure for the plague killing their kind. Nodding my understanding, I waited for her to continue.

"The Donoghues wanted to control my body and use my bloodline to make themselves more powerful."

My stomach churned. "Is that why you gave your womb to the demon? Because they wanted to turn you into a broodmare?"

Her gaze dropped to where our thighs touched. "It was one of the only ways to keep my family safe. If the possibility of having a child was permanently gone, they couldn't use me, even if they managed to find me."

I took her hand in mine, squeezing tight. "That had to be an impossible choice. You're pretty brave, Roslyn Blackthorne."

She sniffed, a tear falling down her cheek. "I think that's the first time anyone's said that about me."

"Then they didn't see you."

After a moment, she lifted her gaze to mine again, moisture filling those eyes I dreamed about. "I know how you and your brother feel about vampires. Gavin's going to be a problem for us, isn't he?"

"I'm not going to lie. We hate that pretentious asshat. It's going to be hard to change a lifetime's worth of bias, especially with him. But for you, we'll try."

"How is it you know him, exactly?"

Fuck. Rosie wasn't the only one with secrets, and I was magically bound not to share this one. "It has to do with that event we went to. I'm not allowed to discuss it because magic, but he was there."

The admission, or lack thereof, sat between us as she

absorbed the information. But she seemed to accept the limitations the spell put on me.

"And what about me? Technically I'm the child of a vampire. I just never turned."

I cupped her cheek. "As far as we're concerned, you're not a vampire unless you've got a pair of fangs hidden in that pretty mouth of yours."

"Funny. Asher implied the same thing the first time we met." She opened her mouth and showed me her teeth. "No fangs."

"Then it's a non-issue. It'd be different if you were a vamp. I don't think Ben would ever be able to get over it."

She shivered. "Then I guess it's a good thing I'll never turn."

I tucked some of her hair behind her ear. "So . . . Gavin is the drunk uncle of the family. The one no one likes but we tolerate. What about the demon? Is he yours too?"

Worrying her bottom lip with her teeth, she sat with that a moment but finally said, "Yes. I think he is. He gets me once a month. Those are the terms of our deal, but I don't *not* want to go. But it's not the same with him. I want him. It's just sex. I don't love him. "

The word *yet* floated on the tip of my tongue. Rosie wasn't one for casual sex. That was clear from the way she connected with all of us. This demon meant more to her than she was allowing herself to accept. She'd given him her virginity, and you never forgot your first. That alone would leave a mark she wouldn't easily get over.

"Well . . . when do we get to meet him?" I asked, trying to picture what he'd look like. The only demons I knew were lust demons, which would explain why she'd be into the idea of fucking one. I really hoped he wasn't one of the other kind, with the fur and fangs and monster parts.

Her eyes went wide. "Never."

"Never? How can he be part of this if he's not . . . part of this?"

"He'll kill you. He's not really into . . . group events."

I chuckled. "Well, that's one less body I need to maneuver around, I guess."

She laughed with me. "Are you really okay with this? I know Asher was easy for you because of your relationship. But the others?"

"It's not like I'm a stranger to group activities." We laughed at my euphemism. "But the mate part is different. My wolf isn't inclined to share, but at the end of the day, all I need is to know I'm yours." My eyes darted to her neck, the desire to mark and claim her nearly more than I could stand.

"You are, Remi. You're mine, and you have been since I first met you."

"I . . ." Fuck, I had to swallow down the lump in my throat. "Rosie, I love you. I'm a fucking asshole for not saying it when you told me, but I was too caught up in how you saying those words made me feel."

Another tear slipped down her cheek. "I know, Remi. You didn't have to say it. I felt it."

Leaning in, I closed the distance between us and feathered my lips over hers. I couldn't help myself. I murmured the words again as I kissed her. "I love you."

Fuck, I'd never told anyone that before. Not until her. I never wanted to stop saying it.

The front door opened, breaking us apart as Ben stood there, eyes blazing a brilliant blue, brows pulled down low. I locked gazes with him, my wolf connecting with his, and I knew exactly what we both needed. Our wolves spoke in unison in my head.

Mate her.

Mark her.

Make her ours.

Ben tore his shirt from his body and tossed it to the floor, focusing on our mate as she stood.

"Ben," she whispered.

His answer was one word, growled low, offering no room for argument.

"Present."

EIGHTEEN

ROSIE

en's voice, combined with that electric gaze, had shivers racing across my entire body. He was here to take what was his. And that . . . was me.

"I . . . I don't know how . . ."

I tripped over my words, unsure exactly how a wolf would present for her mate. Did he want my arse in the air for him the same way Pan had? The last time Ben said the word, I'd been so caught up in a haze of arousal I couldn't remember what I'd done or why. So I did the only thing I could think of. I walked across the room, removing my clothes as I went, until I stood naked before him. Then, holding his gaze, my heart thundering in my ears, I dropped to my knees at his feet.

"Fuck," Remi breathed.

"W-what are y-you doing?" Ben asked, his voice tight and posture tense.

"She's showing you her throat, brother. Can't you see? She wants you to take her, but she's not a wolf."

Remi's explanation sent pleasure coiling low in my

belly. He understood me. It was just another bit of proof we were meant to be together.

"If . . . if there's something special you need me to do, just tell me and I'll do it." I licked my lips, my voice suddenly husky. "I'm very good at following directions."

Ben ran his hand over my head, his expression softening but not quite losing its feral intensity. "Fuck, sugar."

"You can make me cry if you need to."

The way he sucked in a breath told me I'd said something wrong. That I'd scared him. I wasn't good at this. I hadn't had enough practice, but I didn't know any other way to act around an alpha male whose entire being was straining with the need to own me.

"I didn't understand it until just now," Remi said softly, moving to stand behind me to the right. He was just a shadowy figure in my periphery, but he was there, lending me his strength and bridging the gap between what I knew and what Ben needed. "She's a submissive. Gavin is her Dom."

"I'm n-not a Dom," Ben protested immediately.

"I . . . are you sure?" I asked. He exuded such powerful, dominant energy. How could he be anything but?

"I'd n-never hurt you." Conflicted emotions flickered in Ben's blue gaze.

"But . . . you're so . . ."

"Can't you tell? He just wants to take care of you, baby girl." Remi leaned down and brushed his lips over my ear. "He's a Daddy."

I gasped, heat pooling between my legs, but not from the word as much as the rasp of his voice in my ear and the wash of his breath over my skin. "What's the difference?"

"He's dominant, all right, but he doesn't need to hurt you to get off. He wants to give you everything you need. To take care of his girl. Teach you new things. Support you in everything you do. Make you happy. Praise you."

I swallowed. That sounded amazing, and like everything he'd been for me up to this point. My teacher. My rock. My lover. But . . .

"What if I need him to hurt me sometimes? Punish me?"

My question was for Remi, but my eyes were locked on Ben and the play of emotions rushing across his face.

"As l-long as I can kiss away y-your tears after, I can give y-you what you need. I *will* give you everything you n-need."

That same curl of want Gavin caused inside me came to life. The dark parts of me that craved giving over control and needed to follow orders, to please my mate, to make him proud to call me his.

"Then give me your mark. Make it hurt, but kiss it better after." I leaned my head back against Remi's warm thighs. "You too, Remi. I need you both to make me yours."

He tugged my hair, tipping my head back until we were staring at each other. "We might be twins, and I have no issue leaving my handprint on your ass, but I'm not a Daddy."

"I only need one."

He grinned at me. "Good girl."

"Isn't that m-my line?" Ben threaded his fingers in my hair where Remi wasn't gripping the strands.

"I don't hear you saying it. You wanna start waxing poetic? Be my fucking guest, but I can smell how much she wants us, and you're over here wasting time when she's asking us to take what our wolves have been ravenous for."

A twinge of pleasure blossomed between my thighs. I was wet. Soaked, if I was being honest. Positively dripping for these two handsome shifters. I'd had each of them separately, but I could not get the image out of my mind of what it might be like if they both took me together.

It felt right that this moment would be shared between the three of us. Not like what Remi and I had with Asher, but something just as life-altering. These two men came into the world together, and they'd claim the one woman whose soul spoke to theirs . . . together.

"Claim me. Both of you. Now."

"Are you s-sure she's submissive?" Ben teased. "She sure is b-bossy."

"Please?" I added, making them both laugh softly.

"G-get up," Ben demanded.

God, yes. I didn't need him to tell me twice. His command, filled with the dominance Remi had brought to the forefront, ricocheted through me, setting my world on fire. As soon as I was standing, my Alpha wolf slipped his hand around my waist and pulled me flush against his hard body.

Our chests rose and fell in time. It felt like our breathing was in sync. Remi moved in close, sandwiching me between them.

"You can't fuck her with your pants on, Bentley. Have I taught you nothing? All those pornos . . . wasted."

Ben glared at his brother over my head. "I know how to f-fuck my woman."

"Prove it."

Ben's lips came down on mine, hungry and hot, desperate in a way I hadn't expected. He was controlling the kiss, yes, but he was as much a slave to it as I was. I took his head in my hands, clinging to him as my tongue met his in a carnal dance. The pained groan he let out vibrated straight to my core.

Not to be outdone, Remi trailed kisses along the back of my neck, nipping in protest when Ben and I still hadn't come up for air. "Don't take her all for yourself. She wants me too."

Remi's large palms skated over my bare torso, stopping as he cupped both of my breasts, holding me as his teeth gently pressed into the tender flesh at the base of my neck.

"God, you're so fucking perfect. Isn't she perfect, Ben?"

"Sh-shut up."

A low growl slipped into Remi's voice. "Tell her what she deserves to hear, Bentley. Or so help me, I will turn this car around, and we will do this without you."

"Do you ever s-stop talking?"

"Not in close to thirty years. Unless a dick's in my mouth. And even then I like to show my appreciation."

"Or me," I added, recalling how vocal he'd been in his enjoyment while going down on me as well.

"Mmm," he agreed. "And our mate's pretty pink cunt. That's a favorite for sure."

"Jesus."

I didn't give two figs what they were on about; I just wanted them touching me. This was my fantasy come to life. Handsome twins worshipping me? Yes, please.

"How are we meant to do this?" I asked, dragging my nails down Ben's back and relishing the ragged moan that left him in response.

"I n-need to be inside you, sugar."

"Me too."

"At the same time?" I asked, my voice pitched high, but not with fear. The mere suggestion set fireworks off inside me.

"Would you like that, baby girl?"

I licked my lips. "Let it never be said that Roslyn Blackthorne backed away from a challenge."

His hand moved down my belly to cup my sex. "Shit. You're already dripping."

"For you." My gaze flicked to Ben. "Both of you."

The way Ben's eyes flared a vibrant electric blue had my breath hitching. His wolf was on the edge of taking control. I cupped his face between my palms and stared into his fathomless gaze. "It's okay, Ben. I want you to do it. Please . . . Daddy?"

His reaction was visceral, a full-body tremor working its way through him. "Pick her up," he snarled, hands going for the waistband of his jeans as he tugged them off.

Remi wrapped his hands around my waist and hoisted me up. By the time Ben's pants were off, he was back reaching for me. I wrapped my legs around his waist, and we moaned in unison as his velvet length connected with my soaked center.

I could hear Remi undressing, but my focus was fixed on Ben as he nudged the crown of his thick shaft so it brushed over my swollen bundle of nerves.

"Please . . . more . . . I need you."

Ben's fingers dug into the backs of my thighs as he notched himself at my entrance and pressed inside. "You'll fucking have me, sugar. W-whenever you want."

He slid into me in one perfect thrust, robbing me of breath and blinding me with pleasure. He felt so bloody good. Filling me until I could think of nothing but him.

But then Remi parted the globes of my arse with his hands, and his talented tongue was right there, circling the sensitive pucker and making me whimper as he prepared me for his invasion.

"Oh, God," I moaned, unable to speak beyond the torrent of sensation the Mercers were setting off inside me.

"That's right, sugar. Let us take y-you."

My thighs clenched around Ben's hips as he slowly rocked back and forth. Remi's tongue stopped teasing me, and I let out a cry of protest, but he simply chuckled and released me. "Be right back, baby girl. I can't do this without a few necessary things. You'll thank me later."

Ben adjusted his hold so he was supporting me with one arm, gripping my face with the other. "I want y-you to come before he g-gets back. I'm going to h-hold you, and you're going to bear d-down on me, gripping me the same w-way you do when you come."

"Like this?" I asked, flexing my inner muscles.

His response was a grunt of pleasure. "J-just like that." I rolled my hips, but he stopped me. "D-don't move . . . God . . . don't move."

Sensing how desperately he was trying not to find his release, I stilled my movements, instead clenching my walls again, eliciting the same response as before.

"Again," he rasped.

I continued to pulse my muscles around his shaft, the pressure of his erection against my sensitive flesh not as intense as when he'd thrust so hard and deep my toes curled, but no less effective. With each squeeze around him, a build began inside me, the promise of perfect bliss.

Arms around his shoulders, forehead pressed to his, I stared into his eyes as I resisted the urge to ride his erection and chase the easy climax I could feel hovering nearby.

I tilted my hips forward, the pressure on my tender button of sensation as I did so bringing me closer to orgasm than I could control. Tingles raced through me, the goal of blinding euphoria within reach. It wasn't long before we were both moaning.

"Keep g-going. Get yourself off. U-use me." Another low groan. "So fucking g-good."

"Ben, I'm going to—"

"Come for me."

My orgasm slammed into me, making his knees nearly buckle as I clamped down around his thick length and moaned his name. This was unlike any other release I'd experienced. Almost painful, but exactly what I needed.

"Christ, you're so damn beautiful when you come," Remi said, his hands moving over my spine as he rejoined us. "You ready for me?"

"She's dripping d-down my b-balls. She's f-fucking ready."

"Yes. So ready," I agreed.

The sound of a cap clicking open registered faintly as Remi brought his mouth to my ear. "Good, because I can't wait to sink my cock into your tight little ass as I give you my mark."

His breath, minty fresh and delicious, fanned over my face. On instinct, I turned my head so I could kiss him, letting him know I appreciated his attention to my body in all ways. He kissed me back, cupping my cheek with one hand while sliding the lubed fingers of his other along my seam and then pressing up and into me. I instinctively clenched around the intrusion, which made Ben moan.

"Jesus, f-fuck."

Remi pulled away just far enough to whisper against my lips, "It's going to be a tight fit, baby girl."

"You already know I like when it hurts."

"Goddamn, you're perfect."

I was trembling as the blunt head of his erection

pressed into my tight hole, and I shuddered harder as he carefully filled me while Ben held still. I'd never been so surrounded by strong male bodies as they took me. This was different from Pan using his tail. Different from my night with Asher and Remi. The Mercer twins were touching every part of me, and I bloody loved it.

With every inch, it felt like Remi tapped into a new set of nerve endings within me. I was hot and cold. My skin was too tight for my body, but not nearly containing me. I felt alive in a way I didn't know was possible. For a second, I wasn't even sure of my name. All I knew was the feel of my mates inside me, making us one.

"I need to f-fucking mark you, sugar. God. I can't w-wait anymore."

Ben's voice was rough with need, and I couldn't deny him. "Yes. Do it. Mark me."

Remi let out a sharp grunt, then whispered, "What do we do, Ben? How?"

"Th-there's a place on her neck. You p-probably seek it out. Are dr-drawn to it." Ben was panting, beads of sweat dotting his forehead as he struggled against his primal desire.

Remi's lips feathered over the exact place he always nuzzled me. "I know what you mean."

"That's the spot. Let y-your wolf take over. H-he'll see you through."

I felt Remi nod as Ben took up his place on my other side, the mirror image of where his twin's lips were.

Rocking on them both, I came again, out of nowhere, a panicked sound leaving me. Then they both bit down, low rumbling snarls leaving them as they did. The pain was exquisite as it radiated from each side of my neck, the intense sensation sending me over the edge once more, in what seemed like a never-ending wave of pleasure.

Their shafts pulsed in time inside me as they found their own releases, and it was there our connection was forged. The bond I never thought I'd have, shared with two men. It was beautiful, overwhelming, and everything I needed.

The all-consuming magic binding us together was more than my human soul could take. My vision blurred, then darkened as I broke. The last thing I heard were the low growls of my mates.

"Mine."

NINETEEN

The way they writhed together as the three of them found release had my breaths coming in shallow drags. Rosie crushed between them, Ben's face buried in her neck, Remi's powerful back muscles rippling as he shuddered against her . . . fuck. I was so hard it hurt. But I knew I'd witnessed something magical as I watched them like the creep I was from my darkened fortress of solitude.

You're keeping an eye out for the douchecanoe Bridgerton knockoff. Who else is going to look after them?

It might have started as innocent surveillance, but as soon as clothes started coming off, I couldn't look away. It was so easy to picture myself in the moment with them, their fourth. Remi beneath me while he took Rosie's tight little ass and Ben claimed her cunt. That should have terrified me. I'd never been able to picture myself as part of the whole happy family situation, but with them—because of *her*—I could.

You can never give her what they give her.

Any of them.

Well, nothing like crippling self-doubt to kill your boner. But seeing them mark her and give her something that was physically impossible for me to replicate really drove the point home. They were supernaturals. I was a human. What the hell did she see in me? Nothing. All I was good for was helping her perpetuate a lie.

I didn't realize I'd been absentmindedly rubbing at the marks on my wrist and forearm until they started to ache. That ache began to tingle, then burn like the sting of a tattoo needle being dragged across my skin.

"Jesus, fuck." I glanced down, and my gut churned as the goddamned cursed mark crept up my arm while I watched.

What would happen when the constellation, now past my elbow, got to my shoulder? My heart? I was a ticking bomb.

Glancing at the screen again, my gaze ran across each monitor until I found the three of them again. This time, not in the living room, but all cuddled together in Ben's gigantic bed. He'd be so pissed if he knew I had a camera in there. Knowing they were all safe and happy together helped me come to terms with the fact that I'd have to do one of two things in the end. Break this curse, or leave.

Who knew how much time was left on this countdown before I blew? Who would be there when it happened? *What* would happen? I couldn't take that risk. There was no way in hell I'd be the one to destroy what they'd found with each other. I'd leave before letting that happen. It would kill me, but I wasn't living through this anyway, so I might as well give them a fighting chance at the ever elusive happily ever after.

The time for ignoring what was happening was over. I couldn't keep putting a Band-aid on a gushing wound and hope somehow the bleeding would stop. There was only one person I could think of who might know the answer to any of my questions.

It was time to call the witch.

Grabbing one of the burners on the desk, I scrolled for the name which had become synonymous with salvation.

Belladonna.

She answered on the first ring.

"Asher Henry, you fucking *Chad*. This better be good. I was in the middle of dessert." A soft murmur in the background told me exactly who she'd been enjoying.

My lips twitched. The witch had the biggest balls of us all.

"I'm glad one of us is."

The amusement bled from her voice. "What's wrong?"

I didn't see the point of beating around the bush. We both knew I wasn't the guy who called for a casual chitchat.

"It's growing."

"How far?"

"Past my elbow."

"Fuck a duck."

"Might be weird. I've sort of got a thing going with a puffin."

"What?"

"Nothing. Sorry. But hard pass on the duck."

"I forget sometimes what a dork you are. Must be all that time alone. Are you in any pain? Blacking out?"

"Only when I drink too much, but that's normal."

"Asher, that is *not* normal. But it's a different issue."

My arm burned as I flexed my hand. "The pain thing, that's new. It feels like a sunburn. My skin's all hot and tight, but not in the sexy way, ya know?"

"Uh . . . is that a penis thing?"

"No, I just meant . . . never mind." I blew out a heavy breath. "Moira, I'm freaking the fuck out. I don't want to die."

"I know, Asher. We're not going to let that happen. Let me do some research, okay? There's no reason the curse should be able to reactivate like this, but we knew there was always a chance the spell binding it was temporary. If there are any new developments, call me immediately. Otherwise I'll be in touch. Okay?"

I swallowed past the ball of anxiety in my throat. It was choking me, making every breath a struggle.

"Asher?"

Finally working up the courage to speak and risk my voice breaking, I said, "Okay. Thanks, Belladonna."

"We'll figure this out. I promise."

"I know. You wouldn't want me to come back and haunt you."

She snickered. "As if my ghost army would let you. Besides, I'd have Daddy G exorcize you so fast you'd end up in that waiting room of sorry sacks in Beetlejuice."

"Moira, what the fuck are you talking about?"

"You know, with the flat guy and the dude with the—"

"Ohhh, and that beauty pageant chick with the really great—"

"That would be the part you remember."

I snickered. "Like you didn't."

"Hey, I never said it wasn't an extremely educational moment for me." She giggled at whatever her girl said in the background. "Gotta go, Asher. Talk soon."

The line went dead, and I sat back in my chair, staring at the ceiling and hating that I was stuck here with no answers. I needed them. It was part of what made me tick, being the guy with all the solutions to every fucking puzzle. Except my own.

Until now, there was only one other riddle I couldn't solve. The one surrounding my birth. It didn't take Freud to figure out little Asher had mommy and daddy issues. But that's what happens when you're left on the doorstep of a convent, I guess.

No matter how much I dug, I never got anywhere. It was like they never existed. There was no record of them, or me for that matter, before I entered the system.

They didn't want to be found. Didn't want to face the responsibility of what they'd made together. I should consider myself lucky they left me, really. Wouldn't it have been worse to be raised by people who hated me?

I sighed, letting the phone drop into my lap. No orgasm *and* no answers. The night had really gone to the shitter.

Palming my crotch, I let my thoughts drift to Rosie and Remi. It didn't take long before that hard-on I'd had earlier came back with a vengeance.

Flicking the monitors back on, my smile stretched as I took in the figures moving together on the big screen.

"Ah, looks like I made it just in time for round two." At least I'd end the night with one of the two things I wanted. "Orgasm, it is."

TWENTY

A faint mist hovered over the ground in the clearing behind the house. Past the trees at the base of the hill, our favorite lake glittered in the morning light as the sun rose, casting soft golden rays along the water. I loved this place. It was why, even after the horrors we endured, Remi and I stayed.

I was hoping Rosie loved it too. I wanted her to feel at home here, with us. It was part of the reason I'd gotten up at the asscrack of dawn to hunt down supplies for this morning's adventure. After a night spent rolling around in bed—and in her—I knew we'd all need a breather.

Once the final target was in place, I filled a quiver with fresh arrows and made sure the bow was ready to use. I couldn't wait to see her in action. Rosie had lost a lot of herself in order to start a new life, but I wanted to give her ways to find those pieces. We could put them back together as a unit.

Archery course set up, I made my way back to the house, walking into the welcome scent of fresh coffee and the sound of sizzling bacon. Remi was at the stove, finishing breakfast.

"You were up early," he commented without turning to face me.

"I h-had an errand to r-run."

"Such a grown-up."

"S-says the guy w-wearing an apron."

"Any smart man knows not to let bacon grease anywhere near his bits."

Rosie joined us then, looking absolutely fucking radiant as she padded over to me, soft and sleepy. "I woke up, and everyone was gone."

Without a second thought, I pulled her into my embrace, loving the way my chest loosened the instant I had her in my arms. She nestled into me, chin on my pec as she looked up and blinked slowly, still waking up. Fuck, I loved her. I kissed her forehead, a smile on my lips as I did.

"Mornin', sugar."

"Morning, handsome." She sort of melted into me then, her eyes fluttering closed as we just stood there basking in the feel of being with one another while Remi plated up our food.

There was a peace to it. A sense of *rightness* I couldn't remember ever feeling before. I guess that made sense. I'd finally found my missing piece. And she hers. Well, a couple of them, I suppose. Honestly, I was pretty surprised at how much it didn't bother me to know there were more of us. But after last night, that restless feeling that had been plaguing me was gone. She wore my mark and was part of my pack. She was mine just as much as they were hers.

Remi came over to us, two coffee cups in hand. He waved the brew under her nose. "Here you go, sleepyhead."

"Mmm, thank you."

"She's really fucking cute in the mornings, isn't she?" Remi asked me, a smirk curling his lips.

"She's a-always cute."

"And you're . . . content. That's new."

What is this? Are we going around stating the obvious? "And you're d-domesticated."

"And here, we observe the domesticated Alaskan wolf in his natural habitat," Rosie murmured against my chest.

We all laughed. Pressing another kiss to the top of her head, I gave her a tight squeeze. "L-let's eat. I've got a s-surprise for you."

Her eyes lit up. "A surprise?"

"Yeah, sugar. N-now sit your b-butt down and eat s-so I can sh-show you."

"Okay . . . Daddy."

She whispered the last part, and arousal punched me so hard I had to breathe past the need to throw her over my shoulder and take her back to bed. The only thing stopping me was knowing she had to be sore after last night. Thus, the surprise. A way for the three of us to spend time together that didn't involve tangled up limbs.

We ate so fast that I doubted any of us really tasted the food. Which really was a shame because Remi knew his way around a kitchen. But it was worth it when the three of us stepped into the backyard and she saw the course I'd designed.

"Archery?"

"Y-you said you w-were the champ."

Remi clapped me on the shoulder. "Sometimes I think your swoon switch got stuck in the on position. How am I supposed to keep up with this?"

"It's not a competition," Rosie said, slipping her arm around his waist and resting her cheek on his shoulder.

"You say that now," he grumbled, stealing a kiss. "But I already know I'm going to have to step up my game."

"Since I can only benefit, I'm not going to stop you," she said with a grin.

"All right, sugar. Sh-show us what y-you've got."

"You first. I need to see where the bar is set."

Remi and I exchanged a look, speaking in our silent twin way to determine which of us would step up to the plate first.

Remi grabbed the bow, a smirk curling his lips as he teasingly informed her, "You should probably know I also got a blue ribbon. Anchorage County Fair '02."

"Oh, look at you."

"Yeah, if you've got a Robin Hood kink, you probably should prepare yourself with fresh panties."

"Is that a thing?" she asked, looking at me.

"Everything's a k-kink."

"Huh. Good to know. Well then, do your thing, Robin Hood, and we'll find out if it's one of mine."

Taking his time, he hit target after target, most of them making the bullseye, or at least very near it. I could do better. Then it'd be me she called Robin Hood. Remi would never live it down. I couldn't wait.

"Hmm," he muttered, clearly unhappy with his performance. "Guess I'm rusty."

Picking up another quiver filled with arrows, I took the bow and my place. Not saying a word as I took aim and fired. My shots landed in the mirror image spots to his.

"Fuck," I grunted when my last arrow kissed the outside of the bullseye. "Me too."

"All right, lads. Step aside and let an expert show you how it's done."

I handed Rosie the bow and laughed as her eyes shone

with eager anticipation. In minutes, and from one single spot, she hit the center of the bullseye on each and every target.

"Dude, she just spanked us so hard."

Didn't I know it. I was sporting a total competence boner. She wasn't just good; she was amazing. Olympic level for sure. And then, just to prove the point, she grabbed fresh arrows and sank them clean through most of Remi's and mine, splitting them in half.

"Well, slap my ass and call me Suzi," Remi whistled.

"What was that, Suzi?" Rosie asked as she brought her palm to his right buttcheek.

"Oh, do it again."

I snagged her by the wrist and pulled her close. "That w-was hot, sugar."

"Was it?"

"Yeah."

I didn't say another goddamned thing. Instead, I let my wolf do the talking, and he wanted to mount her again. I tossed her over my shoulder like she was nothing more than a sack of flour, then strode inside the house, calling to my brother, "You coming?"

TWENTY-ONE

GAVIN

My wife moved through the Mercers' cabin, picking up a shirt from the floor and pulling it over her head. It dwarfed her, falling down past her thigh and hiding her delectable curves. I resented it more for the fact it wasn't mine.

I followed her from window to window as she made her way into the kitchen and prepared herself a cup of tea. If she sensed me, she didn't indicate it. Did I want her to know I was there? To feel me instinctively and be drawn to me like I was to her?

Fuck yes, I did.

She practically glowed with pleasure and a vibrancy I had never seen in her as she came out onto the back deck and curled up on the wide swing I was sure the lumberjack had built.

She was so stunningly beautiful, I could almost ignore that she smelled of wolf and cum. I would have been content to simply watch her sip her cuppa until the moonlight highlighted a fresh mark on her neck.

No.

I was on her before she could bring her tea to her lips again, gripping her by the throat and lifting her into the air.

"What did you do?" I hissed.

Her eyes widened as the cup fell to the deck, but a flare of hunger lit in her irises at the dominance, the pain.

Her throat bobbed beneath my palm, but I didn't loosen my grip. I didn't need her words to see the truth for myself. She'd let those curs mark her. Both of them. Matching marks adorned her slender throat.

A growl slipped free. This. Would. Not. Stand.

I would not allow my wife to bear the marks of other men unless she also bore mine.

I might not have gotten there first, but I'd be damned if I didn't claim my place in her life. On her body. In her heart.

No. Fuck. I didn't care about her heart.

But I did. I fucking did. I wanted it all.

"Damn you," I snarled. "I wanted to wait for you to come back to me, but now . . . I suppose I'll simply have to escalate my plan."

"Gavin, what are you doing?"

"I'm taking you, petal. One way or the other. It's your choice whether or not you enjoy it, but. You. Are. Mine."

TWENTY-TWO

Gavin didn't give me the opportunity to retort. He simply scooped me up into his arms, and we were gone into the night. It was a trick my brothers liked to play on me, so I was familiar with the sensation of blurring to another location, but it was different when Gavin was holding me.

It was the first time since our wedding night I'd been pressed against all those lean muscles of his. My husband was strong in a way forged by his vampiric nature, all toned flesh and smooth planes. A back that could have been sculpted by one of the masters flashed through my mind unbidden, reminding me how good he'd been with his whip.

He dropped me unceremoniously less than a minute later, his eyes flashing with a hunger that had nothing to do with a vampire's need to drink blood. The intensity had me licking my lips and overly aware that the only article of clothing in my current possession was Remi's discarded shirt. I hadn't even grabbed my knickers.

"Where are we?"

"What does it look like?"

Glancing around the dark space, I fought a wave of unease as I recognized this place for what it was. "The church?"

"And here I was starting to fear for your eternal soul. Very good, Roslyn. Yes, it's a church." He wrinkled his nose in distaste as he looked around at the rafters and dust-coated pews. "Though not a very well attended one. It would seem the good folks of Aurora Springs are not a God-fearing people."

"Why would they be after what came to pass here?" I scoffed. "And for the record, at least I have a soul."

He canted his head. "You think me soulless?"

"If I didn't know better, I'd be sure of it." Only made vampires lost their souls. Those born into the world of night might possess them, but they certainly didn't worry about being damned to hell.

"And what does it say about you, *wife*, that you cuckolded your husband mere weeks after pledging your troth?"

"Pledging my troth? This isn't some historical romance, Gavin, no matter how much you love to play the depraved rake."

He smirked, but there was heat in his stare. "I don't have to play." That dark gaze dropped to my neck, his grin fading and pressing into a harsh line. "Mmm, you disappoint me, petal. I had such high hopes for us."

"So did I. Too bad your parents were plotting to breed me and then imprison me to farm my blood until our children were old enough and I outlived my usefulness. Thanks for that, by the way. Quite the wedding present."

His eyes widened and his nostrils flared, but other than those two slight movements, he showed no reaction to my words. I might say he was surprised by them, but how could that possibly be true?

"Oh, I don't know. It seems you gave me a pair of shifters and a lowly human to bring to our marriage bed. I'd say your gift to me is much worse." The way he paced up and down the aisle as he raked his hands through his hair had my breaths tight. I'd never seen him so worked up, so . . . uncoiled.

"My gift was that case you're carrying. The one you stole since I never actually gave it to you." Well, the case and my virginity. Somehow it didn't seem prudent to mention that part when he was so clearly upset about the other mates in my life. It sort of seemed like Gavin was throwing a temper tantrum. A posh and fairly well-mannered one, but a tantrum nonetheless. Someone had played with his toy without permission, and he was in a right snit about it.

"My *gift* was *you*, Roslyn. All of you. Instead you gave it away and made me think you were dead."

"You can't honestly have expected I would stay after what I learned. I may have agreed to be your wife, Gavin, but never your captive."

He blurred to me and stood before me, our bodies nearly touching, his hips eye level. I could see the outline of his hard manhood beneath his trousers. His finger pressed firmly into the soft space under my chin, tipping my head up to stare at the sharpness of his jaw. "You like to be my captive. You crave it. I know how your cunt smells when you're wet and ready for me, petal. You forget I've been there before. Made you crawl to me. Submit to me."

My lips parted, and my breath caught as my mind was taken over by the memory of our time in the library. Bugger.

Even the phantom of our past had me squirming with renewed need.

"That was true. Once. I won't deny it. I'm not a liar, unlike present company."

"Not a liar? Roslyn, dear, the men you part your thighs for didn't even know your true name until I came to collect you. Do not play coy. It doesn't suit you."

Blast. He had me there. But I couldn't let him see the truth of my feelings for him yet. Not until he agreed that my connection to the others was just as necessary. If he won this round, we'd all lose.

"Why did you bring me here, Gavin? I've already made my position clear. They've claimed me as theirs. You have nothing left."

His hand collared my throat and held me up off the pew I was perched on before I could finish my sentence. "Then I will take it back. Do not start a game you don't want to play, petal. I never lose."

God, I wanted him to take it—me—back, even though I needed my other men just as badly. But I craved his punishment even more. I wouldn't let myself ask him for it, but perhaps I could draw what I wanted from him this way. "You lost me." His upper lip curled, but before he could say anything, I added, "My lord."

He sucked in a breath. "Oh, petal. You naughty girl. If it's the Duke of Tears you're after, I'm happy to introduce you. But once he's unleashed, there's no going back. I will make you cry and relish in your sobs as I lick the tears from your cheeks while you milk my cock like the filthy whore you are. Is that what you want?"

I bit my lower lip, considering the warning in his offer. Did I want that from him right now? The same night Ben and Remi made me forever theirs?

Yes.

I did.

Because I was just as much *his,* and he was the only one who could give me this. The domination I craved. The pain I needed. I couldn't explain it before, but I understand it now. I never felt more alive than I did in the moments I was most aware of my mortality. I liked when it hurt because that was when I felt the most safe. The most cherished. Because in those moments, more than any other, I knew my men would never let anything truly bad happen to me.

I spent most of my life being caged. It was time to learn how to fly.

Instead of speaking, I dropped to my knees and bowed my head, staring at the floor in front of me. I'd done enough research to know this submissive pose was how he'd like to start.

The groan he released told me I'd been correct.

"Get up."

My focus snapped to him. "What?"

"I said, get up."

When I didn't immediately obey, he grasped me by the arm and lifted me. From the tender pressure on my skin, I knew I'd be wearing his bruises come morning.

"I am a sadist, petal. I will not give you what you want simply because you demand it like a manipulative little brat. I revel in your pain. So because it is what you want, it is the very thing I will deny you. *That* is how the game works."

"Then just let me leave."

"Oh, no." A dark chuckle filled the room. "I will still have you. I'll mark you and fuck you until you're crying for me to let you come. But believe me when I say you will only find release under my care tonight. *If* I decide you find it, that is."

I wanted to toss back some pithy dismissive comment, but all that left my lips was a wanton moan. God, no one affected me the way he did. Just a few heated words, and I was melting.

"Prove it."

His grin was savage. A feral promise bordering on violence. My heart tripped over itself in excitement.

Then he ripped my shirt up over my head and spun me around, shoving me down until I was pushed forward over a pew, the wooden panel pressing against my ribs while my hands struggled for purchase on the seat. From this angle, I was a bit off kilter, the bulk of my weight resting on my hands and my feet lifted up onto my toes. It wasn't comfortable, but it wasn't supposed to be.

The rough scrape of wood echoed through the church. Gavin must've shoved a pew out of the way, but before I could verify, his mouth trailed down the line of my back as a crack rang out. His palm connected with my bottom, but not hard enough for my taste. It was a tease. He knew what he was doing to me.

"More."

He fisted his fingers in my hair, roughly tugging back.

"No." The growl was low. Filthy and perfect.

I shivered, my body begging for him to fill me.

"I smell your desire, wife. Tell me who you belong to, and I'll ease the ache." He slid his hand between my legs, cupping my sex but not actually giving me what I wanted.

The way he held his palm over my throbbing center had me wriggling under his touch.

"Who?"

I bit back a curse. "Ben."

The hand holding my hair tugged hard, his erection pressing against my rear. "Wrong."

"Remi," I moaned.

One long finger grazed my needy clitoris before he pinched the sensitive bundle of nerves between two digits.

"Wrong."

The pain had me whimpering as my arousal flooded between my thighs.

"Asher," I whispered.

"Strike three." He removed his hand from my core and wrapped it around my mouth and nose. "Do you smell that?" he asked, his lips at my ear now. "None of them did that to you just now. I think my little wife likes to wind me up."

I licked the center of his palm, hoping to catch him off guard so he'd move it. The scent of my arousal wasn't unpleasant, but I couldn't very well talk back when he'd all but gagged me. Come to think of it, that was probably the point.

"Do you have any idea what you do to me?" he groaned, rubbing himself against my spread cheeks, his mouth still at my ear. "You have ruined my life. Every waking hour, I crave you. I despise what you make me feel. And yet I cannot stay away."

"Why?" I mumbled into his palm.

"Because you are my mate!" He gripped my hip hard as he released my mouth with his other hand. "Fated. Destined. Chosen by the goddess. And you. Left. Me."

"You betrayed me first."

He tugged on my hair again, this time bringing tears to my eyes. "No. Not me. You lay my parents' sins at my feet. I never did anything to earn your mistrust, yet you ran rather than giving me an opportunity to prove my loyalty to you."

"You left me alone on our wedding night to be with someone else."

"Daniel is gone. He was a sorry replacement for what I really wanted."

"But you refused to claim me. I was mortified."

The sound of a zipper was his only response before the blunt head of his shaft slid between my legs, running through the slickness he'd caused. God, I wanted him.

"Then I'll claim you now. But it's not going to be some pathetic, gentle moment between us. I'm not capable of that. You married a beast, Roslyn. Not a prince."

"Good. I never wanted to be a princess."

Except Asher's.

Any further thoughts were ripped from me as Gavin thrust into me in one painful push, the hand in my hair pulling me almost to standing as he filled me. My cry was garbled and strained as he slid one wandering hand up my torso and between my breasts.

"Fuck, petal. I knew you'd be tight and hot."

"Gavi—" His palm left my sternum and wrapped around my throat, cutting me off.

"I'm done listening to your lies. All I want are your moans. Or your tears. Both are more honest than your goddamned mouth. Your body will never lie to me. It recognizes its true master."

As if answering, my walls clenched around him. I was already on the verge of an orgasm. But I wasn't allowed. My legs trembled as I fought against the climax my entire being was chasing.

Still holding me by the neck, Gavin drove into me, his thrusts relentless. Brutal. Incredible. It felt as though he was imprinting the steel of his length inside me so I'd never forget it. As if I could.

My husband squeezed my throat, cutting off my air supply, then released the pressure in a slow, rhythmic pattern until my vision went spotty and my head spun. The rush of pleasure accompanying the sensation was unlike anything else.

He leaned forward, his front pressed to my back, his lips hovering over the nape of my neck. For the first time since he'd started pistoning inside me, his thrusts faltered.

"Fucking shifters," he growled, the hand on my throat clamping down hard as he pulled me up and changed our position.

He released me, large palms gripping my waist hard enough to leave a mark before he slammed me against the nearest wall and lifted me back onto his straining length. I was still so lightheaded from the breath play and shift in my position that it was all I could do to hold on.

"I'll take what's mine now, and you'll never fucking forget me." He slammed home, his head dipping to my breast, and white-hot pain lanced my nipple as sharp fangs pierced my flesh.

"Yes, my lord."

The affirmation was rasped but thick with need. Before I was fully aware of what was happening, his wrist found my lips, a freshly opened wound spilling his blood into my mouth. I latched on, greedily taking what he offered. Completing our bond. Sealing my fate.

I felt it the moment something snapped into place. A connection equal parts magic and instinct. Like he'd always been part of me. Made for me.

Mine.

The same sense of possession swept through him, the primal pleasure flooding my senses as the release I wasn't allowed to have hit me. Gavin shuddered and pulsed inside me, his hot cum filling me even as overwhelming sensation sent my eyes rolling back in my head. I knew this was him, his thoughts, his orgasm, but I felt it all as keenly as my own. It was done. We were mated.

There was no going back.

TWENTY-THREE

PAN

"NO!" I kicked the coffee table filled with vials, only to jump back and grab my toe before hopping up and down. "*Merde.*"

"Are you all right, master?" Juniper Titmouse, chief imp, hurried forward. Her bulging yellow eyes filled with concern as she fell at my feet.

I sneered down at her. The imp, only two feet tall, her skin a mottled gray and covered in nodules that only added to her hideous visage, wiggled her long, donkey-like ears. Each one was weighed down by a row of gold rings from base to tip to indicate her rank. And also a damned convenient punishment method, if I do say so myself. One of my better decisions. Thread a chain through them, and they became the perfect means of control. You could drag, hang, or tug an imp wherever you wanted them to go. Which was usually punted through the air, if I'm being perfectly honest. Which I always am. We don't keep secrets from each other, do we? Only others. (Cough cough, Roslyn, cough cough).

"Of course I'm not all-bloody-right. Do I look all right to

you?" I snarled, stalking to the plate glass window that overlooked the city and resting my fist on the pane as I sulked like some kind of Byronic hero.

"What can I do to ease your suffering?" Juniper approached me, her clawed hand reaching for my thigh in some pathetic offer of . . . sexual comfort?

"Away, imp. You don't have anything I need."

No one did. I stared morosely out the window as an ache built between my ribs. Was I dying? Had my mother given me a plague? I did a quick internal scan, checking myself for any sort of new infection.

My relief was palpable. *No.* Not yet. That's not what this was . . . but it would be soon if I didn't figure out how to fix this mess.

That was Mummy Dearest's plan, after all.

The thought of true death had my stomach clenching in fear. I'd never much considered mortality before. I'd been alive longer than the history books accurately account for, and time held very little relevance to me or my kind. Or at least it did until I was faced with the prospect of my death and found that I didn't enjoy the thought of it.

Go figure.

I quite liked my life. Even if my little pet had betrayed me and bonded with three of her mates. *Three.* They were coming out of the bleeding woodwork. It would only be a matter of time before dear old Mum showed up again and hung me out to dry for that. Unless I could cause a diversion.

Juniper's wrist snapped in my hold, the creature whimpering and making a wicked grin spread across my face.

"Hannah, Heather, Heidi, Catherine, where are you?"

"Here, master!"

"Coming, master!"

All four of them came scuttling in from where they were doing the devil knows what.

"Where's Caroline?" I asked, counting them.

Juniper bowed her head. "You banished her, my lord. Remember? Sent her to work for Heinrich."

"Ah, yes. Fine, never mind her. Send word. Gather the rest of my hellions. I've got a job for you."

"All of us?"

"Did I fucking stutter?"

"This is what we've been preparing for," Juniper whispered, excitement overshadowing her pain. "Operation Wingspan is a go."

Their squeals of delight rivaled that of a thousand tiny nails scraping over a chalkboard.

"I hate that bloody name."

"Well, bird flu was taken."

"Is it ready, master? The plague?" Catherine asked . . . or was it Hannah? I couldn't tell them apart.

"But Pestilence hasn't—" Juniper snapped her mouth shut when my narrow-eyed gaze landed on her.

"It's ready when I say it's ready," I snarled, leaning down until my nose pressed against the hooked end of hers.

"Of course. Whatever you say, master."

"Just for that, you'll go first." I pinned her with my stare before touching my palm to the crown of her nobby head and sending my power through her. With a sharp little gasp, she transformed into an inky black raven with beady eyes the same odd shade of yellow.

Reaching over to the table beside me, I took one of the vials filled with swirling aqua liquid. The cork came free with a tug of my fangs, and I spat it out and then pulled off the ring that had been storing Rosie's precious blood. Just a drop. No one need know. Not like you'll tell on me, will you?

Once my very special ingredient was added, the concoction turned a sickly green. The same shade as my mother's demon form. Wouldn't you know. It stopped sizzling, and I upended the solution over the bird's head.

Juniper squawked unhappily, though I was choosing to see it as a belated thank you. Then I turned my attention to the other four imps watching on.

"Hester, Hannah, Hilde, Catherine, fuck it, I don't know which one of you is which, but it doesn't matter. This might sting a bit."

I released a pulse of magic that filled the room, and soon, rather than five squawking imps, I had an unkindness of ravens staring at me. Dosing them with the remaining liquid in the vial, I watched as they all shuddered, their feathers ruffled.

"Off you go, my pretties. Fly far and fast. Spread sickness to every feathered creature you can find. I'm tired of waiting for permission. The Age of Pestilence has begun. And it starts with a *pan*demic."

TWENTY-FOUR

"I think I sprained my dick," I groaned, rolling over to snuggle into my mate and coming up empty. "Hey, where did the best part of the sandwich go?"

My twin, who was still asleep and snoring like a bear in hibernation, jolted when I shoved at his shoulder. "What th-the fuck, Remi?"

"We're one sweet honey and PB short of our perfect sandwich. Where's Rosie?"

Instantly alert, hair sticking up in every direction, Ben sat up and scanned the room. He gave me a horrified look. "Y-you don't th-think she's making b-breakfast, do you?"

"Oh, God, no. Not again." My stomach turned at the memory of the last time she tried to make us pancakes and we'd choked them down. "How is she even awake? I've never been this sore in my life, and I wasn't even the one getting railed." Slipping out of bed, I tugged on the pair of jeans I'd discarded last night and padded into the hallway. "Hey, baby girl, let's go out for breakf—"

I didn't finish my sentence. Instead I narrowed my eyes and focused on the things that were out of place. The cute little tea tin she'd picked out wasn't in its usual spot, the kettle sat on the counter rather than the stove, and the milk was still out, like she'd meant to return to it but never got the chance. Placing my palm on the carton, I cursed under my breath when I found it room temperature.

"Ben!"

I didn't elaborate beyond a panicked shout of his name, knowing he'd feel the urgency climbing up my throat. Wherever she'd run off to, she'd been gone for a while.

"Wh-what is it?" Ben's eyes were frantic as he came into the kitchen. "Wh-where is she?" His gaze landed on the tea shit lying around. "Sh-she takes her t-tea on the d-deck."

"Yeah, I know. Which would track, but the milk's warm."

Without a word, Ben spun on his heels and headed for the back door, his wolf barely leashed.

I closed my eyes, trying to calm my racing thoughts before they sent me spiraling. *Think, Remi. Where would she go?* The more I focused on her, the stronger this sense of *knowing* became inside me. She wasn't here. The place in my chest where I'd felt her since the moment I marked her was strangely hollow. Like something vital was missing.

I hadn't realized the bond worked like that, but I didn't doubt it either.

The back door slammed as Ben tore through the house, returning with a broken teacup in his hands. "She's g-gone."

Our eyes locked, panic morphing to anger. "Gavin," we said in unison, hints of our wolves slipping into the growled name.

"Can you feel her at all?" I asked, rubbing at my sternum with the heel of my hand. I didn't like this sensa-tion, this emptiness. It was wrong.

"N-not really. M-maybe a little. L-like an echo of her."

Yeah, that was it. A faint echo of our girl flickered in my mind.

She was alive, just not close by.

But then the feeling grew stronger. Sort of like when an object in the rearview closes in. Still far away but looming with the promise that it'll catch up.

"Come on," Ben said, not even stopping to put on his shoes as he went for the front door.

Looks like we're shifting then. I hoped the townspeople didn't mind a full frontal show if we ended up needing to be on two legs for any part of this. They should be so lucky. I really should install a tip jar outside the bar. Then they could pay us for the privilege whenever they caught the Mercer double feature picture show.

My twin nearly ripped the door from its hinges but then stopped dead, his knuckles going white on the wood. A quick glance over his shoulder confirmed why.

Rosie was strolling down the drive, fingers linked with that filthy bloodsucker's.

In broad fucking daylight.

"How?"

A snarl so deep it hurt my ears came from my twin's chest. "Sun blood. Fucker f-fed on her."

It took all of one heartbeat for me to shift as I went for the leech's throat. I leapt from the stoop and landed feet away from the two of them, hoping to God my brother would take care of our mate while I dealt with the dick who hurt her.

"Remi! Stop."

A growl built in my throat, my wolf wanting nothing more than to rip apart the threat to our mate.

Even though I knew she couldn't hear me, I projected

my thoughts to her. *Get out of the way, baby girl. This time he's not walking away.*

"Remi! I said stop it. I'm fine, look. I'm whole. Unharmed. Perfectly happy."

"See, Remington? Now that I've finally claimed her, my wife is 'perfectly happy'."

A whimper escaped. I didn't like that. I didn't want her to be happy with him. Only us. I hated him.

"I'd have her show you her mark, but . . . it's in a private location, and the bruise is still quite fresh." He smirked, and his eyes lit up with devious delight.

That was it. I launched myself at him, not caring one bit if Rosie didn't want us to fight. This motherfucker was going down. I was tired of him playing in my sandbox. No one wanted him here. Except maybe Rosie, but I'd make it up to her later. Asher could help me.

I distantly heard my brother pull Rosie back. "C-come on, sugar."

Gavin went down under the force of my forepaws to his chest. But he didn't stay down. He moved so fast I couldn't track what was going on. All I knew was I'd been on top, and in a blink, I was on the ground, his fist connecting with my muzzle. Stars bloomed in my vision as I slipped briefly into unconsciousness. When I blinked, my very naked human body was still taking a beating by the preternaturally strong vampire.

He landed two more blows before Rosie was there, trying to pry him off. I saw everything happen in slow motion and couldn't do anything to stop it. Gavin's elbow cocking back. Rosie reaching for him. Then it all came into sharp focus and time caught up to itself as he hit her, hard. Rosie's cry of pain and the scent of her blood instantly registered for all of us as she stumbled back.

Gavin was up and off me so fast I didn't even see it happen.

"Petal? Are you all right?" His gaze was intense on her, his hands cradling her face as he inspected the damage.

I spat out a mouthful of blood. "Oh, now he cares that he hurt her."

"Of course I care. She's my mate, and we're not in a scene. I don't go out of my way to abuse her."

"Only consensual abuse," Rosie quipped, though her voice was muffled.

"N-not funny," Ben growled, his eyes a blinding neon. His wolf was trying to take over, but Ben was holding him back. Barely.

Gavin pried Rosie's hand from her nose, lifting his wrist to his lips as he opened a vein. "Drink this. It'll heal you."

"I'm okay. It's just a broken nose."

"Petal," the vampire warned.

"Baby girl, if you don't let him heal you, I'm taking you to the doctor, and Ben's going to practice arts and crafts with vampire body parts in a second."

My twin let out an approving rumble.

Rosie rolled her eyes, far less amused by my description. "You three fighting is what got us into this mess in the first place. Have you learned nothing?"

"Have you?" I asked, pushing myself up and wincing as the world tilted on its axis. Jesus, that vampire hit hard. Thank fuck I healed fast.

"What do you mean?"

"You keep bringing this asshole around, we're gonna keep defending what's ours. You can't tell me you went willingly with him. Not when all signs point to a kidnapping." If it hadn't been for that broken cup, I would have believed she'd chosen to go with him. I knew she wanted him, but I didn't appreciate the way he treated her.

Rosie must've taken a drink of Gavin's blood while I'd been trying to get my head on straight because her nose began healing as I spoke. At least he did *that* for her, the pretentious dick.

"It was more of an abscondment. And she was mine first. But, I'm willing to . . . share if I must."

"Oh, that's big of you. I don't recall extending an invitation for you to move on in."

"Now that she's allowed me to bond with her, I'm part of her, as much as either of you. I belong by her side. Good luck getting me to go anywhere."

"Who n-needs luck?" Ben asked.

It was the crestfallen look on Rosie's face that finally broke through to me. "Ben, stop. We're hurting her."

And we were. I could feel the sorrow pouring out of her and filling me up. Right in that same place that had been so achingly empty only minutes prior.

"Sugar?" Ben asked, turning his attention to Rosie.

"I need you all. None of this will work if you're always trying to kill each other."

"Fuck!" I knew I'd agreed to this, but I really despised this bloodsucker. Dragging a hand through my hair, I strode past all of them, right back into the house. Usually, I didn't give two shits about being naked in my own home, but right now, I needed clothes, order, control. Everything was spiraling. I hated it. Last night was supposed to make things better for us, not worse.

I blindly grabbed a pair of joggers off the top of my laundry basket, pulling them on and turning toward the door at the sound of footsteps.

"Remi . . . are you all right?"

"You're the one who got her nose broken, and you're checking on me?"

She winced and pointed to the still tender spot beneath my left eye. "That looks painful."

Shrugging, I slipped a shirt over my head. "It'll be good as new in a minute. Wolf perks," I added, tossing her a smile I didn't quite feel.

"I know you don't understand my connection to Gavin—"

"Understand? He's the one you ran from. You're afraid of him. Of course I don't understand."

"I already told you, it wasn't him. It was his family. I've always wanted him. In the same way I want you, Ben, and Asher."

I blew out a breath. Why was this so hard for me to wrap my head around? I accepted her need for Asher, no problem. Maybe because I felt it too. But this guy? Accepting him into our home—possibly into our bed—it just wasn't the same. When I looked at his smug face, all I wanted to do was punch it. Twice. Maybe three times.

"Can you at least try? For me? You told me to ask for what I need. This is me asking."

Swallowing hard, I gritted my teeth, then nodded. "I'm not ever going to like him. But I also want you happy. So I guess the best I can promise is that I won't kill him in his sleep."

"I guess that will have to do," she teased, rising up on her tiptoes to feather a kiss over the bruise on my cheek. "Thank you, Remi."

"For getting my ass kicked? I swear I'm usually better at these things. That fucker is fast."

"It's because he just fed."

"So you're saying I might have a chance next time?"

"Maybe we skip next time altogether?"

I leaned forward and kissed her, soft and sweet, my favorite flavor lingering on my lips. "No promises."

My phone rang, the sound sending ice down my spine. Only one person had that ringtone, and she rarely called. I'd chosen the *Exorcist* theme song special just for her.

Aisling.

What did that bitch want now?

"I, uh, have to take this," I said, waving my phone distractedly.

Rosie must have picked up on my discomfort because she nodded. "Sure thing, I'll just pop outside and make sure Ben hasn't killed Gavin. Or vice versa." She laughed, but it was hollow. For all we knew, it was a very good possibility.

"Why are you calling me?" I hissed into the phone.

"Oh, is my wee little darlin' angry? Did Mummy call you at a bad time?"

"Yes, actually."

"Too bleedin' bad." I could practically picture her, dressed like some cosplayer's dream sexy pirate, spread across a chair, a Cheshire cat grin on her face. "There's a fight tonight. I want you both there. And I want you to lose."

"What? No. We never lose."

"There's a first time for everything, love."

"Aisling—"

But she'd already hung up. She never bothered with pleasantries. That'd be too much of a reach for the vampire bitch of the north.

My phone creaked in my grasp before I put it away and prepared to return to my mate and her other two men. As soon as I stepped into the living room, I knew they'd heard everything. Three sets of eyes stared at me, though the emotions in them varied wildly. Concern. Curiosity. Fear.

"What?"

"Why d-did Aisling call? W-we don't have another f-f-fight until next m-month."

Gavin's gaze narrowed as he looked between my twin and me. "So that's how she does it. I wondered what she had on you. Why you two kept coming back without anything to gain. She's blackmailing you. Isn't she?"

"What?" Rosie gasped. "Who's blackmailing them?"

Instinct told me to ignore Gavin, but I wouldn't lie to Rosie.

"Aisling O'Connor. A vampire who seems bound and determined to ruin my life."

"Our l-lives."

"Why?"

"Because I tried to end hers."

Gavin's eyes widened with appreciation. "More balls than brains. Surely you knew better than to go after someone as powerful as her."

"Surely not," I said with a cutting grin. "Seeing as how I did."

"Why would you dare to do something like that?" Rosie asked.

"Wouldn't you, if you found the person responsible for slaughtering your family? Almost every person who meant anything to you?"

Rosie's little hiccuped gasp had Ben and I both approaching her. She held out her arms for us, and we gladly wrapped her up.

"How did you survive Aisling's wrath?" Gavin asked.

"She lets us live so we can win her as much money as possible." I hated to admit the truth of our arrangement.

"Fight night." Apparently the magic that prevented us from mentioning it didn't stop him. "You two have been working with her this whole time?"

Ben nodded.

"You know her?" Rosie asked, her attention laser-focused on Gavin.

"Of course I know her. She's my great-great-several times removed-aunt, on my mother's side."

"You would be related to her," I muttered.

"Help them, Gavin. Get them out of this. She's danger-ous." Rosie's eyes filled with tears as she pleaded with him. "Do this for me."

He held her gaze, then nodded once. "I'm already working on getting you freed from that blasted demon."

"Please, my lord."

I wanted to gag as I watched that Bridgerton mother-fucker melt.

"All right. Consider it my wedding present to you. Since you were so underwhelmed by the last one."

She glared at him. "Careful, husband, or you'll be sleeping alone for the foreseeable future."

He gave her a playful spank. "Doubtful."

And just like that . . . Gavin Donoghue, vampire Duke of Canterbury and royal pain in my ass, joined our wayward pack of misfits. Even if I *really* didn't want him to.

TWENTY-FIVE

"I have a bad feeling about this," Remi muttered as we stepped through the portal and into the seedy underbelly of the supernatural's filthy rich.

"M-me too."

Nothing good would come from Aisling changing the rules on us last minute. First she called us in for an extra fight. Then she wanted us to lose. After ten years of predictability, she was deviating almost overnight. That couldn't bode well.

"Look, there's Donoghue. The sneaky fuck didn't do a damn thing to help us. I knew we couldn't trust him."

I grunted, my frustration growing with each passing moment. I never enjoyed coming to this place, but it was worse than usual. Instinctively, I knew it was because we'd left our newly claimed mate behind. We should be holed up in bed, lost in each other for the foreseeable future, taking turns giving her what she needed from us. But instead we were here, about to get our asses handed to us for no damn good reason.

The vampire bitch was up to something, and I was sure

it wasn't good. It was more common than not for the losers to end up dead and buried, never to be heard from again. That was why most fighters weren't creatures with families. No one to miss them when they didn't come home.

"Do you know w-who we're f-fighting?"

"No fucking clue. But I really hate to lose."

"Ladies and . . . douchecanoes, welcome to a very special edition of fight night," a booming voice said, echoing off the walls.

I couldn't figure out where the voice was coming from until I saw the flicker of light trailing behind a tiny pixie man. He landed on Gavin's shoulder and made himself comfortable.

"I personally wanted to come up with a catchy name for this one, but I got outvoted. Some of my favorites were Supernatural Death Match, Blood Bath, and The Beastly Beat Down. But I guess fight night works. Whatever, so long as I get paid and laid, amiright?"

The five-inch tall faerie elbowed Gavin in the throat, making the vampire snarl as he used his fingers to flick the small man off his shoulder.

He wasn't fazed. The pixie took off in a blur of wings, microphone to his mouth. "I'm your host for tonight, Pip Pickering. Are you bunch of birches ready to tuuumble?"

Remi leaned over, pitching his voice low. "Did he just call us birches? Like the trees?"

I sighed. "Pixie slang."

"Rosie will love that. Remind me to tell her when we get home."

Pip flew in front of our faces, giving me a wink before raising the tiny mic to his lips. Remi tore off his shirt, getting himself pumped and ready to fight. I did the same.

"In this corner, weighing in at . . . I don't fucking know,

a whole lot of muscle and a big swinging dick, the one, but technically not the only, Remington Mercer.”

What. The. Fuck.

And that's when I knew. This was what she'd wanted. To catch us off guard by only having one of us fight. We never fought alone at these things. We were a package deal.

I stepped forward, but the stupid little firefly got in my face.

“Sorry, pal. It's gotta be a one-man show this time. Boss's orders.”

The low growl I let out had his wings turning from the cheerful yellow they had been to a dull gray. “God, you're a scary fucker. Do you have a girlfriend? Boyfriend? Want one? We could get married. I know a guy.”

“P-piss off, p-pipsqueak.”

Before Remi could step into the ring, I grabbed him by his hair and tugged hard.

“Ow! Fuck! What the hell?”

I stepped over the barrier and knew the second I did something was wrong. This wasn't just a magical circle to keep people out. It was a fucking cage.

We were locked in. Well, *I* was locked in.

Motherfucker.

Pip shook his head like I was the stupidest man alive as he flitted over to me. “Your funeral, buddy. You shoulda taken me up on my offer. Maybe it's better this way. I'm not sure I would have made a good widow. I don't look good in black.” Casting me one long look, he flew high above me.

“And in this corner, weighing more than any man has a right to while still being cut as hell, the Nordic Nuisance, the Viking Violator, the Berserking Beast of Novasgard. Tor Nordson!”

A towering wall of muscle stepped into the ring, his

blond hair falling down around his shoulders. His blue eyes damn near glowed with the same pre-fight adrenaline I knew would be in my own. His shirt was also off, and in the center of his chest was an intricate black rose tattoo with swirling vines on either side. It seemed out of place on him. Not like something he would choose, but rather something he'd been given. It almost appeared as if the thorns were digging into his flesh.

Before my eyes, his muscles seemed to swell. He beat one powerful fist into his chest and unleashed a primal bellow that had the hair on the back of my neck standing on end.

Oh. Fuck.

He slammed his fist on his chest again, and this time his skin rippled with scales, turning a sickening charcoal hue that started at his hands and climbed up his arms and finally spread across his chest. A third pound on his chest had thick horns curving up and back from his temples. The rest of his face remained mostly unchanged, except for a sharpening of his cheekbones and his eyes melting into pools of night.

"What the hell is that thing?" my twin shouted.

"Our new reigning champ," Pip answered gleefully. "No one has bested him. You should really thank your brother for his noble sacrifice."

Then, the pixie flew high into the air above the two of us before crowing, "Fight, you fuckers!"

The crowd's cheer was drowned out by the inhuman roar from my opponent as he charged forward. I had no time to prepare against a fighter like him. He was easily five times my size, fast, strong, and crazed. I wasted precious seconds finding Remi's gaze, and the look on my brother's face was tortured, filled with fear.

The beast slashed across my chest with long, razor-sharp claws I hadn't realized existed. Instant pain burned through me as blood spilled down my front. I staggered back, hands instinctively coming up to press against the wounds.

My brain had barely recovered from the shock of his first blow when the second found me. This time as a fist to the face. But as his knuckles collided with my cheek, the resounding crack was like nothing I'd ever heard. It felt like he'd taken a sledgehammer to the side of my head.

My vision swam, black spots dancing in my periphery as I careened toward the blood-splattered floor.

I hadn't even tried to lose. The bastard took me out in two shots. No one had ever kicked my ass so spectacularly. But then, I'd never fought the Beast.

My last coherent thought as the ground rushed up to greet me was that at least I'd gotten to be with Rosie and make her mine. Even if only for a night.

Take care of her for me, Remi.

TWENTY-SIX

GAVIN

Well, this was an interesting turn. In all my years attending these events, I'd never seen one of the Mercers taken out so easily. Or ever, to be perfectly honest. I found that I quite enjoyed the experience until I realized how upset Roslyn would be. That rankled. I shouldn't bloody care. But I did.

Oh well. I would just have to keep her distracted and work her through her grief.

The Beast moved to tear at Bentley's unconscious form, his claws poised to strike, saliva leaking from his fanged mouth as he snarled.

"Oof. That looks like it hurts. Annnnd, let's go ahead and call it before we end up with faces full of Mercer guts. There's only one kind of fluid I like on my face, and it's not that. The undefeated champ, The Beast of Novasgard!" Pip, the ridiculous little shite, flitted around the Beast's head, distracting him. "Can someone ring the bell?"

The deep, resonant sound of a gong signaled the end of the match. The entire thing had lasted at most five minutes. And that was being generous. Poor Bentley. If he survived, he'd never live down the shame. Too bad. He was a good fighter. I'd have a drink in his honor. Straight from Roslyn's vein.

I turned to leave now that the show was over and there was nothing more to see, but the vicious growl from the Novasgardian monster that bounced off the walls stopped me. Remington screamed incoherent nonsense at the Beast, his eyes frantic as he hurled anything and everything he could find at the barrier separating him from his twin.

"The match is over. He's still alive. Let me get him out before that fucking lunatic kills him."

As if intent on doing just that, the Beast punched down into the shredded skin covering Bentley's chest. "He's going to rip his heart out," I murmured. I couldn't say I hadn't had the idea myself at least once.

Okay, fine. Twice.

"Drop the goddamned barrier!" Remington shouted.

"I can't. He'll escape. He'll eat everyone. You know what they say, sacrifice one to save the many. Listen, do you know how hard this is for me? We were basically engaged. He's a hero. All we can do now is remember him fondly. Oh, sweet prince." Pip flew around the crowd, his wings now a sickly green.

"Fuck that!" Remington grabbed the closest wizard by his beard and tugged hard. "Use your magic. Drop the circle."

"Only the owner of the magic can undo it. Safety measures, you see. Otherwise, anyone would be able to take it down at any time. Not very sportsmanlike."

"Great. In the dark underground, where everyone is doing something they shouldn't, I pick the one old fart who's a rule follower. Thanks for nothing, Dumbledork."

I stood in the periphery with a smirk twitching at my lips. Oh, how I loved watching Remington unravel.

The room burst into brilliant, blinding light, all of us flinching away and covering our eyes as a booming voice proclaimed, "Do I really have to do everything around here? Back, Beast. You've conquered this day, but you must not take it any further."

Unimpressed with the speech, the snarling monster rushed toward a blond man wearing motorbike leathers.

"That's quite enough of that."

With a single press of his index finger to the creature's forehead, it was disabled, like a plug had been pulled. The Beast dropped like a stone, his body already turning back into the Viking he'd been at the start. Though it looked like the tattoo on his chest had changed, one of the lush petals now shriveled, appearing to fall away from the rest.

Murmurs of the name Gabriel filtered to my ears from the whispers of the audience. A few even fell to their knees, trembling.

He cut a glance to the pathetic wretches on the ground. "I'll give you to the count of three before I smite the lot of you. Ready? Three . . ."

Every creature in the space ran for escape, leaving me, Remington, and what remained of Bentley. I strode toward my own personal exit, not wanting to give this *angel* the satisfaction of seeing me flee like a scared child.

"Not you. You stay, vampire." Gabriel's tone was the same as a tired and disenchanted school teacher ready for the holiday break to hit.

"Who the hell are you?" Remington snapped.

The angel raised a mocking brow. "Oh, I do love this part." There was another blinding flash, and the motorbike leathers were replaced by a white robe, and a halo appeared above his head. "I am the Messenger of God. But you may call me . . . Gabriel."

"Listen, Gabe—"

"I said my name is *Gabriel,* you insufferable pissant." His clothing changed back to the biker leathers, which must've been preferable to the sheet and sandals. "No respect. None. It's like shifters don't know their place. No one in this community does. Frankly, I'm rather tired of having to explain myself. You come down with the glow and the fire and the booming voice, and you expect at least a modicum of respect. But nooooo, I have to prove myself. Put on this ridiculous toga—a stereotype, mind you—and only then does anyone believe me. I might as well rain down a few miracles while I'm at it."

I simply leaned back against the wall with my arms across my chest, watching the Messenger of God have a full-on tantrum. This was bloody entertaining.

"Well, if you're here to pass out miracles, Leather Feathers, can you do something about my brother? He's dying in there."

Gabriel let out a long-suffering sigh. "No."

"No? Then what the fuck are you even here for?"

"*I* cannot interfere. Rules. Red tape. It's all very boring, I assure you. But nothing prevents *you*"—the bastard's gaze cut to mine—"from doing so."

"Me?"

"Yes. You. Or is that too much to ask of the wicked Duke of Tears?" He cocked a brow, staring at me and speaking very slowly, "You're a vampire." When I stared at him blankly, he mimed fangs with his fingers at his teeth. "Rawr."

I still didn't respond. Was he a numbskull? Of course I was a vampire; I didn't require some half-cocked demonstration. *Does his nurse know he ran away and is roaming unsupervised? I had heard the angels were going senile.*

"Oh, for the love of my father. *Blood,* you idiot. Use your blood and save him. Honestly, do I have to do *everything*?"

I drew back as if he hit me. "You want me to give that dog my blood?"

"Was I unclear? Was my enunciation lacking? Yes, you pompous popinjay. Use your blood and save the shifter. It is not his time." He stared me down. "It's not rocket science."

"No."

"*Yes.*"

"No."

Gabriel's eyes flared with menace. "On your head be it, then. I'm sorry, Remington. There's nothing more I can do." Then the angel dropped his gaze to the once beastly Novasgardian prince. "As for you, I'll see you soon."

The air shifted, making my ears pop as the pressure changed, and Gabriel vanished with much less fanfare than he'd brought upon arrival. As soon as he was gone, the barrier separating us from the ring fell, and Remington raced to Bentley, who was barely breathing. I could hear the painfully sluggish beat of his heart, sense the life leaving him. He didn't have much time.

He should be healing, but the barrier that kept us out must have prevented his magic from assisting him. Part of equalizing the fight or something.

Nasty business.

"You heard him, Gavin. Save my brother."

"Why would I do something so against my best interest?"

"Because Rosie will never forgive you if you could have done something and instead you let one of her mates die."

Oh, bloody hell, he was right. I knew this. I hated it, but I knew it.

Heaving a sigh, I stepped into the ring as I rolled up the sleeve of my white button-down. I knelt next to Bentley's battered form and took in the damage. It was worse than I thought. Blood seeped from his mouth and nose, and his chest was all but caved in, not to mention torn to shreds. It was astounding he was still alive.

Using my fangs, I ripped open my wrist, holding out my arm as soon as the blood began dripping freely from the wound. I didn't press my skin to his mouth. Instead I just let the life-saving liquid splash onto his face. Surely some of it would make its way into his mouth.

"You really are a dick, you know that?"

"I've been called worse."

"Can't you at least pretend you want him to live?"

I glanced at Remington's furious expression. "No."

"I hate you."

"Finally, something we agree on."

"If I hadn't already promised not to kill you, I'd end you here and now."

"Oh, puppy, you could try. But do you really want to insult the only person around capable of saving your brother? Because I promise one Mercer is my quota. You come for me, and I will kill you."

Bentley's soft grunt of pain had us both putting our attention where it needed to be. Him. His brows pulled together as he opened his mouth and let more of my blood drip in, and it wasn't long before he gripped my wrist in his meaty paws and pulled my arm flush against his lips. I'd be lying if I said it didn't feel good. It always felt good, but *he* wasn't the one I wanted.

"Enough," I snarled, tearing myself free as soon as his wounds were healed. "Disgusting dog."

As he sat up, Bentley gave me a terse nod that seemed to be his way of thanking me. Had no one taught these creatures manners?

"W-we have . . . t-to stop her," he rasped out. "B-before she k-kills us."

"Aisling?" I asked.

"Who fucking else?" Remington countered. "The bitch set us up to die tonight."

I weighed my options as I stood. I suppose I could let her kill them. Ridding myself and Roslyn of her unwanted mates had been my plan since arriving, but Remington had a point. My petal would never forgive me. I could deal with her impertinence but not her hatred.

"I suppose I could go to the Council on your behalf," I drawled.

"How big of you," Remington deadpanned.

"Do you want me to intercede or not? Because your behavior—"

"P-please," Bentley said, looking like it hurt him more to say the word than getting punched in the face had. "We c-can't k-keep doing this. It w-will b-blow b-back on Rosie. We c-can't put her i-in danger."

I leveled my gaze on Bentley. "Tell me everything."

TWENTY-SEVEN

Striding through the hellscape I called home, I stopped in at one of my favorite pubs, Screaming Sarah's, named fondly after one of the only witches to escape the Inquisition. Pure legend, that one. Her soul might've been my favorite I'd claimed.

Every eye turned my way the second I stepped inside, a few wise lesser demons scrambling away and offering me their seats at the bar when they recognized me.

I ignored all of them. My kind didn't bother rubbing elbows with the little people unless we needed something from them.

Like my favorite blend of hellfire and brimstone whiskey.

The bartender already had a glass waiting for me by the time I sat down. The lone ice cube was filled with red smoke, giving the drink its name. Wraith's Blood Whiskey. By the time the ice melted, the wraith's blood would fill the liquid and turn it from drinkable to deadly.

"Trying to kill me again?" I asked him before I knocked back the contents.

"One of these days I'll succeed."

A loud cheer went up from a group of lesser demons in the corner, and one of them stood, beaming with excitement.

"Finally! I got my call! I'm going up, boys. Say goodbye to Timmy the minor demon. Once I get this biker's soul, I'll be able to take Aurora Springs by storm. Maybe I'll come home with all their souls."

My head snapped in his direction. The bald, pot-bellied pigman stood, his back to me as his buddies congratulated him.

"It's about damn time!"

"Bring us his eye teeth! I can get them set as earrings. Me missus has been wanting something special for our anniversary, and you know how hard it is to get things from topside."

A third, sniveling weasel with a hump on his left shoulder rubbed his gnarled hands together. "And maybe a set of ladies knickers, too. It gets so lonely down here. I really like the lacy ones. Perfect amount of friction over me boils."

All three of them fell silent as I loomed behind Timmy.

"Mister Pan, sir. H-have you come to wish Timmy well?" the weaselly motherfucker asked, eyes trained on my shoulder since he couldn't bring himself to meet my gaze.

"I'll take that off your hands, Timbo." I snatched the rattling plastic pager out of the crossroad demon's hands. There was no way I was about to let him be the one to answer the summons.

"Oi, you can't just—" All the bluster left him when he looked into my eyes. That could have been because I had the power to burn him to a cinder where he sat, or it could be the fact that my knee was currently crushing his bollocks in the chair.

Without another word, I pressed the long button on the side and was transported directly to the crossroad in question. Somewhere about fifteen miles south of one Aurora Springs. Perfect. I was due for a little field trip; it had been far too long since I'd been free to play.

The cold, crisp air of the little Alaskan town wasn't terrible by any means, but I preferred not smelling the humans when in demon form if I could help it. Their desperation reeked. The only one I wanted to smell was *ma petite monstre*.

But I did love a human making his last stand. And that's what this bloke was doing here on his knees at the crossroad.

"Get up, you pathetic shite."

He struggled to his feet, motorcycle leathers covering his body, dark hair slicked back. "I can't believe it actually worked." His Scottish brogue—Edinburgh, I'd bet my sister's life on it . . . if I had one— took me by surprise. I'd just assumed he'd be American, but the hint of home had my lip curling in a smile. I took it as a sign that destiny was at work.

I did love fucking with fate.

"What do you desire? Tell me so I can be done with this."

"Make me famous. Make me the most famous rock star in the world."

Oh, bloody hell, not another one. We were still dealing with the fallout from the last one. What was his name? Sassy Al Yankabitch? Harry Stylo? Whatever. It didn't matter. They always went a bit nutty in the end.

"What will you give in return? That's a hefty ask."

It wasn't. Pretty basic if you ask me.

"Anything. I'll give you anything. I need to make it big. I need to win her back."

Oh, for fuck's sake. He was doing it for *love*. What a disgusting cliché. He deserved everything he had coming to him.

"I can make all your pitiful dreams come true, but you must give me whatever I ask for."

Idiot.

"Aye. Anything. Name your price, demon."

"Well, you see, it's a tad bit hard to walk around up here without a human form. So I need you to let me . . . borrow you for a while."

His eyes widened. "Borrow?"

"Don't worry, I'll give you your body back in the same condition I found it. Maybe worse. But nothing you won't be able to fix."

"Um . . . I'm not sure."

For Lucifer's sake, I was getting rusty. "Honestly, you said anything. Is she not worth a little lost time? I thought you were in love."

Gag me.

"I just want to shag her."

"Oh, I was wrong. You don't deserve half of what I'm going to give you."

His lower lip trembled, and I was certain he was about ten seconds away from pissing himself.

"Do we have a deal or not?"

He raked a hand through his hair, glancing back at his motorbike before giving me a jerky nod. "Sod it. You only live once, right?"

I grinned, a slow, menacing curl of my lips that wasn't the least bit friendly. "Not if you play your cards right."

"What?"

He was so dense. I couldn't keep him talking because if he said another word, I was going to rip his tongue from his mouth and fry it for my dinner. And that would ruin *my* plans.

"Give me access to your body, and once I'm done, you'll have everything you want. Yes or no? I am a very busy demon. Get on with it."

"Aye."

"Praise Satan." I clapped my hands and then grasped his face between my palms. "Now let me in."

He gave a jerk, instinctively fighting against the invasion as I shoved my demon essence into his fragile mortal body.

The man was weak. He stopped fighting as soon as I was in his mind. It didn't take long for me to get used to controlling his limbs. He was fit, strong, and definitely handsome by human standards. I reached down to cup his undercarriage. Hmm, not bad. It listed to the left a bit, but it wasn't small by human standards. Definitely not an aubergine, but he'd do quite nicely. And it seemed he was a fair bit attracted to me, by the feel of things down below. Bully for Pan.

Striding down the dark road, I stopped when I found his motorbike parked not far away.

"I do love a steel horse."

Swinging my leg over, I settled into the seat and turned the key, conveniently left in the ignition. Throttling the gas, I let the beast roar to life beneath me.

"Hi-ho, Silver, away."

～

THE TIPSY MOOSE might have been the worst dive bar I'd ever been inside. The patrons and the owners could hang. Except, of course, for the one staff member I had my eye on. I was here for Rosie.

The little monster in question strolled toward my place in the back of the bar, a smile spreading her lips, not a shred of recognition in her eyes.

"Hi there. What can I get you?"

Out of reflex, I opened my mouth to answer that her cunt would do nicely, remembering in the nick of time that was not only inappropriate, but she'd recognize my voice instantly. If I wanted to let this little game of mine play out, I needed to tread with care. Inspired by my host's home-land, I opted for borrowing his accent as well, really leaning into it.

"I'm new in town, lassie. What do ye recommend?" I forgot the feel of a Scottish brogue on my tongue.

"Scotland?"

"Aye. Edinburgh." Letting some of my natural smolder shine through, I grinned at her and purposely glanced down at the name tag on her shirt. *Nadia.* My pretty little liar.

"What brings you here?"

"Sightseeing. I like taking in the beauty of this world." I purposely locked gazes with her. The fucking twat who called himself her mate took notice.

Her cheeks turned pink. "The burger is quite nice if you're looking for a meal. Otherwise we've got a local ale on tap and some excellent whiskey. If you're after something more posh than that, you're in the wrong place."

"I'll have a pint. And keep 'em coming, yeah?"

"You got it. One pint, coming right up." She knocked lightly on the bar and spun, grabbing a clean glass and working the tap like she'd been doing it her whole life. Pulling me a pint, she kept flashing her eyes at me, a little wrinkle working its way between her brows.

She was trying to place me. A piece of her, the part that belonged to me, felt my presence. Even if she didn't recognize the face I was wearing.

"New in town?" her hacker boyfriend asked. Did I tell him I wasn't even close to new? That I'd been inside his precious *princess* since the night she set foot in this backwater town?

"Aye. Only just arrived."

He nodded, and not in a friendly, nice to meet you way. In an 'I've got my eye on you, and I don't like what I see' way.

Well, the feeling was bloody mutual.

"Maybe you should keep on passing through."

"What is this, a wee cowboy town? Are we going to draw our pistols at sundown?"

"Do we need to?"

I quirked a brow. "You tell me, laddie. I'm just here for the beer."

And the barmaid.

He grunted. "Get your pint and leave. We don't have room in this town for another outsider. Especially one who doesn't know how to keep his eyes off my girl's tits."

It took everything in me not to bare my teeth and snarl at him that I had her first. That it was my mark on her wrist and my jewelry in her nipple. Short of covering her in my cum right in front of him, I couldn't do much more to mark her. Maybe I'd take her into the back room, shed myself of this stupid Scottish meat suit, and fuck her while I made the hacker and wolves watch. That'd teach them.

"As I said, I enjoy pretty things."

"She's not yours to enjoy. Keep your eyes to yourself, buddy. Or you'll have far worse on your hands to deal with than me."

Stuttering Stanley was nowhere to be found, but her pretty boy hacker frowned at me like he wanted to send me packing with my balls in a takeaway container.

"Here you are," Rosie said, breaking the tension as she set my pint in front of me. "First one's on the house." She winked, and oh, her man did not like that. Not at all.

Sucker.

"Thanks, darlin'."

"What's your name, then?"

"What do ye think it should be?"

She raised one brow. "Scotty, I suppose. Since you're a Scot and all. Or maybe Hamish?"

"Very original. Shall I call you Rosie?"

Her eyes widened. "What? Why would you say that?"

I jutted my chin at her earrings, little red roses. "Jewelry."

"Oh." She fingered the little flowers and huffed out a laugh as she glanced away from me, and bloody hell, I could get used to flirting with her as a human. "Anything else for now?"

"Not yet. I'll give you a shout when I need something."

She gave me another polite but impersonal grin and bounded off to the other end of the bar to lean across from her hacker.

Poison. That would work. I could poison him quickly, and no one would be the wiser. Then I'd just keep this body and toss Rosie on the back of my bike as we rode off into the sunset.

When Rosie pushed to her tiptoes and leaned over the bar to kiss the Clark Kent wanna-be, giving me a great look at her peach-shaped arse in the process, I decided I'd seen enough. Draining my drink, I set my empty glass back on the bar and stood.

"Off so soon? Bummer," the smart arse said, not even pretending to mean a single word.

"Actually, I quite like it here. Think I'll stick around for a while. Might take a walk and see if I can't find a place to hang my hat."

"You're not wearing a fucking hat."

"Metaphor."

"Dumb metaphor."

I glanced at Rosie and offered her another wink. "See you around, *Rosie*."

Those cheeks went red again, and she reached up to touch her earrings. "Bye, Hamish."

I'd take it. Especially with how angry the bloke watching me seemed.

Striding out of the bar, I chuckled to myself as I walked to my waiting bike. Yes, this town deserved a little of my extra special attention. If Rosie was going to deny me, I'd just have to make her want me in a different form.

A perky woman with bountiful tits and big hair walked past me, her bright smile and Just the Tip shirt letting me know she was ready to serve more than beer if I wanted it.

"Hello, handsome. I think you're going the wrong way."

"No. I got what I came for."

She pouted as I stalked out into the night, hands in my pockets and my favorite song on my lips as I whistled my way down the street.

Ring around the Rosie . . .

Spotting an ancient oak, I paused long enough to give it a little Bob's Your Uncle, leaving a scorched handprint in my wake. Don't be a pervert. What did you think I was doing, humping it? It's just an expression.

It wouldn't be long until my present took effect.

The plan was taking shape. My new plan. One my mother could never know about. I'd have my way, even if I had to burn this town to ashes.

TWENTY-EIGHT

Thank fuck that Scotsman left. Something about him wasn't right, but I couldn't put my finger on it. With one eye on Rosie at all times as she worked the bar, I resumed my doomscrolling on my phone.

I liked to keep my finger on the pulse of what was happening in the world. Especially since we were only weeks off one Apocalypse, yet the crazy events didn't seem to be slowing down. The cycle had been kicked off, and the bomb might've been diffused, but that didn't stop the rest of the catastrophes from raining down on us.

It always baffled me how people could bury their heads in the sand and ignore this stuff. How was it the mainstream news was covering this serial killer, but no one was talking about birds literally falling dead from the sky all over the world? Or the fucking lake in Michigan that was still inexplicably filled with blood? But the birds worried me. Avian flus were dangerous and not uncommon, but mankind had never seen one like this.

"What's got your face so stormy?" Rosie asked, sliding a

glass of her favorite Scotch to me across the polished wood bartop.

"Puffins."

"I'm sorry. What was that? Puffins?"

I nodded. "There's a puffin crisis."

She wanted to laugh; I could see her fighting against it. "I didn't realize you were such a puffin enthusiast."

"They're defenseless. I mean, have you ever met one? I have. A whole family, actually. I visit them and check in from time to time. The papa puffin, I named him Toderick, and I had sort of a run in a few weeks ago. Now we're like this." I crossed my index and middle finger. "Anyway, the guy has a wife and like three kids. There might be more, but they sort of come and go, so it's hard to tell. Tammy, Tod Jr., Toby, and Tallahassee. I think there's another batch on the way. I'll have to give them U names. Ursula seems a little threatening, though."

"Asher? Sweetie, you're rambling."

Shit. I was.

"It's a crisis," I muttered, embarrassed.

She rested her palm on the top of my hand. "Why is it a crisis? What's happening to the puffins?"

Finally. Someone else actually cared about what was going on.

"Birds are dying all over. The puffins are next, I just know it. Pigeons are already nearly extinct because of this flu. And I read that the Canadian geese are down to like one percent of their total population—after a few days of the first categorized death. Not even a full week. And those fuckers are mean! There's a legend that all Canadians perform a ritual once a year to send all their anger into the geese. That's why they're such assholes. And if they can go down, how are the poor puffins going to survive?"

"Good riddance," Darla said. "Pigeons and geese are the rats of the sky."

"Don't you see what is happening? It's not just birds. It's going to spread. It's going to mutate and kill everyone!"

"Oh my God, chill out. Who invited the doomsday prepper?" Darla poured herself a shot and downed it as she stared at me.

My heart was racing as a strange sense of foreboding settled over me. I wasn't wrong about this. I could tell. It was the beginning.

"Asher? Look at me. You're hyperventilating."

I blinked and swallowed. My skin was clammy and my breaths shallow. "Sorry. I guess I'm a little stressed out."

"Strung out sounds more accurate," Darla muttered.

"Fuck off, Darla. Go find a leg to hump." I narrowed my gaze at her.

Her eyes widened. "Who the fuck are you? Do I know you, my guy? Because I sure as hell didn't tell you my name."

Crap. I was slipping. Hard. The only person in this bar who'd seen me as my true self was Rosie. Of course Darla wouldn't know me from Adam. But I was tired of hiding in the shadows, wearing fake beards and tattoos. From now on, if I was going to have a tattoo, it'd be a real one. I already had an appointment with Tove at Inkgard. He was some Norseman who'd retired here a few years ago and set up shop. It was just him and his buddy Zak, a bunny shifter, who ran the place.

I had my design planned and everything. Rosie was going to fucking love it. I hoped.

"Hello? Are you deaf? You sure seemed able to hear me a second ago." Darla waved her hand in front of my face.

"Darla, this is Asher. He's new in town. He's my . . .

friend." There Rosie went, saving me. I was supposed to be the one saving her.

"Friend, huh?" Darla smirked. "You sure seem to have a lot of those these days, new girl."

Rosie blushed but shrugged. "What can I say? I'm a woman of sizeable appetites."

Darla cackled. "A woman after my own heart. Go you." Then her smile slipped, and she gave me an unfriendly once-over. "This one's cute, but seems a little off."

"Because I care about the puffins? Maybe you're just heartless. Ever think about that?"

God, what the fuck was I doing? Raving about seabirds was a surefire way to become the resident lunatic of Aurora Springs. This was so not how my first venture into town as myself was supposed to play out.

"Asher knows more about the Apocalypse than most of us. He's human, but very well-versed in the supernatural world, Darla. I trust him more than anyone when it comes to information like this. If he says the birds dying is something we should care about, I care about it."

Darla paled. "Well, shit. Okay."

Pride washed through me to hear my girl come to my defense. "I just think it's something we should keep our eye on."

"Is there anything we can do? For the puffins?"

I leaned over the bar and kissed my girl. "I don't know, but I love that you asked."

God, it felt so good to kiss her in front of everyone. I'd been pretending I didn't exist for so long, I forgot I could be . . . this guy. The one who let myself be affectionate without worrying about being exposed.

"What are you doing?" Rosie whispered against my

mouth. "You didn't tell me *you* were going to be here. Is it safe?"

"Just go with it." I kissed her again and gave her lower lip a soft bite.

Darla snorted. "Friends. Riiight."

"Friends who kiss." My voice was a low rumble, because I wanted to do a lot more than kiss right now.

"And visit the sexy dungeon?" Rosie asked.

I laughed and shook my head. "You just won't let that go, will you?"

"You can't tell a girl a thing like that and then not show her the goods."

I guessed it was a good thing said *goods* were already ordered and on their way.

"You want to see the goods, huh? Pretty sure you already have."

She shoved my shoulder playfully and then rested her chin in her hand as she leaned across the bar to flirt with me some more.

I didn't know how we'd gotten here—from me spiraling over the puffins to this—but I wasn't about to complain.

Was this what happiness felt like? Was I happy?

A tendril of apprehension worked its way through me. *Fuck, don't ruin this, Asher.*

The rest of the night went by in a blur of surreal awareness about my situation. I watched over Rosie as she and Darla held down the bar, proud of my girl for rising to the challenge of her new life. Some people would have buckled under the strain of such a drastic change. Not her. She rose from the literal ashes of her life and became someone she was always meant to be. A fierce, independent, sexy as hell woman. She may not see herself that way, but I sure as shit did. It took balls to fake your own death and leave your old life behind.

"Later, puffin boy." Darla's voice cut through my reverie and pulled my attention back to the present. "I'm clocking out." She blew Rosie a kiss and sauntered to the back, rolling up her apron as she went. "Have fun with your *friend*."

I stood, my gaze immediately going to Rosie. "Are you closing up?"

"Yeah. It's my turn. Did you . . . want to do something after?"

Did I want to do something? Of course I did, and that something involved a bed and no clothes. "How long does it take?"

"It'll be faster if you help me."

I scrunched up my face before snagging the rag from her. "Just don't tell, Remi. Do you have any idea how many times he used that same line on me?"

"And you turned him down?"

I held up my hands. "These are basically priceless. A callus or a paper cut is pretty much a national disaster."

"Oh, you poor baby. Would you prefer to mop the floors?"

"Honestly, I'll do whatever you want if it means I'm inside you sooner."

Heat flared in her eyes. "Lock the door, Asher."

Fuck. Yes.

I dropped the rag and made my way to the door, throwing the lock and changing the sign in the window from open to closed. As soon as I turned, a sharp burning in my arm pulled a gasp from me.

Not now. Please, not now.

Rosie looked up, lips twitching. "Don't tell me you got a splinter?"

I glanced down at the stars climbing up my arm and forced out a laugh. "Cute."

She crooked a finger at me. "Get over here, lover boy. I have another job for you. One that doesn't require the use of your hands at all."

As quick as it began, the pain in my arm vanished. I flexed my hand and shook it out. I was fine. It was fine. "Up on the bar, princess. I want to make sure I do a very good job."

"Oh really? Are you angling for employee of the month, then?"

"Of the year, baby."

Wrapping my hands around her hips, I lifted her until she was seated on the glossy wood, legs splayed, those perfect lips level with my eyes. I tilted my chin up so I could look at her, gauge her expression.

"Anyone ever tell you how damn pretty you are, Rosie?"

She locked her legs around my waist, linking her arms around my neck and pulling our bodies closer. "Maybe once or twice. But it never hurts to hear it again."

"You are so"—I kissed her lips—"fucking"—I kissed her jaw—"beautiful."

My kisses trailed down her throat on the way to my real goal, those perfect tits. She let out a little gasp when my mouth brushed the base of her neck, where a faint raised mark sat, barely visible. Despite myself, a little curl of jealousy built in my chest.

Goosebumps broke out across her entire body, or everything I could see of it anyway, as I gave her mating mark a little lick. "Does it bother you?" I asked.

"Bother me? You mean hurt?"

"No . . . that I . . ."

Dammit, Asher. You're ruining it. Why can't you ever just shut the fuck up?

"That you what?"

"I'm just a human. I can't ever give you something as powerful as they can."

"You're not 'just' anything, Asher."

I couldn't stop myself from rolling my eyes.

"No, I mean it. Do you know what name I first saved you under in my phone?"

The temptation to hack into it had been nearly impossible to resist, but somehow I'd managed, so for once, I didn't have the answer. "No, actually."

"My Black-hatted knight. You might be human, Asher, but you're not weak or useless. You're really quite extraordinary. The one I ran to for help when my entire world imploded." She pressed her forehead to mine. "You're my hero."

I shuddered at the sincerity in her voice, at the wave of emotion that crashed into me in response. Unbidden, the memory of that bright light bursting from my hand came back to me. Maybe I really was a superhero. At least to her.

"We don't need to share marks. It's not like *I* marked them. It doesn't make us belong to one another any less. But if it matters to you, we can find a way to do something special for the two of us. My sister-in-law did that with one of her mates."

"Oh yeah?"

"They got tattoos."

"You would do that? For me?"

"It's no different from bearing their bite marks."

I kissed her then, my hands gripping her waist tightly as I devoured her mouth and let the warm happiness wash between us. No one had ever wanted to claim me like this, and I didn't know how to tell her what it meant to me. So I'd show her instead.

I grasped the material of my shirt behind my neck and pulled it up, yanking the clothing off and making Rosie giggle.

"I never quite figured out how a computer nerd got so fit."

"I'm a dancer," I said, shrugging like it was no big deal. "Can't really go to the gym when you're on the lam, but music is portable, and anything can be a dance floor if you're creative enough."

"Like, ballet?"

Smirking, I reached for my belt. "Like . . . exotic."

"Pardon?"

"Just call me Magic Mike."

"You're teasing me."

"Guess there's only one way to find out."

I backed away from her, snagged a chair, and placed it in the center of the room. Then I lifted her off the bar and sat her in front of me. If I was going to do this, I'd do it all the way. Pulling out my phone, I connected to the Bluetooth sound system before turning on a classic.

Her eyes lit up as soon as the beat dropped. I strolled around the back of the chair, my fingers drawing her hair across her shoulder to expose her neck so I could ghost my fingertips along it. Once I was in front of her again, I straddled her, taking her hands and guiding them down my torso as I rolled my hips against her lap.

Her giggles were quickly replaced with a breathless gasp when her hands found me already hard and aching for her behind my fly.

I leaned in, lips brushing her ear. "You wet for me, baby?"

"I have been."

Standing, I spread her thighs and positioned myself between them as I stared down at her.

"Then take what you want, princess. Stop being such a good girl."

Her fingers played along the top of my jeans, sending ripples of arousal through me as she bit her lower lip and popped the button. God, I wanted her so badly.

As she lowered my zipper, I had to hold my breath in anticipation of her hand . . . or mouth on my dick. Either would be fan-fucking-tastic. The way she was licking her lips, I was betting it'd be her mouth. Yes, please. Sign me up.

"Asher," she whispered.

"Rosie."

"I want you."

"Me too. Go ahead, take what y—fuuuuck." My words cut off and were replaced by a scream of absolute agony as pain ripped through my arm and into my chest.

"Asher? Asher, what's wrong?" Rosie jumped up as the unexpected pain sent me to my knees on the floor.

Cold sweat broke out across my body, and I could barely breathe through the burn of the curse claiming even more of my unmarked skin. A disembodied female voice echoed through my mind.

Ashes, ashes . . .

I was losing consciousness, my vision going gray and hazy. I was dying. The curse was killing me right here, right now. I didn't want to leave. Not now that I'd found her . . . found them. Rosie's hand clutched mine, her body trembling. That random singing continued, scaring the shit out of me. Was this the witch? Had she found me?

We all . . .

"Asher, what can I do? What do you need? Please tell me how to help."

Fall . . .

"Moira. Call . . . Moira."

. . . down.

TWENTY-NINE

Asher writhed on the floor, eyes rolled back in his head, jaw clenched, muscles in his neck straining. I'd seen this before when my uncle Lucas had been poisoned at one of my family's antiquated balls in a failed assassination attempt. He'd nearly died, and this was what he looked like as the silver worked its way through him.

"Asher, what can I do? What do you need? Please tell me how to help."

"Moira. Call . . . Moira."

Shock had me sitting back on my heels. Moira? But that would mean admitting that I was still alive. He wouldn't ask me to out myself if it wasn't serious, but could I really do that? Moira was connected to my brother. There'd be no keeping this from him once I contacted her.

The deathly pallor of Asher's face made up my mind for me. I'd have to deal with the fallout later. Saving him was far more important than weathering my family's fury.

Asher's phone was still sitting on the bar where he'd left it as the sultry beat of the song he'd selected for his performance played in the background. What had started off so promising had taken a terrible turn.

Why is this always happening?

Because you don't deserve to be happy, Roslyn.

Scrambling to my feet, I grasped his phone with shaking hands. I tapped on the screen, desperate to get to Moira's contact information, but the bloody thing wouldn't open for me.

Fingerprint not recognized, flashed on the phone.

Of course he'd have fingerprint security. I raced back to him, dropping to my knees at his side and grabbing his clammy hand. It took me three tries to line up the right finger because Asher Henry wouldn't go for an index print. No, he used his pinky.

The phone vibrated softly as it accepted the fingerprint. Moira was one of only a handful of numbers. And thank God I knew her full name, because she was saved as 'That Belladonna Bitch'.

She answered on the second ring.

"Look, Henry. I told you I'd call you when I had something."

"Moira? It's, um, not Asher. It's me . . . Rosie, that is, Roslyn. Blackthorne," I added lamely.

"Roslyn Blackthorne is dead," she said carefully, her voice not exactly unfriendly, but a far cry from her usual perky charm.

"On paper, yes. But I assure you, I'm very much alive."

"How do I know this is you? Tell me something only Rosie would know."

"You and Ash tried to have a threesome with my aunt Callie, and I walked in on you."

"Shit on a stick, it really is you. Ooh, girl. Do you have

any idea how much trouble you are in? Why the hell are you with Asher?"

"Can we talk about that later? It's an emergency."

She exhaled heavily into the phone. "Of course it is. That's all anyone ever calls me for. Why isn't it ever 'Hey Moira, how's the wife? What are you growing in the garden? Perform any cool spells lately?' But noooo, it's always doom and gloom for me. Well then, hit me with it."

"It's Asher. I think he's dying."

"What?"

"The curse. It's spread. He's unconscious on the floor. He had a seizure or something. He was in so much pain. I need you to come right away."

"Video call. Right now."

I pulled the phone from my ear and pressed the camera icon, initiating the video call. Moira's face with her lime green curls popped on the screen.

"Show me."

I turned the phone so she could see Asher's limp form, panning along his arm and chest to show her the extent of the curse's growth.

"Shiiit. It's almost all the way to his heart. Oh, this is bad. Why is it growing so fast?"

Since I didn't have the answer to her question, I asked one of my own. "Can you help him?"

She bit down on her black lacquered lip. "I can try."

"How soon can you be here?"

"Give me an hour. I need to gather some things."

"Do you know—"

"Don't insult me, babycakes. Of course I know where you are."

Relief flooded me, making my limbs tingle. "Thanks, Moira."

The video went shaky for a second, crackling coming over the line as Moira's face was replaced with one I knew almost as well as my own.

Noah.

My stomach sank.

"Rosie?"

The phone jerked away from him, Moira's voice the last thing I heard as she frantically said, "Gotta go! Bye!"

The screen went black, but I knew it was too late. My brother saw me. My cover had been completely blown.

THIRTY

"Something's wrong with Rosie." My chest ached as her unease shot through our bond. I could feel her panic as if it was my own. It was fucking weird. I'd never been so connected to another person, not even my twin.

Ben rubbed at the area above his heart as if he was feeling it too, and Gavin's eyes were narrowed, his gaze hazy as if focusing hard on something far away.

"We need to get back. Right bloody now," the vampire said, standing and moving away from my brother, who was fully healed thanks to the leech's magic blood, although he still looked like an extra in a horror movie with the amount of red covering every inch of him.

"Asher w-was supposed t-to be w-with her." Ben's fight for his words betrayed how on edge he was.

"We really need to stop leaving the human on guard duty," I growled, my wolf rising to the surface with the need to protect his mate.

Something flickered in Gavin's dark gaze, but he didn't correct me.

Ben strode to where the portal always opened for us, standing there, waiting for our entry to Aurora Springs. But nothing happened. No ripple in the fabric of reality or magical glow. No home.

"What the fuck?" I walked through where it should be, hoping it would just . . . work. It didn't. "What the FUCK? How are we supposed to get home? Where are we right now?"

"No one knows the location of this club. That's part of why we stay safe." Gavin sighed as he pulled a thick gunmetal gray card from his breast pocket. "Once the fights are over, the portals close. The only way in or out is with one of these."

"What's that? Some kind of members-only key card?" I asked, reaching for it.

Gavin pulled his hand back. "Something like that." He pressed his thumb into its smooth surface, and it flared with holographic light, a portal appearing right beside him. "Well, lads, your chariot awaits."

I glanced from Gavin to Ben, waiting for my brother to balk at the offer. Instead, he shrugged and walked through. I followed, because what else could I do?

Instead of the cold, clean air of home, I was slapped in the face by the scent of sex. A lot of it.

Iniquity.

There was nowhere in the world quite like Lilith's club for the supernaturally depraved and adventurous.

"Fuck, Lilypad, keep going." A haughty British accent filled the hall, coming from the door to our left. "Make me your good little poppet."

"Hush, darling. Mummy hasn't given you permission to speak. Don't make me spank you again."

"But I like it when you spank me," the unfamiliar voice crooned.

A yelp of pleasure followed the words.

"Sounds like he got what he was after," I muttered.

Gavin shook his head. "Topping from the bottom. That's not how a good submissive behaves."

"M-maybe not, b-but something t-tells me Lilith is a b-brat tamer."

I cut a shocked glare at Ben. "How do you suddenly know about brat tamers?"

His brow lifted. "R-research."

I should have known. The second Rosie mentioned she was into power dynamics, Ben's need to provide for her would have kicked in. He'll be an expert in a matter of weeks. I risked a glance at Gavin, who was also giving my brother a curious look. I could already see the battle for dominance that would ensue. The Daddy Dom versus The Sadist. Oh, this was going to be fun. A whole other kind of fight night. One with whips and lube. Lots of lube.

My kind of party.

"Wait there, poppet. We have company."

"What? No! Not again." There was a low growl of frustration followed by the rattle of . . . chains?

The click of heels on hardwood was accompanied by the creak of the door opening. Lilith Duval stood in the doorway, her body clad in shiny black leather, a red corset around her waist, tits practically falling out of her top. She was the personification of sex positivity.

"What on earth do you three want? Are you here to give us a show, Gavin? I have to admit, the crowd would love watching you dominate two handsome shifters. And it's been ages since we've had twins."

Gavin was hot, but the thought of pain mixed in with sex really didn't do it for me. Aside from Rosie's nails down my back or Asher's hands in my hair. I filed that idea away for later.

"Hard p-pass," Ben said, nearly at the same time Gavin shook his head. "Not today."

"Then why are you here?"

"I have a favor to ask of you."

"A favor? My, you're making a habit of collecting them, aren't you? Are you sure you can afford me, darling duke?"

"Put it on my tab."

She tsked. "My favors aren't cheap. You already owe me one. Be certain you want to add a second."

"We just need to make use of your portals so we can get back to Aurora Springs. Hardly an expensive request."

She made a throaty purring sound. "Value has so very little to do with cost. Though I must admit I'm intrigued by this Alaskan hideaway of yours. Aurora Springs sounds charming."

"It's . . . small," Gavin grumbled.

"That's what she said." I couldn't resist.

"Remi, w-we don't have t-time for j-jokes." Ben stepped closer to Lilith with his head held high. "What d-do you want from us? I have to g-get home."

Lilith reached out and ran her fingertips across Ben's jaw, then took his chin between her thumb and forefinger as she stared into his eyes. "Oh, you positively reek of her. All of you do. Wait here. I won't be a minute."

"I beg your pardon?" Gavin's voice came out as a harsh growl.

"I'm due for a holiday, and since dukeykins here couldn't wait for me to come to him, I'll just join you now. Helping stop the end of the world was exhausting, not to mention the remodel. Some quality time in a quaint little

Alaskan town will be just the thing." She turned on her heels and strode away, leaving the door open as she called to her partner, "Playtime's over, darling. We're going on a trip."

"But . . . but I haven't come yet," he whined.

"Just remember how hard you came the last time we engaged in a little edging."

"A little? Lilypad, it's been days."

"Oh hush, poppet. Unless you want me to leave you behind."

"You know you can't."

"Oh, I know. I'm perfectly aware of the terms of our arrangement, dearest. I just wanted to give you the illusion of choice."

Ben and I exchanged glances. Mine asking, *What the hell is up with these two?* His a confused, *Fuck if I know.*

"Fine," her pet bit out. "Where are we going?"

"Alaska."

"What in the ever-loving hell is in Alaska?" he demanded over the sounds of locks being undone.

"That's what I intend to find out."

Traveling by portal was one thing. By demon magic, another. My stomach churned as the group of us materialized in the middle of The Tip. If I wasn't so focused on Rosie and Asher, I'd have needed a fucking minute to get my shit together. But the two of them were on the floor, Asher unconscious, Rosie's expression stricken with worry, a phone by her knee.

I couldn't take it.

"What happened to him? Who hurt him?" I practically

threw myself at them both, dropping on the other side of Asher and placing my fingers on his throat. His pulse was there. Faint and thready, but still beating.

"He just passed out. I think it has to do with the curse."

"Curse? What the fuck are you talking about?" My heartbeat skyrocketed, the organ thundering in my chest as panic took hold.

Rosie opened her mouth and then closed it, at a loss. Her gaze darted around the room, taking in our hitchhikers with surprise. "Why are they here?"

"Don't worry about them. Tell me what you mean when you say curse."

She hesitantly reached out and touched Asher's wrist, then followed the tattooed map of stars up his arm, trailing her fingers along the pattern until she reached the place they stopped, right over his chest. "This."

"It's a tattoo."

"Tattoos don't grow, Remi. This is his curse."

Gavin made a sound that might have been, "Ah-ha," but my attention was locked on Rosie.

I shook my head, denial a good friend of mine. "He would have told me about it."

My twin moved over, placing his hand on my shoulder. "When? You t-two were always f-fighting."

"*Are*. We are always fighting. No past fucking tense about it."

Lilith tutted. "It's killing him. I can feel the life draining from him. These sorts of things always hit hybrids the hardest."

Rosie's head snapped to her. "Hybrid? What are you going on about? Asher's human."

"Part of him is."

"Enough games, Lilith. If you know something, you better fucking share it," I spat.

"Or what, puppy? You're going to hurt me?" She laughed, a dark rumble that rolled through the bar. "I think not."

The dark-haired man with his silver eyes took an aggressive step forward. Power coiled between the two of them, and I swallowed, rethinking my stance. I didn't know who he was or what he could do, but now didn't seem like a great time to find out.

"Besides, I can't tell you. I don't even think the boy knows what he is."

Fuck. Asher wasn't human. He was cursed and dying. And my girl was hurting because of it. Hell, I was hurting. I needed him.

Shaking him, I leaned close and whispered, "Wake up, you nerdy fuck. We have some serious conversations ahead of us about you not keeping things from me."

His eyes shifted beneath his eyelids, but he didn't make any other move or sound. Feeling helpless in a way I hadn't since I was a kid, I took his hand in mine and squeezed. "You better not die on me, you fucking asshole."

"Romantic," Gavin snarled softly.

Lilith's head turned, her gaze on the door. "Oh, goody. Company."

"What?" But the way Rosie tensed as she got to her feet told me everything I needed to know. "What did you do, baby girl?"

"Before he passed out, Asher asked me to make a call. Someone he, uh, thought might be able to help."

"Well then, what the hell are you waiting for—"

"Interesting choice of words," Lilith murmured.

"—open the goddamned door."

But we didn't need to. Whoever was behind it blew the heavy wood off its hinges. Shit.

A tiny woman dressed in leather and lace strode in. She looked like a little punk rock Barbie doll with both sides of her head shaved and a long mane of vibrant orange hair running down the center.

"Belladonna," Lilith said, a smirk in her voice.

"Lilith? What are you doing here?"

"I'm just the delivery girl. But I had to stay and see what all the fuss was about."

Rosie glanced at the doorway, then to the little witch. "But I thought . . . He saw . . ."

Relief flickered in her eyes until a tall man strode into the bar, his dark hair slicked back, his pristine clothes something I would have seen on a model in a magazine. Another vampire. But when he turned his molten amber gaze on us, I realized he wasn't just a leech. He was a Blackthorne.

"Noah," Rosie whispered.

"Rosie? It's true? You're alive."

Oh, shit. No wonder she was so nervous. My loyalties were torn between holding on to Asher and protecting her from the shitstorm that was obviously heading her way.

Thankfully, Ben and Gavin had no such issues. Ben stepped up until he was beside Rosie, his arm curled protectively around her shoulders.

Noah's eyes tracked the move. "Who the hell are you?"

"Her mate."

Not a hint of stutter. Good job, Benny boy.

Noah looked like he had something to say to that, but then Gavin stalked forward, and Noah's expression turned murderous. "You."

Ever the insufferable prick, Gavin plucked at his cuffs

and drawled. "Yes, me. Glad to see my reputation continues to precede me, Blackthorne."

"You knew? It doesn't make sense. We thought she was dead. We buried her. You mourned her, and you knew all this time."

"You buried something, but it definitely wasn't her," Lilith's pet offered helpfully.

Before anyone had a chance to respond to that, yet another newcomer jogged into the wide-open door. His sandy blond hair wind tousled, his lips curled up in an easy smile. "Sorry I'm late." He patted his flat stomach. "This dad bod is really slowing me down."

"Kingston?" Rosie asked, looking torn between shock and laughter. "Why are you here?"

"I couldn't let Thorne have all the fun. Someone has to watch his ass. Sunday would have my balls if anything happened to him—and not in the fun way. She would have come herself, but she can't leave Eden."

"She had the baby," Rosie said, her expression softening. "I'm an aunt."

"I told Asher the Apocalypse ended. Goddess, no one listens to me. It's like I'm talking to a bunch of pretty walls." Belladonna, or whatever her name was, threw her hands up and huffed.

"Look, I don't give two shits who you all are right now." I locked my gaze on Asher and then focused on the witch. "You. Fix him. Now."

"I need you to take your hands off him first," she said gently.

Surprising myself, a low growl escaped. She wanted me to step away from my injured . . . Asher?

"Please, Remi?" Rosie begged as Ben shifted his hold so he had her against his chest, his arms around her waist.

I hated it, but I backed away, going to my twin and our mate for comfort. I couldn't be alone while I watched the witch work on Asher.

Noah's shrewd gaze found where I'd linked hands with Rosie, but I didn't say anything.

"Hey, look at that, Thorne. Your little sis has more than one too. Maybe multiple mates runs in the family."

"No. It doesn't. I have one mate. Sunday has more." Noah stared hard at me, then turned his attention to Rosie again. "Is this why you ran? Did you really think we—I—wouldn't understand?"

"It's . . . complicated."

Noah's gaze shot around the room, landing on Gavin. "I can see that. Want to tell me what your fiancé is doing here?"

"Husband," Gavin corrected.

Kingston breathed in, choking on his laughter. "Fuck, I need popcorn. This is better than that soap Sunday has me watching."

"You mean the one you never miss an episode of and watch alone?" Belladonna quipped as she held her hand over Asher's bare chest. "Now, hush. I'm trying to concentrate."

"Shut it, Sabrina."

Ah, so her name was Sabrina.

"For the last time, Kingston. My. Name. Is. Moira. Do you need me to tattoo it on your dick for you?"

"Leave Jake out of this."

"Who the fuck is Jake?" I whispered, thoroughly confused but as invested in this little drama as I was in Asher's. These people knew my mate, were her friends and family. I wanted to memorize every detail.

"His member," Rosie murmured.

"H-how do you know?" Ben rumbled.

"He won't shut up about it," she said so dryly any trace of jealousy evaporated.

"Still can't say cock, huh, princess?" Kingston teased.

Moira huffed again. "Everyone, shut up. I'm trying to save Asher's fucking life, and you're distracting me. Honestly, this is what they mean when they say too many cocks in the kitchen."

"I don't think that's the—" Kingston started, but Moira shut him up with a withering glare.

Noah's menacing stare at Gavin was impossible to ignore. "That's fine. Donoghue and I need to have a conversation anyway."

"And that's my cue," Kingston said, stepping up next to Rosie's brother.

"What are you doing?"

"We're gonna duel, right? I'm your second."

"Jesus. You have to stop watching Bridgerton."

"Eden loves it. The music puts her to sleep."

"And you really need to stop blaming our newborn daughter for your binging habits."

I heard all of this, but my eyes were still trained on Moira, watching her lips move silently as she muttered the words of whatever spell she was performing. I wasn't sure what I was expecting. A flash of light, some glowy hands, but it sure as fuck wasn't Asher gasping and sitting straight up like he'd just woke from the dead.

"Fuck."

I honestly didn't care what he said. I just loved hearing his voice. My eyes stung as the emotional weight crushing my chest was lifted. I might never have heard him talk again. The thought made my knees weak. Never releasing

Rosie's hand, I pulled her with me, and the two of us went to Asher.

"What's . . . with the . . . long faces?" Asher asked through labored breaths.

"You almost died," Rosie whispered.

"You fucker."

"Oh. Yeah." He rubbed at the back of his head. "That. What's a little case of near death between friends?"

"Mates. We are mates, you tosser."

"Oh, look, there's the fourth one. She's got a full set."

"Can it, Kingston." Noah's admonishment was soft and barely audible as the blood rushed to my ears.

"Why didn't you tell me?" The hurt I didn't want to admit to was in my voice as I forced Asher to meet my gaze head-on. What I found there devastated me. Relief. Panic. Regret. Love.

"Why do you care?"

I growled. "Because you're mine."

"I thought he was hers?" Kingston stage whispered.

"They're a throuple, you twinkie."

"A what-ple?"

"Oh my God. Rosie loves all of them. They all love Rosie. But Asher and Remi love each other, too."

"Fuck, I need to take notes," Kingston said.

"Wait, what?" Asher said, his eyes wide as he looked over at Moira.

My heart ran wild. Is that what this was? I knew I needed Asher, couldn't give him up. But was what I felt for him the same as what I felt for her? Was that even possible? Could I have two mates?

"Oops. Spoiler alert," Moira said, hand up to her lips.

"But . . . Rosie is yours." The disbelief in Asher's voice had my heart doing this weird squeezing thing.

But as I looked at them, I realized the truth. Moira was right, even if I wasn't ready to say the words. "Both of you are mine. This doesn't work without you. I can't . . . I can't lose you."

"Neither can I," Rosie added, taking my hand as she held Asher's with her other. "We're a unit. All of us."

"Oh, I get it. Throuple. Like a couple. But three of them," Kingston announced, breaking through our moment.

"Can we get rid of him?" I muttered.

"No. Unfortunately. He's here to stay. Trust me, I tried," Noah grumbled as I helped Asher to his feet.

"So, is he okay? He's fixed? You magicked it away?" I asked, looking at Moira, who was now sitting on a barstool, her face pale and her eyes ringed in dark circles, her hair now bone-white and in a sloppy bun.

"For now," she said on a sigh. "It's like putting a bandage on a sucking chest wound, though. It's going to happen again. I just don't know when."

"That doesn't make me feel very confident, Moira." Asher leaned on me as we stood together.

"It shouldn't. You need to break the curse, not try to stop it."

"How long do I have?"

"What part of I don't know did you misunderstand? It could be weeks. Days. Twenty minutes. I. Don't. Know. What I do know is this is bad, and you are running out of time."

Asher was pale, but he managed to keep his voice steady. "Well, I guess it's a good thing we called in the calvary then. You can help me end it. For good this time."

"I'm not staying. I've got a wife at home waiting on me. But I'll do what I can from there." She pulled a little blue ball out of her pocket and held it up. "Kingston? Noah? You coming?"

"No. I have a few things to discuss with my new brother-in-law. Don't worry about me, Moira. I can get home just fine on my own." The expression on Noah's face said his discussion was going to be more like a fistfight.

"I'm staying with Thorne. Jake's happiness is on the line. I won't let him suffer because Thorne got himself hurt," Kingston said.

Noah ignored him and walked to the doorway. "Gavin. Outside."

"Noah . . ."

Rosie's brother looked back at her. "You and I can talk after. I've seen enough in his depraved mind to know you deserve so much better than what he's done."

Oh, shit. I forgot about the vampire mind reading stuff.

Gavin removed his jacket and smirked as he neatly placed it on the back of a chair. "That's only a glimpse of what I plan for her."

Noah's lip curled in a sneer. "Outside."

Rosie let out a long-suffering sigh as she released her hold on Asher and followed. Only then did Ben's brow furrow as he looked behind me.

"Where did Lilith g-go?"

THIRTY-ONE

I wondered how my wife would react to me killing her brother. Likely not well. She'd punish me for it, but this was a matter of honor, and Noah Blackthorne had challenged me. I couldn't let it go unanswered. I stalked out of the bar, following after him until the two of us stood in the middle of Main Street with nothing but a single light shining down on us under a cloud-filled sky.

"Where shall we do this?" Blackthorne asked, glancing down the empty boulevard. "Here?"

"The venue doesn't matter. I'm going to wipe the floor with you regardless."

Kingston positioned himself next to Noah, his posture tense and ready for a fight. "Will the townspeople care if there are pieces of this asshat all over their street when they wake up?" He snorted. "Oh, never mind. Whatever's left of him will be ashes by the time the sun rises. No problem. He's like a self-cleaning oven."

"He's had my blood. He won't burn." Roslyn's voice coated me in pride and pleasure all at the same time. She wasn't quite coming to my defense, but she acknowledged what had passed between us.

Blackthorne didn't like that. His jaw tensed, and retribution flashed in his amber eyes, so like his sister's.

"You gave him your blood?"

Roslyn brought herself directly between her brother and me, glancing from me to him. "He's my mate, Noah. Please tell me you don't need me to explain this to you, or I'm going to need to send Sunday a heartfelt apology note on your behalf."

Remington snickered from where he was leaning against the facade of The Tipsy Moose with Asher on one side and Bentley on the other. "Our girl doesn't take shit from anyone. Not even her brother."

"Especially not her brother," Noah tossed out. "Much to my dismay."

"So how does this work?" Kingston asked, bouncing from foot to foot, shaking out his arms like a boxer in the corner of his ring. "Do we need to drop a flag? Count down? Does someone bust out dueling pistols? More importantly, when do I get to kick some ass?"

"No pistols," Roslyn said. "Vampires tend to deal in breaking minds rather than bodies. It's too easy to spill blood."

The wolf deflated as though someone had popped a hole in him. "What? Thorne, you really should have told me that before you asked me to be your second."

"I never asked you to be my second."

"It was implied."

"How? I don't recall even asking you to come."

Kingston's expression fell. "Never mind. It's not important."

"If it makes you feel better, Donoghue doesn't even

have a second," Noah offered. "That makes you the best second here."

"Damn straight," Kingston said, recovering some of his bravado. Then he slapped Blackthorne on the shoulder. "All right, buddy. You got this. Go twist his mind or . . . whatever."

I rolled my eyes. How pathetic. I couldn't believe this one had been allowed to procreate. I pitied his children. They were doomed.

"First one to their knees loses," I grumbled. "Anything goes."

Blackthorne steeled himself and nodded. "You've taken advantage of my sister. I saw what you did to her. What you made her do. She deserves better than a man who'll make her crawl."

Roslyn stiffened, her cheeks flushing pink. "You were rooting around in his mind?"

"No. I was in yours. Honestly, Rosie. This is who you want to be mated to?"

"You had no right." Her hands balled into fists, and she looked all but ready to fling herself at him.

"Hey! We don't kink shame. Not cool," Remington called out.

"If it's consensual, you shouldn't care, man," Asher added.

Kingston pointed in their direction. "The throuple has a point."

"Sod off, Kingston. Stop trying to help me."

"I'm just saying, man, if your sister's into it—"

"Stop it, Farrell. I don't need you speaking to me of my sister's bedroom habits."

"Are you sure? Because it sounds like maybe you're taking the big brother protective thing a little too far."

"This? From you. What if it was Tessa?"

"Oh, enough," I snapped, over whatever the fuck this was. "You have a problem with me, Blackthorne. Fine. Let us deal with it like vampire males should."

I lashed out at his mind, burrowing deep and catching him off guard if his hiss of pain was any indication. I went straight for the kill, twisting memories of his mate, showing her dead and bloody on the altar of some church I'd never seen before, the world ending around him.

He cried out in pain, clutching his head, but he didn't fall.

In a surprising display of mental fortitude, he lifted his eyes, slowly meeting and holding my gaze, before he latched on to my own secret shame. Danika. Still. Lifeless. Her throat marked by my hands, face mottled, eyes open and unseeing.

But that wasn't all. On its heels came others. My father beating me. Every hateful world he hurled in my direction, swirling around me like a swarm of angry wasps.

A cold sweat broke out on my skin, my stomach rolling as nausea followed the memories he wasn't even twisting. These were my truths, and *he* was witnessing them. I'd opened my mind and exposed myself like the arrogant duke I was.

"You should be locked away in the Council's dungeon," Blackthorne snarled. "My sister should never have been forced to marry you."

"Perhaps not, but she's mine now, and there's nothing you can do about it. 'Til death do us part, Blackthorne."

This time I was more creative with my attack. I spun image after image of his daughter and mate, twisted, bloodied, damned. I recycled the nightmare of Death coming for his family. Though his sister's screams for mercy were nearly unbearable to hear. I blame that chink in my armor for what happened next.

Noah screamed in agony but came at me full force, the visual of Roslyn's charred remains assaulting me. The funeral, her casket, open and displaying her unmarked face, and with them the blame for all of it on my shoulders. Except this time, in his fabricated vision, she hadn't faked her death, and she wore my mark on her neck, the very spot it should have been placed the night we were wed.

"Stop," I gasped before I could keep the words held inside.

"What was that?"

"I said stop, you fucking wanker!"

The assault on my mind ceased, but the aftereffects lingered as I dropped to my knees and conceded. I was trembling, disturbed beyond anything I was used to feeling. I didn't understand why what he'd shown me had me reacting this way, but the end result was undeniable. I hadn't been able to withstand it.

She'd been my undoing.

Again.

"Is it just me, or was that pretty underwhelming?" Kingston asked, causing everyone to turn their gazes on him. "What? Is it so wrong that I expected blood? I mean . . . vampires."

Blackthorne's outstretched palm was the first thing I could fully focus on. His expression was telling. He was the only other person who knew what I'd seen and experienced. This was why vampires rarely dueled. We were opening ourselves to each other, experiencing the truths hidden deep in the recesses of our opponent's mind. Now I knew his weak points, and he knew mine. Apparently, his sister was mine.

I took his offered hand and got to my feet, legs still shaky.

"At least that answers one question," Noah said, his voice softer than I'd heard it thus far.

"What's that?"

"I know now it isn't a charade. You really do care about her."

Roslyn came to me, curling her body into my side and offering me her silent support.

I fucking needed her, and I hated to admit it. "I do."

"Gavin," Roslyn breathed.

"This is over," Noah said, running his hand through his hair.

"What? Excuse me, but I was promised a duel. I came all the way out here with your ass. I could be balls deep in—"

"Stop it, Kingston. I need to talk to my sister, and then we'll go home. You can do whatever you like then."

Bentley stepped forward, his blue irises focused on Roslyn. "The o-office is open. Or th-the apartment."

Roslyn extricated herself from my hold and went to her brother. "Come on, big brother. You're right. We need to clear the air. I have a lot to answer for."

Still inwardly reeling, I watched as the siblings walked back into the bar, leaving the rest of us standing out in the middle of the street like the pathetic wretches we were.

Kingston was the first to break the silence. "Well . . . I've got to admit, that was a letdown."

"Were you hoping to get your ass kicked?" Remington asked, pushing off the wall to join us in the street. "Because we can still make that happen."

"I'll pass. I'm too pretty to get punched. But I'll settle for a race."

The way Remington's eyes lit up, I knew the shifters

would be gone in moments. Good riddance. They were a nuisance I could do without.

The cockiest of the Mercers glanced back at Asher, who had slid down the wall and was sitting on the pavement. "I'm fine. Just tired. Go. Run, wolf boy."

"I've g-got him. He'll be okay. Just be b-back before sunup," Bentley called as he helped Asher to his feet and they made their way into the bar.

"Yes, dad!" Kingston and Remington both shouted as they headed around the bar and into the alley. Two peas in a fucking pod.

Seconds passed before two wolves bounded past me, leaving me in the middle of the street with my heart cracked wide open by the emotions assaulting me. I was more than mated to Roslyn. She had a hold on me no one else could ever claim, and I didn't know what to do with the newfound understanding.

The one thing I did know was I couldn't stay here.

With Roslyn safely inside the Tipsy Moose and the threats to all of us managed, for the time being, I slipped away into the night.

THIRTY-TWO

The tension rolling off Noah as he paced the floor of my old apartment weighed heavily on me. While I couldn't read his thoughts, I could sense his emotions, even if he wasn't telegraphing them so strongly.

More than once, he opened his mouth, and I braced myself for his tongue-lashing, only for him to close it, grunt in annoyance, and resume pacing.

"You're going to be bald if you keep tugging at your hair like that," I said lightly, finally breaking the silence.

"That's the least of my worries." He wouldn't look at me, his shoulders tight and jaw clenched. Then he turned his luminous amber gaze on me. "I watched you die, Rosie. Over and over. I was forced to endure it and know there wasn't a damn thing I could do to save you."

"W-what? How?"

How's that possible? I didn't actually die. There was nothing for him to witness, even if he was home. Which he hadn't been.

"It doesn't matter. I just . . . I'm having a little trouble coming to terms with the fact you're sitting in front of me. I can't decide if I'm grateful, relieved, or bloody furious. Do you have any idea what it was like for us? Burying you? Mourning you? Only to find out none of it was real."

"I should hope you're more relieved than anything. Unless you'd like to go back to thinking I'm dead?"

He leveled me with an exasperated look only an older brother could manage. "Of course I'm relieved. I just don't understand how you could willingly allow us to believe you were ever dead."

Crushing waves of guilt assaulted me with each word, but he continued, the need to get everything off his chest eclipsing his awareness of my mental state.

"Father is beside himself. He's lost everything, you, our home, and . . . Mum."

Ice filled my veins. "But she's fine. She was hurt in the fire, but Father healed her."

Right? Come to think of it, I never really got much detail from Gavin about the extent of my mum's injuries. I'd just assumed . . .

"She's different now that she's been turned," Noah said.

"Turned? What?" My stomach rolled. Mother had been staunchly against becoming a vampire. She'd refused our father's requests time and time again. "Father wouldn't do that to her."

"It was that or let her die."

My blood ran cold. She would never forgive him if he changed her without her consent. "Did she . . . ask for this?"

"She gave her consent. But it's been difficult. She'll never quite be the woman she was now that she's a vampire."

I gripped my hands tight, my eyes trained on my knees. "I'm sorry. Faking my death was the only way, Noah. You have to know I never would have done it otherwise."

He exhaled heavily and took a seat beside me on the

sofa. "I know, but couldn't you trust us with your secret? It must have been so hard doing all of that on your own."

"I knew you'd take my secret to the grave, Noah. That was never the issue. There could be no doubt it was real, don't you see? The Donoghues would never have left you alone otherwise. They . . . had plans for me. For any children I might bear Gavin. And if I didn't, they were going to do unspeakable things to you all to keep me in line. I just . . . I couldn't allow it to happen."

"And they would've taken the knowledge from our minds if given the chance . . ." he said, the thought trailing off as he stared into the distance.

I nodded. "Noah, I'm sorry. For all of it. It didn't even matter in the end. Gavin found me anyway."

"You don't have to stay with him."

"You know as well as I do that mate bonds are stronger than will. Especially when we're fated."

"That implies he's forcing you, Rosie. You should still want to be his, mate bond or not."

Letting out a heavy sigh, I stood and walked into the kitchen, just to give myself something to do as I admitted this next part.

"I do want to be his. I crave it. I never really wanted to leave him behind, but there wasn't another way. He was as entrenched in his family, his bloodline, as the Blackthornes are."

"Do you trust him?"

Did I? That was a difficult question to answer. With my body? Yes. With my secret? He'd kept it so far, so that was promising. With my heart? That was less certain. I wanted to. I guess only time would tell.

"Rosie?"

"Yes. At least, I think so."

"So . . . you feel for him the way I do for Sunday? The pull is that strong?"

Would I run to the ends of the earth for Gavin? I wasn't sure. I'd done the opposite at the first sign of trouble. I'd run away. But after a moment, when I gave myself the chance to close my eyes and picture my mate in danger, I realized I'd do anything to save him. Just as I'd done for Ben by striking a new deal with Pan.

I'd felt the mate bond calling to me before Gavin fully claimed me. I knew we were connected from the very start. It was why I'd volunteered to marry him in the first place. And seeing him in his element, dominant and strong, unlocked a part of me as well.

I'd always wanted Gavin Donoghue to be mine. But not at the expense of his life. And make no mistake, that's what I'd done when I left. I'd saved him from his family and the war they'd eventually cause. Not to mention the monster he'd become if he didn't have someone to help him out of the dark.

"I do," I finally answered.

Noah nodded like he'd expected as much. "Then I guess it doesn't really matter what I think."

"No, but it would be nice to know I have your support, if not your blessing."

"If this is what you want, Rosie, then it's what I want for you. All that's ever mattered to me is that you are happy and safe."

I looked at my brother, sitting with his head in his hands, shoulders slumped as he processed everything. It was the same thing I'd do if I were in his situation. Sunday hadn't been menacing or the enemy of our family. She hadn't actively tried to harm us. But if she had? I would've been the first with an arrow notched and aimed at her heart.

Tears swam in my vision as I watched him, then my lower lip wobbled. Bloody hell, I didn't want to start crying, but when his own watery gaze found mine, I lost it.

He got to his feet and blurred to me in an instant, pulling me into his arms and holding me tight.

"I've missed you so much," I sobbed into his chest, my words muffled by tears as much as his shirt.

He tightened his embrace, his lips at the crown of my head. "Not as much as I missed you. I'm so fucking glad you aren't dead."

"You understand why we can't tell anyone? The damage this could do . . . if the Donoghues tell the Council I ran from our arrangement . . ."

"They could demand restitution. Again."

"They could take your head, or West's."

"I know." My brother sighed as he released me. "As far as the world's concerned, Roslyn Blackthorne will remain dead. For now. So long as the threat remains, my sister must remain in the ground."

The relief I felt knowing that I didn't have to be completely cut off from my family, but also that Noah would help me protect them, was immense. It was as if a weight I hadn't even realized I'd been carrying was finally gone.

"Did you really have to marry him without any of us present?"

"They sprung it on me. They were going to keep me as their little captive breeder."

"Bastards," Noah snarled. "Still, you could have said something."

"When? While you were off trying to rescue your mate

and stop the Apocalypse? Excuse me if my troubles seemed insignificant by comparison. Especially since I'd brought them on myself. I handled it my own way."

"As you always do." Shoving his hands into his pockets, he frowned. "I have to go back home. Sunday is expecting me, and Eden will be wanting a bedtime story."

"Is she just the most beautiful baby?" I knew she had to be. Any child made by my brother and his mate would be.

"She is." He pulled out an old pocket watch. "This is my favorite photo of her."

I took the offered trinket and opened it. On one side was the fully functional clock face. The other contained a picture of Sunday holding a chubby-cheeked infant with a shock of curly black hair and multicolored eyes, one the Blackthorne amber and one blue. "What a perfect little cherub. She's stunning, Noah."

"She's a little bit of us all. You should see her when she's angry, though. Alek calls her his little valkyrie."

I laughed. "How's the priest handling fatherhood?"

"Taken to it like a duck to water. You'll never get me to admit it to him, but I think he's the best of us."

"I might be biased, but I find it hard to believe anyone is better than you."

My brother blushed a little and knocked me under the chin. "I had lots of practice with a hellraiser of my own."

"I was a perfect angel, thank you very much."

"So was Lucifer. Until the fall."

I feigned a nip at his finger.

We smiled at each other for a second, both lost in a childhood filled with shared memories.

"Call me if you need me, yeah? Day or night, it doesn't matter. We aren't getting much sleep these days anyway."

"I will, but please don't be cross with me if I stay

quiet. I'm settling in here, finding myself, and these guys are helping me. I'll be fine. The end of the world is over."

Something flickered in Noah's expression. "For now."

Dread curled in my belly. "What do you mean, for now?"

"There were four of them. Four horsewomen, and they told Sunday they were playing a game. I don't think this ends with War."

My blood ran cold, and the hairs on the back of my neck stood on end. "Well, that's just bloody brilliant. What do you expect me to do about it?"

"Just do your best to stay out of trouble. But keep an eye out. Trust your gut."

"Have any more cliché advice to offer, big brother?"

My brother laughed, hooking an arm around my neck and pulling me in for another hug. "Just be careful. I already lost you once. I'd rather not have to do it again any time soon. Or ever, for that matter."

My lip quivered again. "Don't make me cry like a bloody schoolgirl again. I'll be on guard, all right? No Apocalypse here."

"Good." He hugged me once more, then looked at his watch. "Kingston and I have to go if we're going to make it home in time for Eden's story."

"Where is home these days?"

"Colorado. The Farrell pack has been surprisingly accepting of us all."

"I'm happy for you. All of you. Please extend my congratulations to Sunday and the rest of your family. Maybe once this is over, I can come for a visit."

"I'll hold you to that." He walked to the door but paused and fished something out of his other pocket. "I forgot. I brought you this. In case you want to have a reminder of your old life."

My heart lurched as he handed me the necklace I'd cherished since the day he gave it to me. It had been more painful than I'd expected to use it as the magical talisman that disguised the body posing as me.

"I never thought I'd see this again." I ran my fingers over the black rose pendant.

"I'm glad it's back where it belongs." Noah opened the door and let out a sharp laugh. "Possessive shifter mates. Why am I not surprised to see you here?"

I leaned around to peer past him, finding Ben and Remi waiting just outside the door. Ben looked sheepish, Remi wearing his trademark smirk.

"I think you mean protective," Remi said. "There's a difference."

"So Kingston loves to remind me."

"Yeah, I kinda love that guy. He's a real wiseass."

"L-like you?" Ben asked.

"There's only one Remington Steele Mercer. But he's a close second."

"Your middle n-name is Elijah." I couldn't help but laugh at the exasperation in Ben's voice.

Remi shot Ben a horrified look. "Hey, you promised never to speak that name again. It's Steele. I changed it when I was like seven."

Ben raised a brow. "D-deciding it's t-true doesn't m-make it true."

"Okay, Bentley Malcolm."

Ben winced.

"Another Kingston. We're all doomed," Noah groaned. "I'll leave you here, then, Rosie. But I'm serious. Anything you need, I'm just a call away."

Remi slipped past him and wrapped me up in an embrace. "Don't you worry, big bro. We're not letting anyone hurt our girl."

"You'd better not. Or you'll answer to me."

I opened my mouth to chastise him, but he was gone before I could utter a word. Damn vampire speed.

"So that's your brother, huh?" Remi asked.

"Yes."

"Can't wait to meet the rest of the in-laws."

THIRTY-THREE

"Oi, let me out. You promised! This isn't our deal. You great bloody wanker."

I chuckled darkly as I turned on the top of the stairs, which led into the dark, dank basement where I'd chained up my meat suit.

"Oh, settle down, Hamish. It's not nice to call people names."

"That's not my name."

"It may as well be."

"You said you'd give me what I wanted after I let you use me."

"And now you know how every disappointed woman you ever slept with felt. Don't think of this as your prison. It's more like a closet."

"A closet?"

"Well, *my* closet. A wardrobe. Except for you, it doesn't lead to Narnia."

His eyes widened. "Where does it lead?"

"You'll see. Eventually."

"What about our deal?" he demanded.

I pulled out the phone I stole from him last time and did a quick Google search. Yes . . . I am intimately familiar with the internet. Who do you think invented it? Viruses aren't just for humans, are they?

"Here. See? You're the world's most famous musician, as promised."

"Missing. Missing musician, you bloody liar."

"Am I a liar? Or are you just terrible at making a proper bargain? Maybe next time you should read the fine print, eh, mate?"

"What fine print?"

I imitated him as I spoke, making hand puppets to reenact our conversation.

"What will you give me in exchange for your desire?"

My right hand, the stupid one—I'm a lefty—yapped in a Scottish brogue. "Anything. Just make me the most famous cocksucker in all of music. I want to fuck women and toss them aside and die of a preventable venereal disease by the time I'm thirty."

"That's—I didn't—you're making that up!"

"Am I? Huh, funny, I have perfect recall. Pretty sure that's exactly how it went. Next time, be more specific. But for now, I need to make use of you once again, so pony up."

"And if I say no?"

Truth was, that ship had long since sailed. He never set any time limits on his willing participation, but no need to rub it in, so I shrugged. "I'll eat your heart and use your fat to make candles."

"Are you ever going to let me go?"

"Perhaps. One day. Once you're no longer of use to me."

He closed his eyes and refused to look at me.

I crossed my arms over my chest and sighed. "Oh, for pity's sake, you are as bad as Henry VIII. He never wanted me to take control, but let me tell you, those were the only times anything got done."

Elton Joan blanched, eyes going wide. "What?"

"Gotcha. Now, let me in, Tedward."

"Tedward?"

That was that Sheeran twat's name, wasn't it? Or was it . . . "Edward?"

"What?"

"Oh, fuck it. I don't care what you call yourself."

"Shouldn't you know my name if you're going to bum a ride in my body?"

I rolled my eyes. "Narcissistic to the core, aren't you?"

"Are you seriously a demon? You can't even remember a name."

I knew his name. I just didn't care to use it. It was more fun this way.

"It doesn't bloody matter! You don't exist anymore. Now shut up and let me in before I turn your mind to liquid."

He slumped against the wall, defeated and resigned, just the way I liked my humans. "Can I at least know what we're doing this time?"

"We're going for a walk."

"Are you having me on?"

I pressed the palm of my hand over his mouth to cease his incessant rambling and stared into his eyes as I poured my essence into him.

This time, he fit less like a glove and more like a soggy pair of Wellies. I really didn't care for it. I had hoped to use him for a while longer, but we'd see. Maybe we'd settle into a better dynamic. Rosie seemed to like his form, at least a little.

Grabbing the leather jacket I'd left on a hook behind the

door, I made my way out of the basement, stopping just before walking outside to give my armpit a cursory sniff. Ugh. Humans were vile. Maybe I'd go for a swim and launder my Scottish suit before hanging him back up to dry.

Popping the collar on this arsehole's ridiculous leather jacket, I swanned right down the main road of this little town, hoping maybe I'd run into my favorite Blackthorne princess. Instead, I wandered aimlessly with ever-growing annoyance gnawing at my gut. I had a task. I had an entire plague to continue spreading. If everyone was dead, no one would be in my way when I reclaimed Rosie.

Instead of walking down toward the harbor, I'd gone inland and stumbled upon a wee loch of sorts. With my attention focused in front of me, I didn't notice the grass blackening beneath my feet or the flowers withering on their vines until I turned back to ensure I hadn't been followed.

I stripped bare, dropping the leathers in a haphazard pile on the dirty forest floor before I did my best impression of John the Baptist and walked into the water. Almost immediately, fish floated to the surface, the pristine glacial water turning a murky algae-infested green.

"There, mother. Even you should be pleased with my day's work."

A deer who'd been drinking at the water's edge fell to the ground, twitching as its eyes rolled back in its head.

"I was going to put up a sign or something, Bambi. I'd apologize, but . . . I really don't care."

I looked around at the pretty landscape, which now showed advanced signs of decay. "Well, David Tennant Bowie, our work here is almost done. One last task and we can call it."

Placing my palms on the water's surface, I closed my

eyes and actively sent a little bit of me out into the wilds, allowing my mother's DNA to infect the once untouched land. Every root system of every tree in this area would soon soak up my plague. The blight would infect this land with a creeping sickness there was no cure for, and before long, all the animals would begin to die off. Plague didn't need a great deal of opportunity to spread. All it took was the right opening and a little bit of negligence.

I'd infect everything around the people of this town before they knew what was happening.

And then, with the aid of Rosie's blood, Pestilence would ride, and no one would be safe from her reign.

THIRTY-FOUR

BEN

The pass-through between the kitchen and bar was clear rather than crowded with tickets for food orders, which wasn't great news for The Tip, but it sure as shit helped me see Rosie. She was chatting with the gargoyles, our only steady customers since my arrest. With the appearance of Whalen Scroggins, back in town after a weeklong fishing trip, today was practically booming by comparison. We'd see if he was a repeat customer once the gossip mill reached him.

I kept an eye trained on the deep fryer, making sure the fish and chips I was cooking up for him didn't burn, and the other on my mate.

In the three days since her brother's unexpected visit, she hadn't gotten around to telling us what they talked about. I was sure it was personal, and probably painful if the tear tracks down her cheeks when they'd opened the door were any indication. Which was why I hadn't pushed for details. She'd tell me when she was ready.

I pulled the fish out of the grease and laid each perfectly

crispy piece on a sheet of newspaper as I waited for the chips to be ready.

"Have I ever told you how much I fancy a man who is good in the kitchen?" Rosie's sweet voice had the tension in my shoulders loosening.

"Th-that's just because y-you need someone to c-cook for you, sugar."

"Doesn't make my appreciation any less real."

I smirked. "Then c-come here and sh-show me your appreciation."

"Mister Mercer . . . at *work*?"

I dumped the basket of fries onto the paper, then stepped toward her, diminishing the distance between us. "I'm the b-boss."

"You are."

"So w-what I say goes."

"Noted."

"Come. Here." I pointed to the spot right in front of me, biting back a smile when her cheeks went pink and her eyes just a touch glassy.

Licking her lips, she practically skipped over to me. "Sir, yes, sir."

My God, the way I wanted her. I kept my cool, though, and leaned down, my mouth at her ear. "I thought it was Daddy."

Her lightly hitched breath sent a twist of anticipation through my stomach.

"K-kiss me, sugar."

Tilting her face up, she rose on tiptoe and brushed her lips over mine. She pulled away too soon, though. A growl rumbled in my throat as I wrapped a hand around her waist and yanked her closer. "More."

A little hum of approval escaped her as I claimed my mate's kiss.

"Should we leave?" Dick shouted through the pass-through.

"What do you mean, leave? I'm waiting on my food!" Whalen shouted in response.

"I can take over in the kitchen for ya, if ya need tae head upstairs for a wee shag," Tom chimed in.

"N-nothing about it would be *wee*." I winked at Rosie, who let out a soft giggle as she palmed my erection through my apron.

"No. Definitely not."

I'd never been more thankful for this half wall separating the kitchen from the rest of the bar.

"Fine. If you're not going to shag her senseless, can you come out here and pour me a refill?" Harry grumbled.

"Looks like my break's over," Rosie said with an exaggerated pout as I plated the food for Whalen.

Taking the dish towel off my shoulder, I snapped it and smacked her right on her plump ass. "Go on then. I'll d-deal with you l-later."

"Can't wait." She picked up Whalen's cone of fish and chips, making a hum of approval. "Just like home."

I returned to the bar, a good-natured glare aimed at the gargoyles. "Three?" I asked, gesturing to their mostly empty pints.

"Aye." Tom smirked as he assessed me. "For a murderer, you're certainly in a good mood."

"Didn't you hear? He's not. That's why they let him go," Harry said, slapping Tom on the back of his head and knocking his cap askew.

"That's what he wants ye tae think. Jack the Ripper

walked around happy as you like between his murderous rampages."

"I'm n-not a m-murderer."

"What do you mean, murderer?" Whalen asked, a little panic in his tone.

Fuck. I snagged the pint glass out of Tom's hand mid-sip and leaned in close, menace in my tone as I whispered, "Are you t-trying to sc-scare away m-my only c-customer?"

"What are we?" Dick asked, face twisted in offense.

"A d-damn nuisance."

Harry laughed. "He's not wrong, lads."

"Well, to be fair, we are gargoyles. Our kind has built a reputation out of scaring the masses. Comes with the territory, I'm afraid," Dick added.

Whalen cast a worried glance at me, then looked to Rosie, who was placing a bottle of malt vinegar on his table. "I think I'll take it to go, thanks."

"Don't let the door hit you on the way out," she said, giving him a smile that was none too friendly.

He shook his head and bolted for the exit after tossing a few bills on the table. "Keep the change."

"Oh, goodie. Fifty pence. How generous."

"Good riddance," Tom grunted as he lifted his fresh pint to his mouth.

But I was worried. How could I provide for my mate if I didn't have any money to do that?

Good thing she has others to help out.

That little reminder was not appreciated. If anything, it only reinforced my feeling of inadequacy. Gavin was wealthier than more than a few small countries, but I still needed to know that I was able to give Rosie everything she could ever want or need. She was mine to care for and protect. In every way.

"Hey, it's going to be okay. Your customers will come back. I promise. They just need some time for things to blow over." Rosie smoothed her thumb along the wrinkle between my brows. "Besides, you're the only bar in town. Where else are they going to go?"

"Th-thanks for the vote of c-confidence."

Tom, Dick, and Harry began yammering among themselves, but I didn't pay any attention. I was too busy looking at the beautiful woman who continued to show me what having a pack really meant.

"I'm sure we could get Remi to go drag people in."

"A-are you offering t-to threaten people into d-drinking here?"

"Uh-huh. Whatever it takes."

"Nah, things will settle down once the sheriff gets off his lazy arse and makes a new arrest." The interruption from Dick reminded me we weren't alone. The gargoyle was right, though.

"W-we'll see."

The door swung open as if on cue, letting in a gust of wind and rain, bringing with it a familiar blond-haired hacker. It was startling seeing him walk around without one of his costumes, but not unwelcome.

"See!" Harry crowed. "They're comin' back to you already."

Rosie's face lit up, and she bounded over to him, wrapping him up in a tight hug that nearly knocked him over.

"How come we didnae get one of those?" Tom asked.

"We're not fucking her," Dick offered.

"And he is?"

"Probably. Look at the way he's cuppin' her arse." Dick waggled his eyebrows. "That's the grip of a man who's seen her naked."

"Or at least wants to," Harry chimed in.

"Enough," I snapped.

But the gargoyles weren't threatened. They simply pressed their heads closer together and dropped their voices as they continued with their whispered conversation.

I shook my head and sighed, pushing away from the bar and grabbing a fresh towel to start my hourly wipe down.

The door opened again, another rush of wet leaves and blustery wind coming with the patron. As one, the three gargoyles gawked as Lilith and her pet, Crombie, walked inside. It could not be more obvious she did not belong in Aurora Springs. She was leather and dominance; this place was flannel and desperation.

She trained her gaze on them and narrowed her eyes, a low hiss leaving her before she said, "Leave. Now."

Without so much as a grumble, the three gargoyles hopped off their benches and scurried for the door.

My brows lifted in surprise. Why were they so scared of her? Those three had seen me do far worse, and I couldn't get them to do a damn thing I said. But the succubus walks in and has them tucking tail with two words.

"Lovely. Now we can get to business."

THIRTY-FIVE

Fuck, she smells good.

I pressed my nose deeper into Rosie's neck, inhaling her sugar cookie and citrus scent. "I could fucking devour you."

She giggled and held me tighter. "You might want to wait until we're somewhere less public. Unless audiences are your thing."

"Are they *your* thing, princess?"

The way she tilted her face up to stare at me, blinking those big eyes innocently . . . goddamn. "Only when it's you who's watching."

"We could take a little trip to the back alley and recreate the other night."

Her cheeks flamed, and she bit her lower lip. "Later."

"Promise?"

Running her fingertip across my chest, she drew an X over my heart. "Cross your heart."

I snagged her hand and brought it to my lips, pressing a light kiss to her fingertips before biting down gently. "That's not how the saying goes."

"I don't care."

"Me either," I admitted, so wrapped up in her and the spell she was weaving around us I didn't notice the newcomers until they were almost on top of us.

My spine stiffened as realization dawned on me. The succubus, Lilith Duval, stood in the doorway within arm's reach of where we were still standing wrapped up in each other, a man I didn't have intel on at her side. Who the fuck was this guy? Why didn't I know him?

The idea that I could've missed someone connected to a powerful demon who had her fingers in all the supernatural pies irked me. She was one of those creatures I always had in my periphery. You never knew what kind of mischief she would make. Whether she'd use her power for good or evil.

When her eyes landed on me, every hair on my body stood on end. Thank fuck for my beanie, or I was pretty sure I'd look like I just stuck my finger in the light socket. It took everything in me to play it cool and pretend I didn't know how dangerous she was.

"Well, this is a surprise. A half-breed and a demon-marked. Aurora Springs is just filled with all sorts of delicious secrets."

My blood roared in my ears. What the fuck was that supposed to mean? Rosie was technically a half-breed, though the preferred term was hybrid—something told me Lilith didn't care about harmful language—did that mean I was demon-marked? Is that what this curse was?

I flexed my tattooed arm and fought a wince at the tingles that raced along the stars etched into my skin.

"Everyone needs a place they can exist without their secrets being spilled, demon," I grumbled.

"That's Mistress demon to you, *human*," the man at her side snarled.

I raised a brow. "I was under the impression those sorts of titles had to be earned."

The dark-haired man sneered. "She's the bloody queen of demons. I'd say it was more than earned."

Lilith pressed her hand to his chest and licked his cheek. "I do so love it when you defend my honor, poppet."

"He's being petulant and disrespectful. I'm the only one allowed to do that." He gave the thin gold chain linking them a little tug, as if he was emphasizing the point.

What. The. Fuck?

Beside me, Rosie's eyes had glazed, and she gave a little shiver. "Is it hot in here?"

Lilith closed the distance between us, the movement making Ben tense as a low growl rumbled in his chest.

"Look into my eyes," she murmured, training her stare on me. A little furrow developed between her brows as she assessed me, then her forehead smoothed and she snatched my left hand, inspecting my mark. "Oh, you poor soul."

My mouth went dry. "You know what this is?"

"Of course I do," she murmured, her thumb lightly rubbing circles on my palm.

"Can you stop it?" Rosie asked, her voice hopeful.

"Stop what?"

"The curse."

"Oh . . ."

Her fingers traveled up my arm, sending tingles shooting through my entire body, my dick growing painfully hard. This chick was *potent*. Fucking succubi.

"That's what we're calling it? A curse?"

"What else would you call it?"

"Your burden. Your legacy. Your destiny. Take your pick. And no. I can't stop it. Fate is . . . inevitable."

"Well, that's just great. Thanks a million for all the help. Can you stop touching me now?"

Her crimson lips twisted into a smile. "Darling, I never said I came here to help."

"Why are y-you still here?" Ben asked, finally in control of his wolf enough to speak. I'd seen him trying to work through the situation from the corner of my eye. She's lucky he didn't attack.

"You never know when you'll find the perfect investment opportunity."

"What?" Rosie asked.

"I've been considering expanding my empire, darling. This sleepy little town might just be the perfect place for a second club."

"Here? You can't be serious, Lilypad."

She jerked on the thin chain wrapped around her wrist, and he sucked in a sharp breath. "Think of the possibilities. A town composed solely of supernaturals. They feed me so much better than mere humans ever could. I am sure, if our Roslyn is anything to go by, the people of Aurora Springs are . . . in need of a place they can get their freak on—as the kids say."

The kids. This chick was a trip. Not at all what I expected the first demon to be like.

Her companion made a grumpy sound in the back of his throat. "But I hate it here."

"I'm certain I can make it worth your while, pet."

"Promises, promises."

"Sweetheart, you know I always keep my promises."

His eyes went molten. "Thank fuck. It's the only thing that makes our arrangement bearable."

"The only thing?"

His eyes dropped down her body, and his lips curled in a smile that not even I was immune to. "Maybe not the *only* thing."

"Now," Lilith clapped her hands together. "We are famished. Who do I have to get off to find a meal around here?"

"No one," Ben grumbled right before her plaything made a disgruntled choking sound.

"Perfect. We'll have two of your night's special."

"W-we don't have a s-special."

"Oh, for pity's sake. No wonder you have no customers. If you need tips, handsome, I'd be happy to offer you a trade. My business expertise in exchange for your . . . lust."

Ben's brows drew together. "Pass."

"A hand pie will suffice." Lilith rolled her eyes as she and her friend strolled across the floor and hopped onto two of the barstools usually occupied by the gargoyles.

Ben kissed Rosie's cheek and then muttered beneath his breath as he stalked back into the kitchen.

"Do you guys even serve hand pies?"

"No," Rosie said with a little laugh. "I'm not even sure Ben knows what they are."

"This ought to be interesting," I said warily, keeping my eyes on the demon. I wasn't talking about the food.

"Don't worry, she won't hurt us. My brother knows her well. Lilith is infamously neutral and self-serving. It's how she's stayed alive for so long."

"That and the fact she's a demon. They're kinda hard to kill."

Lilith snapped her fingers. "Roslyn, darling, I'm parched. Pour me a pint, will you, love?"

Rosie gave me a wide-eyed look and then smiled. "Duty calls." She pressed a final kiss to my lips and flounced away.

Lilith trained her blue eyes on me, then patted the stool next to her. "Come, love. Sit by me. We have a lot to discuss."

THIRTY-SIX

I kept one wary eye on Asher as he paced the bar and stared Lilith down. Noah's stories about her left little to the imagination. She was a demon who fed on sexual energy. Asher had that in spades.

I pulled a pint for Lilith and another for her . . . friend? No one had introduced him, and I definitely would have remembered if my brother had mentioned anything about a dark and dangerous fae prince literally attached to Lilith by a thin chain.

He smelled like nighttime and thunderstorms, and I was as intrigued by him as I was by the succubus herself. They were an interesting pair. Not quite a couple and yet obviously connected. It seemed like more than just a relationship of convenience, but I couldn't quite put my finger on their situation.

"It's all right, love. You can look. He is handsome, isn't he? My sweet brat prince." Lilith ran a hand along her pet's jaw. "Crombie, be a love and give the little Blackthorne princess your best smolder."

He glowered at Lilith.

"Ah, perfect," she teased.

"What brings you here from the fae realm?"

"A mistake or twenty."

"And the Hunt, don't forget them."

He tossed Lilith another dark scowl. "Some secrets are best kept among the two of us, wouldn't you agree, Lilypad?"

Lilith rolled her eyes. "I don't see what the big deal is. Everyone knows you belong to me now. No one would dare cross me."

"Not. The. Point."

"Fine. Have it your way. Crombie is my submissive until such a time as I decide he's served his sentence. End of."

"Lilith!"

Instead of responding to him, she snatched my wrist and pulled my arm close to her face as she inspected my skin. I knew what she'd find there. Pan's mark. Unease skittered along my spine. If she was a demon, could she tell he marked me?

"Oh, my, my . . . what's all this, then? Roslyn Blackthorne, you have been a naughty girl indeed." I tried to tug my arm back, but she held firm. "I do hope he made it good for you."

I could feel the blood rush to my face. "It's a business arrangement, nothing more."

She hummed, but I could tell she didn't believe me. "Your body betrays you, love."

The answering wash of arousal had me clenching my thighs and biting back a moan. "What are you doing?"

"Succubus, remember? Now, tell me what sort of dark

desires he unlocked in you. Let me taste a little of your power."

"I don't have power."

One perfectly shaped brow lifted as she connected her gaze to mine. "Don't you? The blood of the sun is one of the greatest powers in existence, my sweet. Vampires the world over would pay a pretty penny to have a single drop. No wonder your father kept you hidden away as long as he did. Now that your mother's blood has been tainted, there's only one pure source." She walked her fingers up my arm, following the blue vein visible through my fair skin. "You."

"What are you talking about?" Asher asked as he finally took a seat at the bar on the other side of Lilith.

"Didn't you know? Our Roslyn is a unique blend of vampire, human, witch, and now . . . demon. It's a heady combination, and it's made her blood even more powerful."

"What? I'm not a demon."

"No, but you've been touched by one. Our kind leaves a mark," she emphasized, pressing hard on Pan's sigil and making my clit throb with need.

I couldn't contain the ragged moan that escaped. Asher mistook it for pain, his hand lashing out and wrapping around her forearm.

"Stop."

She lightened her hold but didn't release me. The woman leaned forward, gaze raking over my exposed throat and grinning wickedly. "And marked by two shifters as well. Lucky girl. Yes, your power is nearly irresistible. I'm surprised more haven't come for you already. Or . . ." Her gaze turned considering, lips curving up in a devious smile. "That was your deal, wasn't it? Pan hides you away here, keeping you for himself. Smart. Devilishly so. He has you right where he wants you, and no one else can steal a taste."

"How do you know his name?"

"Darling girl, I know all my relations." She tapped the sigil again, and it was as if she'd trailed her fingers along my aching core.

An undeniable urge to justify my stupidity took hold, and I blurted, "I . . . I was desperate."

"Of course, darling. They always are. Tell me, has he had you?"

"What?" I wouldn't sit here and tell her about my sexual exploits.

"Your blood? Has he tasted you?"

"Y-yes. That was part of the deal."

She released me, then sighed. "It's always that way with men. Fucking patriarchy. Well, I would caution you to be more careful. You are more valuable than you know. It never ends well when a woman allows a man to steal the source of her power."

Why did those words send anxious shivers along my skin?

"What am I supposed to do? I have to go to him and allow him to drink from me once a month."

Lilith frowned, her attention focused inward. She seemed to be thinking through something, but I couldn't begin to guess what.

"Isn't there something you can do?" Asher asked. "You're the first demon, can't you"—he waved a hand—"undo it or something?"

"It doesn't work that way, silly sausage. A demon's mark is not something easily wiped away. It will stain her forever."

"You said it's not easy to do. That means it's been done." Asher was intense as he leaned closer. "Or are you really not strong enough? This male demon is more powerful than Lilith, the original demon?"

Her eyes flashed with contempt. "No. He's not even close to more powerful. But one bargain cannot be erased without something replacing it."

"Like what?" I asked, my heart thundering.

Lilith trained her shrewd stare on me once more, as though she'd come prepared with a solution. "A deal with a stronger demon."

My tongue darted out to wet my suddenly dry lips. "What would you ask of me?" I'd already given so much, I didn't think there was anything I had left to bargain with.

"Lilypad . . ." Crombie's voice was a warning.

"Quiet, poppet. The grown-ups are talking."

"But you're meddling."

"And you're about to be on the wrong end of an edging session."

"I already am," he muttered. Then looking at me, something shifting in his silver gaze, he added, "Tread carefully. One does not enter into a bargain with Lilith without sacrificing something they can ill afford to lose, trust me. She's the first of her kind for a reason. It always seems like a good deal at the time, but that's only because she's so skilled at making it feel good. When the bill comes due, there's usually hell to pay."

"Oh, you're so dramatic. You knew exactly what you were getting into and why, prince. Besides, the price is dependent on how inconvenienced I am by your request. You, Drystan Abercrombie Nightshade, are beholden to me by your own doing."

"I told you never to use my full name again, Mistress."

"And I told you to stay out of this."

She held his stare well past when I would have been

able to before he let out a rumble that I would have sworn was echoed by a crack of thunder in the distance.

"Fine," he huffed, stealing her drink.

"Now then, back to the matter at hand. Of course I am strong enough to replace Pan's pathetic attempt to own you. But are you willing to give up your connection to him? From your reaction, it seemed you rather enjoy your little visits."

I swallowed. If Lilith could free me from Pan, I had to take her up on it. Didn't I?

"Rosie . . . be sure," Asher said. It had been his idea, but I could see that the thought of me tying myself to the succubus didn't sit well with him either.

She was the devil we knew . . . sort of, which had to make her the safer choice. At least she didn't seem to want my blood.

"What do you want in exchange?"

Crombie opened his mouth, but Lilith pressed her index finger to his lips without looking away from me. "That is the million-dollar question, isn't it?"

"I won't agree to anything until I know your terms, succubus. I entered into one deal wearing rose-colored glasses. I will not do so again."

"Good girl."

"Nothing sexual between us. My dance card is full."

"So's mine. Though I could make you scream, I'm certain of it. I'd much rather . . . watch. That's it. I'll take from you your privacy. You and that broody duke of yours can repay me in the form of a show at my club. How's that?"

"That's all?" Crombie blurted.

"As I said. Price is predicated on my pain. Helping sweet Rosie doesn't hurt me nearly as much as helping *you*."

"What kind of show?" I asked, already knowing the answer.

"A session with the Duke of Tears always draws a crowd. I'm sure you know about his . . . preferences."

As her words registered, I waited for embarrassment or hesitance, but found neither. This would bind me to her, but she wasn't trying to steal anything from me. I would be free of Pan. I had to do it.

"When you're ready, the two of you can join me at *Iniquity* and repay your combined debt. No rush, of course. Until then I'll simply feed from you as I see fit."

"Feed from me?"

"Just little sips of your pleasure. Nothing you can't spare. You won't even know I'm there. Promise."

"Why so lenient, Lilypad?"

"Something tells me she has bigger fish to fry, as they say."

Before any of us could respond to that, Ben called, "S-speaking of f-fish, order's up."

"I didn't order fish."

"We d-don't have fucking p-pie."

"I like this fellow. We should keep him," Crombie said, grinning as he snagged a chip and dunked it in the container of ketchup.

"He's already spoken for," I said, surprising myself with the possessive growl in my words.

"Oh, the little kitten has claws," Lilith said with a smirk. "I wonder if she'll learn to use them." Plucking something out from her bountiful cleavage, she set it in front of Asher and me on the bartop. "Speaking of learning, use this. I think it will awaken something inside the both of you that needs . . . addressing."

"Just the two of us?" I asked.

"Perhaps you might want a third." Lilith's focus landed on Ben. "Not him, though. That one isn't ready for something like this."

"You aren't trying to poison us, are you?" Asher asked, giving the baby pink liquid a suspicious once-over.

"Why would I damage my new property?"

"I'm not yours. We haven't made any kind of deal."

"Haven't we?" She glanced down at my mark, which was no longer Pan's and was now a lip print in the same shade of red as her lipstick.

"But . . . I didn't agree . . ."

"You did. In your thoughts. Remember, darling, I can see what you truly desire and give it to you without you giving voice to a single word." She winked. "Don't worry, Mummy takes good care of her pets, doesn't she, poppet?"

Crombie grunted.

"I asked you a question," she said, voice taking on a dominant edge that had my libido perking back up.

"Yes, Mistress."

Lilith smiled. "Now. Drink your tonic. Sooner rather than later, I should think."

"Are you going to be in my head like he was?" I asked, kicking myself for not clarifying earlier.

"Not unless you want me there. As I said, I will be able to feed from you, just a sip now and then when I need to, but you'll never miss it. You won't even know."

"But not on my blood?" I asked, just wanting to hear her confirm it out loud.

"No, sweetling, I'm not a vampire, and I have no use for your blood. I'll feed on your emotions. Desire specifically. It seems you have plenty to go around."

I swiped at the kiss on my wrist, wondering if I would experience the same toe-curling rush I did with Pan's. As expected, the red didn't smear. As for reaction, I felt a delicious tingle roll through my belly, but that was it.

A roll of thunder so loud it shook the walls filled the air, making us all flinch. All except Lilith.

"Must dash. It's been lovely doing business with you. You're welcome, by the way, Asher. Best of luck to you." Then she leaned in close to him and whispered, "Hold onto who you are even if you lose yourself."

Before either of us could question her on the advice, she snapped her fingers and stepped through a portal, dragging a furious Crombie behind her.

Lightning arced through the sky as a torrential downpour hammered the roof.

"I didn't think it was supposed to storm today," I said.

"It w-wasn't." Ben shoved the basket of fish and chips at Asher. "Here."

Asher lifted the little vial and gave it a shake. "What do you think this does?"

I bit my lip and shook my head. "I'm not sure, but she just bonded with me. She isn't going to do anything to hurt me. Not before she collects her payment." Knowing who and what she was, I was willing to bet it was an aphrodisiac of some kind. She did say she wanted to feed on my desire. Only made sense she might give me something to induce it.

Asher popped off the little cork and gave a cursory sniff, his pupils dilating as a low groan escaped. "Oh," he said, shifting in his seat. "I think it's time to go, princess."

Lust flared to life in my belly. "We could close up—"

As I spoke the words, the door opened, and three gargoyles plus two soaked bear shifters stumbled inside, one right after the next.

Harry glanced nervously around. "Is she gone?"

"J-just left," Ben confirmed.

The three sentinels let out sighs of relief.

"In that case, Ben, be a good lad and get us a few pints each," Dick said. "It's a fucking nightmare out there."

Tom glanced at the mostly untouched plate of food. Pointing at it, he asked, "You going to eat this?"

"All yours, buddy. I have an appetite for something else," Asher said, his eyes on me.

Ben smirked. "Go on, you t-two. I've g-got this. But it's m-my turn when I get h-home."

THIRTY-SEVEN

PAN

"**M**otherfucking son of a whore!" I grabbed a stone from the stupid fucking zen garden Lilith had given me as a joke and threw it with all my might. It hit the mirror across from me, and I watched as the glass cracked into a spiderweb, then reformed good as new. Bugger. I still didn't feel any better.

I don't know how she'd done it, but she'd severed our connection. Rosie, *ma petite monstre*, was gone. Just fucking gone.

"Holly, Harper, Hayley—"

"I'm right here, my lord," Hyacinth murmured, dipping into a deep bow.

I wanted to toss her across the room, she annoyed me so, but I didn't. Because I was merciful. I was a good leader. I took care of my hellions. Just like I took care of that ungrateful little Blackthorne who'd abandoned me.

"What in Satan's name have you been up to? I sent you on a very important mission, yet here you are, moping about."

"My lord, we've executed our orders to the letter. The birds are dead."

"*All* of them?" I asked pointedly.

She cast her gaze at her little knobby feet. "Not all. There are still a few puffins who seem impervious to this sickness. And the ravens, of course, per your orders."

It was true, I had asked the ravens be spared, such majestic birds. Excellent portents and messengers. But… "Puffins. Bloody fucking puffins?"

"Yes, sir."

"Try. Harder."

"Yes, sir. Of course, sir. Right away, sir."

My miserable hellion scurried off, ears flopping obscenely as she rushed to get away from me and my black mood. I didn't blame her. I was as liable to fling her into the abyss as I was to give her any sort of kind word. More so, truthfully. I didn't do kind words.

What was this aching, gnawing hole in my chest? I couldn't put my tail on it. Dragging a hand through my long locks, I heaved an angry sigh. Who did she think she was? She couldn't simply erase me as though we hadn't shared something. As if I was just some common crossroads demon.

I was a fucking Prince of Hell.

Okay, not really. But I might as well have been. The seven princes were a bunch of pansies anyway.

I was the son of a fucking horsewoman of the bleeding Apocalypse. She should be so lucky to have me. To wear my mark.

That fucking unfaithful bitch.

"Pan, darling, whatever is the meaning of this?"

Not immediately answering my mother's question, I looked down at the pillow I had unknowingly reduced to a pile of feathers and dropped it with a huff. "She found a way to remove my mark."

"So? You've gotten everything we need, haven't you? Why do you care?"

If I'd been in my right mind, I might have stopped to consider the question before shouting, "Because she's MINE!"

My mother blinked at me. "Well, then . . ."

"I wanted to—"

"Did you think you were going to get to keep her? Oh, my boy. She was never yours to keep."

I growled, low and menacing.

"Fine, if you want her that badly, we will get her back for you. It's no matter to me. I only ever needed her blood to make my plague. Do with the Blackthorne princess what you will. Soulbind her if you must. But please, for the love of Lucifer, stop this tantrum."

Breathing heavily, I strode to the window, not willing to let my mother see the frustration on my face. What was this? Was it hurt? How could Rosie hurt me this many times in such a short span of weeks? But the bigger question was, how could I let myself get so entangled with her that she was able to make this happen?

I slammed my flattened hand against the window. It gave a warning shudder but did not break.

"Pandemic, you stop it this instant. You are a demon of the first order. What is this nonsense? How could you allow yourself to fall apart over a piece of ass?"

"She's not just a piece of arse," I bit out before I could stop myself.

"She is. No mortal is worth this level of self-abuse."

"You don't understand. I—"

"You're weak. You're pathetic. Just like your father.

There is no room for love and devotion in our plan. If you want her more than you want to help me reach my goal, I'll turn you into a human man, and you can try your luck with the bitch. So help me, I'll cut off your horns here and now and leave you out in the middle of nowhere, naked, bleeding, and destitute. I've done it before. Do you remember your sister Plague? Is that what you want? To end up like her?"

"No," I said, my voice lacking conviction, so I cleared my throat and said it again. "No. That won't be necessary."

"Good. Don't make me regret giving you so many chances, Pan. I could have done this by myself if I wanted. But mommy decided to include you, and that means you are allowed a few . . . missteps. I wouldn't be a good mother if I didn't let you fail at least a few times before helping you."

"What do you mean?"

"Do you really think I had you as my only ally? Roslyn Blackthorne has been doomed since the day I set my sights on her. Once my sister's failure was assured, I knew what to do. I've had this set in motion for months. You were only part of this because I said you could be."

So it was a pity task. My mother included me because she felt she had to. Bloody brilliant. And I'd even cocked that up.

"I . . ." Didn't know what to say. How was I supposed to swallow this pill? Here I believed I was the fucking linchpin, and I was as irrelevant as a single bloody screw. "Why use me at all?"

"Because you are my son," she said, coming over and cupping my cheek in her palm. "And you will carry our legacy. Besides, it's ever so much more fun working together."

"It's a riot." My deadpan reply didn't escape her notice.

"Don't be a spoilsport. She's lucky you gave her so much . . . attention. I would've strung her up by her nipples and bled her slowly."

The thought did have appeal. Too bad my little masochist would enjoy it.

"It's not too late for that option, is it?" I asked, my temper leaking into the words.

"It's never too late for torture, darling." Mother patted me awkwardly on the shoulder. "Now, tell mommy what the mean little bitch did to you."

"She broke our deal. Removed our mark. Found a way to cut herself off from me."

My mother's gaze turned shrewd. "That fucking succubus."

"What?"

She shook her head, refocusing on me. "Why haven't you just reaped her soul if she broke the deal?"

My humiliation knew no end. "Well . . . technically . . ."

"Pan!"

"I had her on a technicality. She met the terms of our first bargain, and we hadn't yet . . . figured out the terms of this—"

"I knew I should have put you in demon school as a child."

"Mother . . ."

"Son . . ."

We held each other's stares before I finally sighed and looked away. "I want her back," I admitted, hating myself for my weakness, but knowing that my mother might be the only means of making it happen.

She grabbed me by the chin, smooshing my cheeks

together as she did a baby voice that made me want to die. "Then you shall have her, my darling."

Before I could respond, my mother disappeared, leaving nothing but the scent of antiseptic in her wake. But for the first time since this began, instead of dread, I felt utter relief.

I'd get her back. Roslyn Blackthorne would be my *petit monstre* again.

Even if I had to drag her to hell with me.

CHAPTER

THIRTY-EIGHT

REMI

Fresh from the shower after a long run in the woods, I padded naked through the empty house, a towel in my hand as I dried my hair.

I forgot how nice it was to walk around in my birthday suit. These days someone was always around, and they tended to frown on the freeballing. Well, Ben did. Rosie didn't mind all that much. Usually, it ended with both of us naked, touching, and . . . doing stuff.

A low thump against the front door had my arm dropping, towel protectively hanging in front of my crotch. Rosie and Asher stumbled in, little more than a tangle of limbs as they made out like a couple of teenagers. His shirt was already half off, and one bra strap hung down Rosie's arm. Her lipstick was a sexy smudge across her lips—and his— her hair wild. Her mischievous giggle made me think of that time Scarlett had dosed Rosie with pixie dust. Fuck, that was a fun night. Kind of. Okay, it was until she got attacked.

"Should I drop the towel or . . ." I asked, my erection tenting the white fabric as I held it in front of me.

They pulled apart, and it only took a single look at her face to tell Rosie was definitely on something.

"Weren't you at work?"

"Yup."

"So why are you flying high as a kite, baby girl?"

"Lilith," Asher answered for her.

"As in, the succubus?"

"You know more than one?"

"Not the point."

"Yeah, the succubus. She gave us a special pink drink. I haven't had any yet, but Rosie had a taste, and I kissed her. It's . . . potent." Asher's words were lust filled and hungry. "You should have some."

I dropped the towel without hesitation. No one needed to invite me to a succubus induced sex party twice.

Their gazes raked my body, heating my skin without even touching me. Fuck, they were ravenous. I didn't stand a chance—and I didn't want to.

"Show me this fancy drink. Did you save any for me, baby girl?"

She pulled it out from between her breasts with a flourish. "I kept it safe just like she did. In case it needed to be warmed by body heat or something."

I laughed at the ridiculous explanation. "Hand it over."

Before she could, Asher snatched it from her and pulled the cork free with his teeth, spitting it out and then taking a sip for himself. Holding my gaze, he dropped the empty bottle, took my face in his hands, and shared the potion with me. His lips burned mine as the magic worked its way through us, and before long, I understood why Rosie was so spun up. It tasted like cotton candy and sugar cookies with just a hint of citrus. Like them.

As I kissed Asher, he grabbed Rosie by her nape and

pulled her close until she was against our sides. Then he broke the kiss, but only so he could share the remaining elixir with her.

A guttural moan escaped as heat swept through my body, desire unlike anything I'd ever known taking hold. "What the hell was in that?"

"It's from a succubus. Do you really need more specifics than that?" Asher asked, pulling his shirt the rest of the way off.

I had a sneaky suspicion I knew what it was. But I wasn't going to ruin the mood. "My turn with her." I kissed the side of her mouth, brushing Asher's lips as I took over.

Fuck, that was hot. Kissing them both at the same time.

"Any idea why she gave us this magic potion?" I asked Rosie.

"She said it would help us address some things we needed to open ourselves up to by giving us ... something."

"Like a massive hard-on?"

"I don't bloody know, Remi. Are you really complaining right now? I'm uninhibited and ready to bang your brains out." The edge in Rosie's voice had me fighting a laugh. Even turned on this much, she wouldn't use any bad language.

"You mean, fuck my brains out?"

"Yes. That."

"Baby girl," I laughed between kisses, "you're forgetting that we're the only ones who do the fucking."

"Not true. Sometimes I fuck you," Asher offered. "And you like it."

Yeah, I really did. Hell, I just liked it when they touched me, looked at me, fucking smiled my way.

"Can we do less talking and more of the ... forking?"

"Nope. No way. If you can't say the word, you aren't allowed to beg for it."

"You. Are. Ruining. This," Asher growled.

"I just want her to own her sexual appetite. She shouldn't need a potion to be uninhibited around us. She should always be comfortable enough to use any words, to ask for what she wants, to know that we will give it to her."

Rosie grabbed my dick, a long slow stroke from base to crown, making my eyes roll back. "I don't have to say the words, but if I must . . . I want you . . . on my bed, Remi. Please. I want you to . . . fuck me."

Christ, I wasn't expecting the sound of that word on her lips to affect me this much, but lust exploded inside me, along with pure pride. "Bedroom. Now."

Asher took her from me, picking her up and tossing her over his shoulder, ass in my face, hair hanging down his back. "Got her, boss. Let's go."

"Boss? Does that mean I'm in charge for once?"

Asher tossed me a smoldering look over his shoulder. "Don't waste it."

"But if I'm fucking her . . . who's going to fuck you?"

Rosie pulled herself up, purple hair falling over her face as she met my gaze. "I have fingers. Does that count?"

"Oh, Jesus. Yes, that counts." Asher's palm connected with her ass, a loud crack filling the air, followed by her yelp of surprise and pleasure.

As we walked through the bedroom door, I stopped, my gaze catching on a black box with a crimson ribbon tied around it. *Iniquity* was embossed on the top.

"What the fuck is this? Are you expecting a delivery, baby girl?"

Asher set her down so she could walk over to the bed

and untie the bow. She let out a little gasp as she lifted the lid. "Perhaps I won't have to use my fingers after all."

"What?" Asher asked, peering over her shoulder.

She reached into the box and lifted out a leather harness and a thick purple dick. A very familiar dick. "Is that . . . me?" I glanced down at my cock and back at the dildo in her hand. It matched, down to the veins. "How the hell did Lilith get my measurements?"

"Good fucking question," Asher grumbled.

"Oh, look, lube! And it sparkles."

She had to be kidding. But no, there it was, sparkling glitter lube.

"No. No way. That is not going in my ass," Asher protested.

"Oh, come on. You can dish it out, but you can't take it? I'll have you know, I have an exceptional dick."

"Not the dick. That's fine. It's the lube. I draw the line at looking like I got railed by a pixie. I'll have glitter coming out of my ass for weeks."

"It's called Uni-Porn." Rosie's words were almost impossible to understand through her laughter.

"I definitely draw the line at looking like I let a unicorn rail me."

Asher letting anything rail him was a concept that really fucking excited me. I looked him up and down and made my decision. Rosie would take his ass, not me, but I'd be in control of this whole thing. My lips at her ear, giving her commands, telling her what to do, how to touch him, when to thrust. I would be a damn composer, and our fucking would be my masterpiece.

"Fine, we'll use regular lube, but if I don't get inside someone soon, I'm going to have to rub one out right the hell now."

I glanced over to the bed where Rosie had already started without us. Jesus, she was sliding the dildo over her already naked body. How had I missed her taking off her clothes? This magic potion had me intensely focused on what I wanted rather than my norm of being a passenger on a very sexy ride. Was this what I was supposed to discover? How to take control of both of them?

Only one way to find out.

I let out a low growl and stalked over, snatching it out of her hand. "You have two perfectly good cocks at your disposal. Don't you dare waste your cunt on an imitation."

"You're the one who said it was a perfect imitation."

Fuck, she had me there. I leaned down and nipped her bottom lip. "Stop being so fucking smart, and get the strap-on . . . on."

"Can you do it for me? I don't know how to use it."

Jesus, fuck.

"Of course," I managed, voice strangled by the overwhelming lust consuming me. I knew the bulk of what I was feeling was from Lilith's gift, but part of it was just my reaction to having Rosie at my disposal. Knowing Asher was right here with me. No matter how many times I had them, it would never be enough.

"Get naked, Asher. I'll get her ready."

Trusting in the man to do as I told him, I helped our girl, taking my time as I slid the harness up her thighs, my hands teasing as I ensured the leather laid correctly against her soft skin. And when I brushed against her soaked center, teasing her as I stood and kissed my way along her spine, she whimpered with need.

"You're so fucking gorgeous, Rosie. Do you know that?"

"No."

"Well, you are. You get me hard even when you're not

around. All I have to do is think about you, and I'm aching." I cupped her breasts as my lips found the mark on her neck. The one I gave her. "And the way you watch Asher, it gets me off every time."

"Me too," Asher agreed, taking her face and stealing a kiss.

"How do I look at you?"

"Like you want to fuck me."

"I do."

"Then do it."

THIRTY-NINE

Was I really doing this? I wasn't sure what had come over me, but somewhere between drinking the potion and moving into my room, this tigress I didn't recognize had taken over my body. I was confident and intrigued by the shift in power dynamic, which was something I'd never had before. In most ways they were still calling the shots, but I was the one who was going to get to take Asher. That sent a thrill through me.

It was curious, this newfound urge to be on top. I'd been perfectly content submitting to Gavin. In fact, I craved that from him, and from Ben . . . and Pan. But this triad we'd built within my group of lovers was different. Now I understood why. Lilith was right; something needed to be discovered between us, which was an equal footing for us all. No one in this trio was more dominant than the other. It felt right, just thinking it. When the three of us were together, we were true equals. No games . . . unless we wanted them.

"All fours, Asher. It'll feel better that way. I promise," Remi said, a gentleness in his voice he usually reserved for me.

"I've been fucked before, Mercer. No need to treat me like a blushing virgin."

"Not by me," Remi said with a cocky smirk as he took his erection in his hand and gave it a long leisurely stroke.

I had to bite back a moan, my body lighting up like a Christmas tree as if I was the one being caressed. Asher rolled his eyes. Despite the front he put up, when his focus landed on me, his gaze was hot with need, but a spark of vulnerability was there too.

"That's true. It's been a long time since I've been the one on my knees for anyone."

"Tonight, we're changing that. Let our little princess fuck you with my fake dick until you're sobbing both our names." Remi nipped my shoulder. "Then, maybe later I'll give you the real one."

Oh, my stars and stones. I didn't know what it was about a thick shaft bobbing between your legs, but it really did fill me with power. I giggled.

"Are you laughing at me right now, princess?"

"No. I'm . . ." I glanced down, then pushed on the tip of the shaft jutting out of the harness. It bounced back like a springboard. "I understand why they call it being *cocksure* now."

Asher and Remi both laughed, though they were short-lived. The need to claim, and be claimed, by each other was too high for all of us. Remi placed his hands on my shoulders, his body pressed to mine, his erection nestled against the small of my back.

"Remember how Ben and I got you ready for us?"

I gave him a jerky nod.

"We need to do that for Asher. But probably for longer. He looks like he's a little tense. We need to make sure when you slide inside, all he feels is pressure before you rock his world."

My breaths came in sharp gasps as my skin heated. Asher's head dropped between his arms, hair hanging down in his face, the muscles of his arms coiled and tight.

"Touch him, baby girl," Remi whispered, his lips brushing my ear as his words flooded me with arousal. "Make sure he knows how much we want him to feel good."

"Jesus," Asher panted, Remi's words affecting him every bit as much as me.

Reaching down, I ran the tips of my fingers along Asher's spine, tickling and teasing as much as soothing. By the time I reached the seam between the muscled globes of his arse, we were both shaking with need.

"Touch me. Please, fuck, just touch me."

I moved to part him, but Remi stopped me. "No. Not like that. Arch your back, Asher. Open up for her."

As my hacker did as he was bade, my wolf uncapped a bottle of non-sparkling lube. "Put this on your fingers, then circle his hole. Just tease him. Don't push in yet."

"Is this a rim job?" I asked, for once not letting myself think as I did as Remi instructed.

His answering chuckle was part groan. "No."

"That's what I did to you in the shower," Asher said, his voice tight and strained as my thumb brushed across the puckered ring of muscle. "With my tongue."

"Do . . . you want me to use my tongue?" I asked, not put off by the idea one bit, which surprised me. I just remembered how it felt, that sensation waking up all kinds of nerve endings I didn't know I had.

"Fuck, I . . . maybe . . . I don't know."

Remi bit the lobe of my ear. "He's not ready for that yet. We'll work him up to it."

I nodded, leaning into his touch when he started to massage my breasts. "What do I do now?"

"Did you lube your other hand? Oh, you did. Good girl. Reach around and stroke him. We want him to focus only on how good you're making him feel."

"So good. So fucking good," Asher said on a harsh groan as I ran my slick palm up his length.

"Now push your finger inside him. Nice and slow."

Barely breathing, I did as he said, my whole body alive in a way that didn't make sense. Asher was the one being touched, but his pleasure was my own. Every moan, every shudder, I felt right alongside him. "Oh God," I whimpered.

"In and out, baby girl. Make him writhe for you." Remi's hands were everywhere on my body. His hard length had slipped between my thighs as he continued guiding me.

"I want you to feel good too, Remi."

"Taking care of him is just like taking care of me. Don't worry."

"Are you sure?"

He nipped my shoulder. "You know that feeling you get between your legs when you make him moan? It's the same for me."

"R-really?" I stuttered as he pinched and rolled my unpierced nipple.

"I get off on making you come. Just like I've seen you do."

I continued pumping one finger in and out of Asher as I slowly stroked his erection with my other hand. He was hard as stone, the tip leaking. And then, on reflex, I curled the digit inside him, and he let out a sharp bark of surprise as I brushed a special spot I hadn't realized he had.

"Fuck, do it again."

Remi whispered. "Ding ding, you found it. Pull out and

add a second finger. Then beckon him home. He'll come like a fountain if you do it long enough."

The idea excited me, and Asher and I groaned in unison when I added a second digit.

"Fuck." His back glistened with sweat, and he was trembling, but not from pain. He looked back at us over his shoulder, his eyes hooded, face flushed, totally lost in what Remi and I were doing to him. "What is happening right now?"

"Has no one ever played with your prostate before?" Remi asked. "What a shame. Don't worry, Asher, we're going to take good care of you."

"Just . . . don't stop."

"Why is this so hot?" I asked, more to myself than anyone else.

"Because you're making it happen for him. You're taking care of him. You love to do that. I've seen it in everything you do, Rosie. You make us so happy. You make us feel good. You love us."

"I do," I admitted, my heart near to bursting. I'd never thought about it in those terms, but when he set it out there, it made sense. I liked to show the people in my life how much they meant to me by doing things for them. Taking care of them made me happy. Or, as Remi said, pleasing them pleased me.

"Stop, stop, stop. Oh, fuck." Asher's voice was panicked and desperate.

"Am I hurting you?" I instantly pulled my fingers from him, horrified I had ruined everything.

"God, no. I just don't want to come until you're fucking me, princess. That's what we're here for."

"We'd better give him what he wants, then, shouldn't we?" Remi asked, his palm cracking down on my rear. "Arch that ass again, Asher." Once he obeyed, Remi poured a liberal amount of lube along the seam between his cheeks, then his mouth was at my ear, "Palm out, baby girl. You need to stroke your cock for me."

I opened my hand and waited for him to drizzle the clear liquid onto the center of my palm.

"Root to tip," he whispered. "Just like if you were doing it for me."

Asher craned his neck again, watching me as I curled my hand around the purple shaft and lubed it up.

"Fuuuck, that is so goddamn hot."

Asher's reaction was shorter but no less fervent. "Jesus."

"Okay, beautiful, now line the tip up with him. Press in just a little. Let him get used to how big my dick is."

Asher made a sound that might have been a laugh, but as I lined myself up and slid the crown of the shaft along his entrance, it turned to a wanton moan.

"Please," he begged, his hands fisting into the blanket.

I wasn't sure I'd ever heard anything as beautiful as the sound of Asher's ragged plea.

Is this what Gavin feels like when he makes me beg?

"That's it," Remi rasped, every brush of his lips against the edge of my ear echoing in my core. "Push your way inside him. Make him yours."

My hands went to Asher's hips to steady myself as I thrust forward, the strange sensation of such a powerful move setting me ablaze. I couldn't feel the penetration, but the base of the shaft pressed hard on my needy button too, providing me with delicious friction.

Asher was trembling, his skin already slick with sweat. "More, Rosie. Please."

"He likes it," I whispered, not really knowing why I was surprised.

"Of course he does. It's us." Remi cupped my breasts and tugged on my nipple piercing. "Now sink all the way to the hilt. Then stay there."

"Yes. Fuck. I can take it."

I knew how good it felt when one of my men slammed into me, but I was too worried about hurting Asher to try anything more than a slow, steady slide.

"Ohmyfuckinggodyes," Asher moaned in a single breath.

I couldn't believe how close I was to my own climax just from bringing him to the brink like this. I'd never felt more powerful in my entire life.

"Don't move a muscle," Remi warned. "I need to fuck you both now."

"Okay," we both said simultaneously, a little frantic.

Remi placed his palm between my shoulder blades and pressed until I was curled around Asher. Then he gripped each of my thighs in one hand and lifted until I was kneeling behind Asher on the bed.

"Fuck!" he barked. "This is moving. You said no moving!"

"Don't you dare come yet." Remi's voice was teasing, but there was a hard edge to it. "I need inside her before you shoot."

"Then get in-fucking-side her, Mercer. What are you waiting for?"

Out of the corner of my eye, I saw Remi's hand slip into the box I'd left on the other side of the bed. He pulled out a small black rectangular bit of plastic.

"This," he whispered as he thrust his hard length deep inside me, making both Asher and I cry out.

I didn't immediately register the electric hum; I was too busy trying to breathe around the vibration sitting right on top of my clit. From the howl torn from Asher's lips, the buzz was doing things to him as well.

"That thing vibrates?" Asher said as the humming stopped. "I'm never going to make it through this. I think the succubus might be trying to torture us."

"She said she needed to feed. Maybe she wanted to make sure there was enough to go around," I said with a breathless laugh. "Do it again, Remi. Please."

FORTY

God, I didn't think this was going to feel so good. But it did. When Remi moved, Rosie moved, and I took it with a sob of pleasure in my throat. The only thing that would make this better would be if I could watch them.

"I want to turn over," I gasped, desperate not to come before Rosie.

"Will that work?" Rosie asked.

Remi chuckled. "We can always make it work. It's actually even better, if you like to watch your partner fall apart."

Rosie made a happy sound, and I glanced back at them just in time to watch Remi take her hips and pull her out of me.

I missed her presence inside me immediately. There was something electric about letting her own me this way. Despite what I'd said to Remi, I'd only been topped once, and I hated it. Not the physical act, just the loss of control. But with her—them—it was a totally different experience. I felt whole in a way I'd never imagined could even be possible.

Rolling over, I waited, legs spread, chest heaving as Remi guided her to my waiting entrance once more. This time, he grabbed me by the knees as she held my thighs, and together, they widened my stance.

"Now, baby girl. Make him sing for us."

Rosie angled inside me like a fucking pro. This time her eyes were trained on my face, watching my reaction as she gave me inch after inch of Remi's perfection. Christ, he really did have a perfect fucking cock. I could see why Lilith used it for inspiration. How she got that visual, I didn't ever want to know.

"Fuck, yes," Remi groaned once she was fully seated inside me again.

The sight of their faces, both of them staring at me, both of them loving me at the same time, had my dick jerking on my belly. My balls kept brushing against Rosie's pelvis with each thrust, and when Remi hit that little button on the remote to start up the vibrations again, I cried out like I was in agony. Because I kind of was. I wanted to come, and I was desperately trying not to all at the same time.

I knew this was supposed to be about me, but I refused to come until she did. I needed her orgasm more than I needed my own, which was really fucking saying something.

"Please, princess. I need you to come."

She bit her lip, looking torn. "But I want to make you feel good."

"Oh my God, you two," Remi laughed. "Asher, grab your dick and stroke it."

I jerked my head in the negative. "Can't do it." I'd go off like a damn rocket, and the goal was to wait, not finish.

Heaving a sigh, Remi pressed a kiss to the nape of her

neck, then murmured, "When I say go, you better go. Got it?"

She nodded, and he upped the intensity of the vibration against her clit. That made her squirm and me practically weep from the effort to hold back. I could feel every hum against my overstimulated nerves.

"If you won't stroke your dick. I guess I'll do it for you." Remi said, leaning forward, pressing her deeper inside me, and encircling my cock with his big warm hand.

I cried out when he gripped me tight, using my own precum as lube as he shuttled his fist up and down my length. I was utterly at their mercy, and I loved every second of it.

"Now," Remi gritted.

Rosie's face was twisted in pleasure as she pulled out and drove back in like a champ.

"Jesus, fuck." I didn't even know what I was saying anymore, only that the combined effort of her fucking me and him jerking me had me seeing stars. I had seconds at best before I blew all over.

"I'm . . . Remi . . . Asher . . . I'm coming," Rosie whimpered.

"God, yes, you are. Milk me for everything I've got, baby girl. And watch what we're doing to Asher while you do it."

She got two more deep drives in, and then I was gone. I couldn't stop the orgasm even if I wanted to. I came hard and long, the waves of release almost painful as every part of me seemed to contract and expand over and over. Rosie's cries melded with mine, and Remi's were shortly behind.

By the time we'd all ridden out the last vestiges of plea-sure, my cum painted my chest, so fucking much of it. My balls were drained. Goddamn, I was going to have to do this again.

I was relaxed. Euphoric. And . . . still fucking hard.

"How?" I rasped.

"Lilith," Rosie said, just as Remi answered, "The succubus."

"Maybe I don't hate *all* demons."

Rosie whimpered as Remi pulled out of her, and I did the same when she left my body. I wanted us all to be connected again. There was nothing like the three of us being joined this way.

"This reminds me of something," Remi muttered. "But neither of you are shifters, so that can't be what it is."

"What?" Rosie asked, unbuckling the harness and letting the strap-on fall to the floor with a soft thud.

"It's like what I imagine the rut, or heat in the female's case, is like."

"Rut?" Rosie asked.

"It's supposed to be like an insatiable need to mate. All very primal and instinctual. You just sort of black out and fuck each other boneless."

"Sounds amazing," she whispered.

"Count me in," I added. "Although, my ass is probably done for the night."

Rosie's lips quirked in a grin. "That's okay. It's not your arse I'm after. Not anymore."

"Are you still wet, baby girl?" Remi didn't wait for her response; he slipped his fingers between her legs and sank them inside. "Yes, you are. Coated in my cum and ready to ride his dick."

She bit her bottom lip.

"What is it?" I asked, sensing the question she was holding back.

"I read something once . . ."

"Oh?" Remi asked, wrapping his arms around her and trailing kisses along her mark. "You feeling adventurous?"

She nodded. "I think you two might be my only chance to test this out."

"I'm all for experimentation." I sat up, sliding my palms over her hips as Remi continued working her over.

"Both of you."

"You have us." Remi nibbled her shoulder.

"In the same hole."

"Jesus," I whispered, taking one hand and wrapping it around my erection because when she talked like that, how could I resist?

Remi's eyes found mine over her. "Think you can handle that?"

"Your cock rubbing up against mine while we're fucking our girl? Uh, yeah. Dibs in."

He smirked, and I couldn't stop myself from surging up to kiss him. Rosie's hands explored my body as I devoured Remi. Her body was soft and smooth while his was hard and ridged with muscle. It was the most perfect combination.

"How do we do this?" I asked, finally breaking the kiss.

"Well, erm . . . in the book, one of them was on his back, and the other behind her."

Remi shoved me hard until I fell backward. "Done."

"And then she rode one while the other prepared her for him to join in."

"You already know I'm an expert at prep," Remi said. "Hop on and take our boy for a ride, baby girl."

Rosie straddled me without another thought. She rose up on her knees as I gripped my cock to hold steady for her. I was long, I knew that, and from this angle, it might be too much for her.

"Slow, princess. If it hurts, just say something."

"Good idea," Remi said. "This is going to be intense. We need a safe word."

"Like what? Stop and go?"

"Red light, green light," Rosie corrected. "Green means good, yellow means proceed with caution, red means everything needs to stop."

"Works for me," Remi said, and I nodded my agreement.

"Green light, Rosie. Green-fucking-light."

She sank down on me, the heat of her slick cunt so perfect I moaned, and my hands fisted the sheets. She murmured happily, her eyes fluttering closed before she leaned forward and blindly pressed her lips to mine.

"Love you," she whispered, making my heart flip over.

"Love you too."

She smiled, her eyes luminous as they gazed into mine.

"I'm going to add a finger now, you two. Make sure you tell me if we venture into any territory but green, okay?" Remi surprised me with the seriousness of his tone, but I also knew him. The last thing he wanted was to hurt either of us.

"Green," Rosie said, squirming on me and drawing out another desire-filled groan.

"So green. The most green of any green. Kelly green," I said, threading my fingers through her hair and tugging her down so I could kiss her while also giving Remi better access to where we were joined.

Then I felt it. His lube-slick finger ran up my balls, along the exposed base of my shaft, and inside her. Each rock of her hips had him rubbing the thick vein on the underside of my dick.

"Oh, that feels fucking weird and amazing."

"It's a delicious stretch," she whispered.

"More?" Remi's voice trembled on the word.

"More," Rosie and I said in tandem.

Another generous application of cool lube slipped over me as Remi added a second finger. This time he scissored them slightly, working to stretch her tight hole even further.

The moan that escaped her couldn't be confused for anything other than absolute pleasure.

"Fuck yourself on his cock and my fingers. Open up for me. I don't want to hurt you, and you know I'm not small."

Rosie lifted up and then rocked herself back down, chasing her pleasure. There was a little furrow between her brows, but nothing that spoke of pain.

Remi slid his fingers out, gruffly demanding, "Lift up. Make room for me, baby girl."

Oh, fuck, this was it. Two experiences I'd never had checked off the list in one night. Lilith had been right. We'd needed this. The three of us had already belonged to one another, but tonight made it real in a way I hadn't known was possible. Each of us had taken the other. Together. Separately. We were undeniably a unit. Three pieces of a bigger whole. I was part of something greater than me. I was safe. I belonged.

I was loved.

It was . . . everything.

She rose until just the tip of my dick was inside her, then Remi's hand was there, coated in yet more lube, stroking me as he placed our lengths together and gripped as much of our combined girths as he could.

"Slide down us, Rosie. Nice and easy. Take us until you can't anymore."

Her heat enveloped us with painful slowness, but from the way she was panting, it was as fast as she could go.

"Yellow," I warned, watching the furrow between her brows deepen and her mouth set in a tight line. She was hurting.

Her eyes opened, and she stared at me. "Green."

Oh. Okay.

"My bad, green."

She gave me a tight smile. "Pain makes the pleasure more intense."

I raised a hand to brush away a damp lock of hair on her forehead. "Just be careful with yourself. We're trusting you not to make us do anything that will cause serious harm, all right?"

She nodded. "I promise."

Then she slid down our shafts and cried out as she took us all the way to the hilt.

Oh. My. Fuck.

The way Remi's dick rubbed against mine as she rode us, her cunt clamping down on us like a goddamn vise, was more than I could take. This was so much better than fumbling together for a quick rubdown. Look, I liked a good bit of frottage between the two of us, but replace our hands with Rosie's hot, slick walls around us, and I was in heaven.

Remi leaned forward, sandwiching Rosie between our bodies. He reached out, weaving his fingers through mine and holding on tight. Our eyes locked over her shoulder, and we didn't say a word, but I knew exactly what he was thinking because I was thinking it too.

I love you.

"I'm close," she whispered. "So close."

"Ride us to the finish, baby girl."

"We're right there with you."

I could feel his cock expanding, that rush of blood that came with finding climax. My balls tingled and tightened, already pulsing with the need to release.

As soon as she clamped down on us, I lost it. My fingers tightened around Remi's, and I grabbed her hair hard with my other hand, needing to hold on to something as we rode this out.

Remi must have felt the same, because he sank his teeth into her neck, biting her the way he did the night he marked her. As if his wolf was just beneath the surface and wanted to hold onto his mate as well.

Rosie's lips sought out mine, her kisses desperate and breathless as she floated through wave after wave of her climax. It could have been a side effect of Lilith's tonic, or it might have just been a result of the most intense sex of our lives, but it felt like we rode that wave together forever. The three of us locked in the aftershocks of our joint orgasm.

I loved her, she loved me, and now I knew, even without ever hearing the words, that Remi loved me too. Maybe that was what we needed to discover. But why did Lilith think it was so important? What game was she playing?

Shaking my head to clear those intrusive thoughts, I sighed and helped Rosie off us, rolling her over along with Remi until the three of us lay tangled together on the bed.

Remi's voice was the last thing I heard as I drifted off in a sex-hazed stupor. "So . . . we should probably change the sheets."

FORTY-ONE

PAN

"I've had about e-bloody-nough of this nonsense, *ma petite monstre*." I glared at the disgusting display on the other side of the window. The three sweaty bodies were no more than a tangle of limbs as they . . . snuggled.

I shuddered.

She looked so sated. Satisfied. Dare I say it, happy. These men were ruining all my plans, and I was not interested in continuing on this way. I deserved to keep her as my prize for a job well done. The last thing she should be doing is lying happily in the arms of two men.

A vague thought flashed in my mind. She needed two of them to offer her even an ounce of the pleasure I could give. My tail alone took care of that. And then there was my tongue. She should be missing me. Instead she tried to erase me.

"Foul play, little Blackthorne."

When I got my hands on her . . .

The tenting at my trousers told me I needed to put a

stop to those sorts of thoughts. Revenge was on the menu tonight, and it was, as they say, a dish best served ice cold.

I prowled through their pathetic town, smirking at every living thing I touched, because soon, they'd be dead or dying. The Andersons'—bloody idiots had their family name painted on their postbox—perfectly manicured hedges were already nothing more than diseased shriveled sticks now that I'd touched them. But, for good measure, I grabbed onto the tall, beautiful Japanese maple, its promise of deep crimson leaves in the fall already showing as buds. *Not this year, Mr. Anderson.* I tore it from the ground, the roots clinging to the earth for dear life, but as soon as my power infected the bark, the tree lost the war.

I javelin-tossed the worthless hunk of firewood into the middle of the street, hoping a lumberjack might come along in his truck and have an unfortunate accident. Then I turned the corner, my steps gaining speed as I neared my secret wardrobe. Also known as the Stevensons' house. The deer shifters were dead now, rotting in the attic. Smallpox might be rare, but it was a killer. My little Ringo Spar was still in the basement, safe from the corpses if not from me.

I heard his coughs before I descended the stairs, wet and ragged. Settled in his chest already then. Unfortunate. I needed him for at least a little longer, but he'd be no use to me if he was a sack of skin and bones, emaciated and hideous. How would Rosie ever leave those mates of hers for him if he looked like the walking dead?

There was no use for it, sadly. I either had to leave my toy alone and hope he recovered, or I used him one last time and killed him for good. That was the price for being possessed by one such as me. Without my mother's blood to neutralize it, infection was damn near inevitable.

It was in the name, after all.

"Still alive, I see," I offered, tossing him a bottle of water and wincing as it hit him square in the chest. "You need to be quicker on your feet, man. What if I'd hit you in the face?"

"Kill me. Please. Put me out of my misery." He coughed, foamy bits of blood spraying from his lips.

"Which one of my mother's gifts did I give you? Let's see . . . bloody pieces of lung in your cough, fever, exhaustion . . . looks like consumption to me. Why couldn't you have gotten one of her more attractive plagues?"

Come to think of it, there really weren't any attractive ways to waste away.

He was pale, his eyes bruised, skin covered in a sheen of sweat. I wouldn't be affected by his . . . affliction, but a weak vessel was still weak. And I needed to be at full strength for what I had in store.

Oh, well. I could do what needed to be done from my plane. It wasn't as satisfying as watching it unfold firsthand, but if the alternative was a second-rate outbreak, then it really wasn't worth my time or energy. I was Pestilence's firstborn. I was a damned sight better than a wet cough and sniffle. Turning, I took a couple steps away from the miserable lump of flesh.

"Wait! Where are you going? Don't leave me like this. Please. For the love of God, kill me."

I glanced back at him. "I shan't."

Opening a portal to my realm, I stepped through and left the stench of illness and rot behind me, replacing it with the familiar scent of my home. The ember of jealousy still burned brightly, and it was picking up steam.

"Hortense, Halifax, Holly! Come to me." I stood in front

of the large mantle made of the bones of great rulers of the world who'd sold their souls to me. Patting the skull on the rightmost corner, I smiled fondly. "You're looking well, old friend."

"My lord, Pan. You called?" One of the three imps said as they materialized in front of me.

"Which one are you?"

"Hannah, sir."

Blast, I really was terrible with names. "Where's Titmouse?"

As if on cue, she scuttled in. "Juniper, my lord. I'm here."

"Have you killed all of the birds yet?"

"Most of them. Save the ravens and . . ."

"And?"

"Puffins, sir. They're surprisingly hardy."

It took a second for my mind to conjure up an image of the silly little aviators with their obnoxious beaks and webbed feet. "Really? The puffins? Aren't they just fatter penguins?"

"Not really, sir. No."

"Never mind about them. They're not important. In fact, don't waste any more energy trying to sicken them. It's the ravens we must focus on now."

Her eyes widened. "Ravens? I thought you wanted them spared."

"Yes. Exactly. They will be my eyes in the sky, my warriors."

"Oh, who are we fighting?" Excitement colored her tone.

"Americans."

Her ears drooped. "What?"

"Three in particular. They've taken what's mine and broken her. I intend to fix it."

Julep tilted her head and studied me. If I'd given a rat's arse about her opinion, I might have said her look was filled with censure. "We are here to serve you, sire. Whatever you require, it will of course be done."

"Perfect. Wake my hellravens."

"Hellravens?"

"Remember? I turned you all into great winged creatures? Am I the only one here who pays attention to anything?"

"Oh! Yes, sir. Right away." She gestured for the other three imps to join her and proudly stated, "Ravens assembled, my lord."

I frowned. "Is this all that's left? I remember there being quite a few more of you."

"Well, it was a one-way trip, milord. Most of the hellions didn't make it."

"That's a shame. Must make more, I suppose. Now, you are to gather all the ravens you can and send them on the attack. Her mates can't see her if they don't have eyes."

Holding up my hand, I conjured the image of Rosie's house, the window open and the forms of her and two men still snuggled together—gag me—appearing first.

"Would you like us to use—"

"Any means necessary, but not a hair will be harmed on her head, or you'll answer to me."

Before they could respond, I waved my hand and changed their forms, thankful I didn't need to bother with that potion again after one dose. I thought I might like my hellions better this way. No one talked to me like this.

"Go. Fly and gather your forces. Don't come back

without their eyes. I intend to use them as garnishes for my cocktails."

Watching them take to the air and fly through the freshly opened portal I created, I settled back in my armchair, holding myself as if it was my own personal throne.

"How's that for initiative, Mother?"

FORTY-TWO

I was dead on my feet as I got out of my truck and walked the gravel path up to the house. The hairs on the back of my neck stood on end as the sense of someone watching me tickled my awareness.

Someone or some*thing*.

Without allowing much of a chance to talk myself out of it, I shifted, letting my wolf take over. There were too many weird things happening in this town, and we had too many enemies for me to let this slide. *Trust your wolf. He's always right.*

I heard them as soon as I took wolf form. Soft chittering noises. The rustle of wings and feathers.

Birds.

A sharp, harsh caw echoed through the air as a huge raven dive-bombed me, coming directly for my head. Rolling away in the nick of time, I barely escaped its assault. The bird slammed into the window, cracking the glass and breaking its own neck. As it crashed to the ground, a trail of blood dripped down the panes of glass.

My hackles rose, my wolf warning me that something

was very fucking wrong. I padded back to its feathered body, sniffing deep, and then jerked my snout back. The urge to sneeze hit me hard, my nostrils itching and filled with the bird's foul scent.

Tainted. That's what it was.

Diseased.

Warily eyeing the other looming birds, I bounded for the door, wanting to warn the others.

I had just shifted back into my human form when the door swung open.

"What the hell was that?" Remi asked, eyes wild as they dropped down to where I was crouched.

"Get inside," I ordered, voice still more wolf than man.

Asher hovered protectively in front of Rosie, all eyes trained on me as I silently telegraphed my thoughts to Remi. *Danger. Protect our mate.*

"What's going on?" Rosie asked, her voice holding an edge of panic. "Ben, tell us."

"B-birds. They attacked."

"Multiple?" Asher asked.

"Just o-one, b-but it's s-sick. Blood s-smelled off."

The color left Asher's face as he muttered to himself, "Puffin crisis."

"What?" Remi asked, cutting a dubious glance at the hacker.

"The birds are dying."

"Th-these aren't. They're m-making a stand."

Rosie had crept to the broken window while we talked. Before I could get my fucking throat to work so I could shout for her to get back, a blur of obsidian crashed through the weakened glass. Asher was there when I should've been, his quick reflexes getting her out of the way as the crazed fowl landed on the floor.

"Get away f-from the w-windows!"

Asher pulled Rosie to stand near Remi and me as we watched the bird in its final death throes.

"What kind of birds are they?" Remi asked, making the hair on the back of my neck lift as I instinctively knew what he was getting at.

"R-ravens."

His eyes locked with mine. "Aisling."

"You think she sent birds after us?" Rosie asked.

"It's her calling card," Remi said as two more distinctive thumps hit the door.

"But why? Why birds instead of her other minions?"

"She's making a point? How the fuck should I know? Maybe she found out about Gavin going to the Council."

Rosie frowned, her lower lip pulled between her teeth as she let that sink in. "It doesn't feel like a vampire's first choice. Birds. My father would simply stride in and destroy everything in the wake of his revenge."

"Remind me never to piss off your dad," Remi muttered.

"Too late. You already fucked his daughter," Asher said. "Pretty sure he's going to hate all of us on sight."

"How many more were out there, Ben? Do we need to board up the windows?" Rosie asked.

Asher nodded. "Yeah, I've seen *The Birds,* and if these are anything like Hitchcock's imaginings, we have to wait them out."

"You really think a couple of birds can hurt us?"

Asher gave Remi an exasperated look. "Have you really not been paying attention to the news? Something is wrong with them. They are falling out of the fucking sky all over the world. When birds get sick, humans are sure to follow."

"But we're not human."

"I am, you selfish fuck. And so is Rosie."

Remi turned an interesting shade of greenish-white. "Fuck."

"Now he gets it," Asher muttered, raking his hands through his hair. "Let's board this place up and head back to mine. I have a bunker."

"Of course you do."

Rosie snickered. "And a sexy dungeon."

Her joke added necessary levity to the situation, and we all seemed to loosen up just a little. Until the pounding started. The sound of shattering glass filled the house, and the walls shook. Hammering on all sides had the four of us crowding closer together.

"How are we supposed to run when we can't get through the door?" Remi asked. "Do we stay and fight?"

"We c-can't touch t-them," I reminded him as I snagged a pair of sweats I'd left on the back of the couch and tugged them on.

"You can't, but I can," Rosie said. She darted to the door to where her bow and quiver of arrows had called home since the day I'd surprised her with her archery course.

Huge birds began flying in through the holes in the panes of glass, their squawks filling the crowded space and all but drowning us out. One after the other, they fell, arrows taking them out straight through their chests. But Rosie only had so many. This wasn't a permanent solution.

"W-we have to g-get out of h-here."

"We're sitting ducks," Remi agreed.

"I have an idea." Asher stared hard at me. "I'm parked around back, so you'll have to sacrifice your couch."

"Done."

"Remi, you take one side, Ben, get the other. We can use it as cover while we make a break for it."

I snagged a hoodie and some shoes, pulling them on as

my brother and I each moved to separate sides of our couch. As soon as we reached the back doors, we flipped the big piece of furniture over to act as a shield.

Asher pulled out his keys and hit a button, the sound of an engine turning over barely audible over the cries of deranged ravens.

"Okay, my truck is unlocked, running, and ready to go. As soon as we get to it, we need to ditch the sofa and make tracks. Get inside and shut the door as fast as you can," Asher warned.

With Rosie sandwiched between Remi and Asher, we took off.

"Oh my God," Rosie breathed.

"W-what is it?"

"The trees. They're all dying. Do you think the birds did this?"

That couldn't be right. I'd been out here just the other morning, taking my usual route around the lake for my run. Everything had been fine . . . hadn't it?

"I don't know, princess, but we're in a hurry. Come on, keep up."

It took a few feet before the birds noticed us, but it was enough time to get close to the truck. Thank God. They began pummeling the back and underside of the sofa as we ran.

"Now!" Asher shouted, and we tossed the couch at the attacking feathered fiends.

Then we hauled ass to the truck. But the birds were fast, and there were so many of them. I didn't know how we'd get away unscathed. One flew right for Rosie, and Asher threw himself in front of her as Remi opened the passenger door of the truck.

Bright light exploded behind us, turning the night into

day as we climbed into the truck. Before I could figure out what caused it, Asher grunted.

"That should buy us some time. Come on."

I glanced over my shoulder anyway, a whole wave of dead birds arcing out over the ground.

Had *he* done that?

"What the fuck was that?" Remi asked as soon as everyone was in the cab. "Asher . . ."

"I don't know. It just . . . happens sometimes."

"W-we can t-talk about this l-later. Let's move."

Asher hit the gas, and we tore out of the clearing, the truck's offroad wheels thumping over an uncountable number of bird carcasses.

"Someone needs to call Gavin and tell him where we're going." Rosie's words were soft but strong.

"Why?"

"Because he's going to come back, and the last thing I want is for him to find this."

FORTY-THREE

My search for blood had led me far from town and my borrowed residence. Borrowed might be a loose term, but at least I hadn't killed its former occupants. I compelled them to let me stay here. They went about their merry way on an extended vacation in Arizona. I had a nice cabin in the woods, and Jan and Fred got to work on their tan. Everyone was happy, and they still got a tax break. Bully for everyone.

I puffed out my chest. Roslyn would be so proud of me for showing such growth. Just last week, I would have simply drained them and buried their bodies in the back garden. Not that we were talking much since my little revelation. I'd needed some time and space to process all these . . . feelings.

I shuddered, disgusted with myself. I was the bloody Duke of Tears; I was not equipped for *feelings*.

The snap of a branch in the distance had my eyes narrowing with focus. Oh, good. Another deer. Blurring across the forest floor, I caught the doe in my hands and took her down, ready to feed. But as I brought my lips to her throat, I stalled. Something was off. Her scent was . . . wrong.

I dropped her, not willing to risk ingesting tainted blood. Odds were it wouldn't cause more than a bit of discomfort, but I shouldn't have to settle for a bad vintage. Also, now that I'd mostly come to terms with everything that'd happened, I didn't want to find myself out of commission when it was time to rejoin my mate and her merry band of arseholes.

Standing, I sighed and ran a hand through my hair.

"Roslyn, the things I do for you."

As if on cue, my phone rang, my chest deflating a little when it wasn't my petal. I frowned down at the screen, not recognizing the number.

"Fuck off," I answered.

"Is that any way to greet one of your bed buddies?"

Remington.

I snarled at the phone. "We are not now, nor will we ever be, *bed buddies*."

"Aw, that's a shame, man. You're gonna miss out on all the puppy piles."

"I don't like dogs."

"You are *the* definition of a grumpy dick, aren't you?"

"I think you mean duke."

"I said what I said."

Over the line, I heard Roslyn's soft admonishment, and everything in me sparked to life. "Let me speak to her."

"No. She's . . . recovering."

Alarm sent my nerves jangling. "From what? What happened?"

I heard Asher's distinct murmur in the background. "Puffin crisis."

"What the hell was that?"

"We were attacked."

My heart stalled in my chest. "What? By who?"

Whomever it was, they were dead men walking. No one went after my mate and lived.

"Ravens."

That caught me off guard. "Ravens?"

"A whole army of them. It was one big orchestrated assault."

Aisling.

This had her name written all over it. Who else would send a flock of birds to do their dirty work? Ravens have been her calling card for centuries. The lazy bitch. She'd send them to do her reconnaissance, like some evil queen from a fairytale. If I wanted information, I went and got it myself.

"Where are you? Your house?"

"No. We're heading to Asher's place. I can text you the address."

"No, you will not!" Asher shouted over the line. "Sacred fucking information, Remi. Jesus."

"I don't need it. I'll meet you there."

I'd tailed the bastard the night after his little light show. No way would I let a threat like that exist without knowing how to rid the world of it.

Thanks to my vampiric speed, I was already on the porch and waiting for them when the truck rolled up, nary a hair out of place. As was befitting a vampire of my station. Roslyn would likely fall at my feet the moment she saw me. I was sure she'd missed me something dreadful.

"How did you know where I live?" Asher strode toward me, suspicion in his question.

"I followed you."

"I didn't see you on any of my cameras."

"I disabled them."

"You . . . wait, you did what?"

I shrugged. "I simply re-routed the video feeds."

"Do you know how dangerous that is? I could've gotten killed."

"Pity you didn't."

"Gavin," Roslyn said, a frown marring her lovely face. "Not nice."

And that was news to her? "When am I ever nice?"

"Guys, can we continue this somewhere not surrounded by fucking trees, please?" Remington asked, glancing up at the looming branches.

"Th-they're watching us." Bentley took Roslyn's hand and headed for the front door. "I d-don't trust th-them."

I would have thought him a paranoid fool if I hadn't seen Aisling's birds in action. I could only imagine what they'd faced at the Mercer's cabin that had left them in such a disheveled state.

Asher pulled out his keys, but I simply reached behind me and broke the lock as I opened the door.

"Dude! Was that really necessary?"

"I thought you were in a hurry."

"Not that much of a hurry," he muttered.

See? This is what happens when I try to be nice.

A harsh caw echoed in the air outside, and Bentley pushed us all forward. "I-inside, n-now."

"She's following us." Remington's usually jovial or sarcasm-laced tone was filled with trepidation.

"Not for long."

"What do you mean?" Roslyn asked, heading into the living room with her shifters flanking her.

"Bentley and I have an appointment with the Council."

Every set of eyes locked onto me. I smirked at their surprise. I did so love keeping people on their toes.

"No need to thank me all at once."

"Th-that's news to me."

My brows furrowed. "I don't see why. You did ask me to intervene on your behalf, did you not?"

"I d-didn't r-realize I'd h-have to m-meet th-them in p-person."

His stutter was about the worst I'd ever heard it. I didn't blame him for his fear. It was wise to fear the Councilmembers. It showed that he had a brain in that thick skull of his after all.

"Of course. You'll have to testify against her."

"W-will I h-have t-to s-s-speak?"

"That is usually how one testifies, yes."

Remington stood tall and leveled his gaze on me. "Take me instead."

"Y-you didn't s-see anything, R-Remi."

"I'll tell them the story you told me."

Bentley shook his head and heaved a sigh. "I l-left out a l-lot."

"You what?"

"Y-you w-were j-just a kid. You d-didn't n-need that sh-shit in your h-head. Y-you s-still d-don't."

"So were you, you fucker. We. Are. The. Same. Age."

Bentley shrugged. "I-it w-was too l-late for m-me."

Roslyn moved until she was curled against his side. He visibly relaxed as soon as she touched him, clearly steeling himself with her strength.

Oh, fine, I suppose he deserved some mercy. "Technically, you don't have to speak. They can look into your mind."

Bentley visibly paled. "Fuck," he whispered.

"You couldn't have led with that?" Roslyn chastised, staring at me with frustration flashing in her eyes.

Bloody hell. I couldn't win.

"It d-doesn't matter. Th-they're all the s-same."

I bristled at that. "We are not." Some of us are vastly superior. It was like they'd never heard of a Nosferatu.

Remington raised a brow. "So you're not a blood-crazed psychopath?"

"Sociopath. And I didn't say that." Although I was even questioning that label nowadays.

Roslyn frowned at the shifters, seeming to take my side for the first time. The stupid mutt didn't realize he'd just insulted her entire family. It was easier to pretend she was fully human rather than to accept the half-vampire part of her. This was going to be the thing that ruined them. Their Achilles heel. Until they could accept her fully for who and what she was, this would always be an issue between them.

I bit back a smile, already anticipating how I could best use that to my advantage.

"What are you grinning about?" Remington asked.

I schooled my expression. I guess I hadn't bitten back that smile quite well enough. "Nothing. Just thinking of how this blood-crazed sociopath is going to enjoy feeding from his mate in a moment."

As expected, both wolves grimaced. Surprisingly, it was the human nightlight who came to my defense.

"Oh, come on, like the two of you don't bite her."

"Whose side are you on?" Remington asked.

"Hers."

"I th-thought you f-fed on animals while y-you were h-here."

Bentley crossed his arms over his chest. He wasn't wrong. I'd only fed on Roslyn the once, and that was so we could bond. And of course, there was Darla . . . but he didn't need to know about our arrangement. I was trying. Turning over a new leaf, so to speak. Less killing. More team-playing.

"I tried to hunt tonight, but had to stop."

"Why? Bad at it?" Remington snarked.

Refusing to let him get under my skin, I blurred across the room and wrapped my hand around the wolf's throat as I pressed him into the wall. "Would you like me to show you how skilled I am, pup? I'll even make sure it hurts."

The thrill of Roslyn's arousal shot through me. It was just a spike, but there was no mistaking it. My sweet petal liked the idea of being hunted . . . and caught. I slowly turned my head to look at her, giving her a wicked, knowing grin.

That was a game we would definitely be playing later. Once Aisling had been dealt with and it was safe for her to roam freely in these woods once more.

Releasing Remington, I stepped back and adjusted my cuffs. "The blood was tainted, if you must know. I've been traveling further away from the town for the last few days, but whatever's infecting your animals is moving fast."

The others exchanged worried looks.

"Whatever's affecting the birds is spreading," Asher said. "I fucking called it."

"It's not just birds. All the animals I've encountered have been sick. They all smelled the same."

"Well, that's just great. We have killer birds attacking us and the start of a goddamned plague."

Roslyn's expression tightened. To anyone else she looked merely concerned, but connected as we were, I felt the spiral of sheer panic. *What aren't you saying, petal?*

Asher threw his hands in the air and went to the bar

cart in the corner of the room before pouring himself a drink. "Anyone else?"

We all shook our heads. I needed to drink, but not from a bottle. "Roslyn, I need to feed before I face the Council. If I show any signs of weakness, they'll take advantage. I need all my strength to help protect your wolf."

"Of course."

"You're just going to open one of her veins right here?" Remington asked, disgust thick in his voice.

"No. I prefer my wife and I go somewhere more private. Not everything needs to be a group activity."

"Asher, can we use your sexy dungeon?" Roslyn asked, a little playfulness in her tone.

A curl of desire swept through me. "No. No dungeon."

She raised a brow. "Really?"

I leaned in close, my lips brushing against her ear as I breathed, "I don't have the time to do all that I'd crave to do to you, petal."

She shivered and leaned into me. "Good point. Asher, can we use your room?"

He looked between us and waved a hand down the hallway. "You know the way. Make yourselves at home. Just don't get any blood on the sheets, okay?"

I grinned, but my smile was aimed at my mate. "Oh, trust me, I'm not going to waste a drop."

CHAPTER

FORTY-FOUR

ROSIE

G avin's cool fingers encircled my nape and squeezed lightly. "Lead the way, petal," he growled in my ear, sending a wave of tingles down my back. There was no denying the effect this man had on me. I'd given up trying.

Needing no further encouragement, I hurried down the hall and pushed open the door into Asher's master bedroom.

Gavin didn't spare the room a glance, instead pushing me up against the nearest wall. His dark eyes bored into mine, his hand still collaring my throat as we shared each other's air. A little rumble sounded in his throat as he slowly ran his nose along mine, refusing to close the distance between our lips as he drew in a ragged breath.

If I didn't know better, I'd say that he'd missed me.

"Hungry, husband?"

"Fuck, petal. I'm starved."

"What are you waiting for?"

"Can't a man enjoy a quiet moment with his wife? I so rarely get you to myself."

Guilt hit me hard and swift. I hadn't considered how the group dynamic may negatively impact my individual relationships. Cupping his cheek I brushed my lips over his. "I'm sorry."

"Show me how sorry you are."

How did he want me to do that? I stared into his eyes and had to fight the urge to bring our mouths together before another idea flickered in my mind. My knees bent as I began to slide down the wall.

"What are you doing?" he rasped, excitement coloring his tone.

"Taking care of my mate," I said, my eyes on his as I began working at his belt.

He gripped my wrist, halting my movement. "I'm in a hurry."

"So I'll be quick."

For the first time, he seemed uncertain.

"Pull my hair," I whispered, immediately wishing I could walk the order back. "Please, my lord?"

His upper lip curled. "I don't take orders from you, petal. But in this case, our desires are aligned." He fisted his long fingers in the hair at the nape of my neck and pulled until tears pricked at the back of my eyes.

Instantly the bulge behind his fly grew even larger. I gasped at the perfect pain and traced my palm up his thigh, avoiding the one place I wanted to touch more than anywhere else. Hips rocking forward, he let out a soft groan.

"Fucking tease."

"Please, my lord, tell me what you need."

"Technically that's another order, petal. Have you forgotten how we play?"

"It's been too long."

In an uncharacteristic display of tenderness, he skimmed his knuckles down one of my cheeks. "It has. Allow me to refresh your memory on how this goes. You are going to free my cock, and then you are going to fucking choke on it. I want your tears, petal."

Gavin had a way of making the word 'want' sound a lot like 'need.'

"Yes, my lord."

He tightened the grip on my hair, bringing a burning pain with it. An instant flood of arousal between my thighs was my body's response. By the way his nostrils flared, he'd scented me.

My hands trembled as I pulled his member free from his trousers. He was so hard and warm, my mouth instantly watered. I loved pleasing him, but I loved it when he used me more. With Gavin, there was something about being reduced to my basest state that made everything that much sharper.

"Kiss it while you look up at me. I want you to watch my eyes as you suck me into your mouth and worship your duke."

Oh God. I didn't respond. I simply did as he told me, pressing my lips to the head, licking away the salty drop of his essence from the slit. "Like this?"

He yanked my hair, drawing a gasp from me. "I said suck me into your mouth, wife. Since you could not obey the simplest order, I shall have to do it for you." A wicked grin twisted his lips as he stared into my eyes. "Open."

As soon as my lips parted, he drove inside, all the way to the back of my throat, until I fought the urge to gag. But I was practiced by now; I knew exactly how to manage a man of his size thanks to Pan. Breathing through my nose, I loosened my throat and let him in. He thought he could choke me, but I knew better. I swallowed around him and made him grunt in response.

"I asked for your tears, petal. Do you think to deny me?"

I moaned around him, and his eyelids dropped lower over blazing eyes. "Silly girl, I have no problem working to earn them."

Why did that make me so wet?

"I'm going to fuck your throat now." He stroked my hair, then murmured, "Three taps on my knee if you need to stop."

I hummed my understanding, squirming when he seemed to thicken further in my mouth.

"I won't be gentle."

Good.

His hold on my hair was so tight I was sure my scalp would be bruised as he began to thrust deep. Tears sprang to my eyes almost immediately, and it took everything I had not to look away from him so he wouldn't see how quickly he succeeded. His hips pistoned so fast that my face came into constant contact with his lower belly. Between his hold on my hair and his length down my throat, I was helpless to do anything but take everything he gave me.

This was supposed to be about pleasing him, but as he chased his release, it only spurred on mine.

I reached between my legs, needing relief from the building ache, but Gavin stilled, pulling out and locking blazing eyes on mine.

"Did I say you could make yourself come, petal?"

I whimpered. "Please." My voice was hoarse and my lips swollen.

He took my cheeks with one hand and lifted, pulling me up until our faces were inches apart. "No," he breathed against my lips.

With a firm grip on the collar of my shirt, my husband shredded the fabric in two down the front. He smirked as he did it, the wickedness in his gaze only ratcheting up my need. He was going to torture me, and he'd love it.

Then he pushed me to my knees again, but when I opened my mouth to take him, he took himself in his hand and stroked from root to tip. "You lost the privilege of getting me to spill myself down your throat. Now you'll wear it instead. I've always thought you'd look fetching in pearls."

Oh. God.

His breaths came in harsh pants as he worked his length. I'd had him more on edge than I thought. That made me smile. From one moment to the next, he went rigid, and those tight muscles in his abdomen rippled as he came. His grunts of pleasure sent little shocks of my own through me as hot jets of his climax landed in stripes across my chest.

He smirked as he sank to his knees in front of me, painting his release into my skin. "Now there's no hiding who you belong to, petal. You're mine."

"Yes."

He leaned in close, running his fangs along the side of my neck as his teasing fingers worked their way down my stomach.

"My." He licked the place I wanted him to bite down. "Little." His teeth grazed my skin again. "Slut." Without warning, his fingers slid past my waistband and pinched my clit.

Then his teeth sank into my throat, and I exploded in a burst of pure euphoria.

I didn't realize I'd wrapped my arms around him or threaded my fingers into his hair to pull him closer. Nor did

I realize he'd worked his hand lower, until he thrust not one but all four of his fingers inside me, pumping them in and out as I rode out my climax. The sting of pain from his bite, along with the delicious stretch, initiated a second wave.

"Christ, Gavin."

He stopped feeding long enough to murmur, "That's right, petal. Take the pleasure I give you."

I wanted him to take more from me, and he did, reattaching his lips to my skin and drawing from me in long pulls. The moans of pleasure he let out added to my own. I wanted to serve him in this way, just as he was serving me the pain I craved. My only mate capable of giving it to me. The only one who truly understood why I needed it.

I couldn't exist in this world without him and expect to feel whole or happy. Just as I couldn't without the others. I needed all of them.

He broke the seal on my neck and surprised me by kissing the wound, then licking along the punctured skin. "You are perfection, Duchess."

"When can we do that again?"

"Soon. But first we have to get you up and moving. While I'd love nothing more than to leave you this way, I need to clean you up and deliver you to the safety of the others before I go." He stood and held out a hand for me. "I need to ensure you're fed and comfortable. I can't leave you without nourishment after all you just gave."

What was this tenderness he suddenly tapped into? Gavin was hard and cruel, cold like stone. Did this have something to do with the mind battle he and Noah waged? Or was this the mate bond? Either way, I didn't hate it. Knowing Gavin cared even a little settled something inside me.

He must have sensed my confusion because he cradled

my face again. "We've done everything backward, you and I. But once things are settled, I'll fix that. We will borrow that dungeon you mentioned, and I will finally introduce you to proper play, and then I will teach you about the importance of aftercare. And then . . . we will play some more."

"Do you promise?"

"I do."

Gavin laughed, his gaze trailing over my shoulder to the door behind us. "She's fine, hacker. Just boneless from pleasure. You can stop listening now."

The soft footsteps leading down the hall proved Gavin right. A thrill shot through me at the knowledge that Asher had heard everything. Perhaps he'd want to watch us play together? The idea did things to me.

"You like him listening in?"

"Yes, my lord. Asher likes to watch. And I . . . like knowing he's there."

"Noted." He pulled me into him, not caring I was covered in his spend and my blood. "Now, kiss me, wife. Let me taste your lips before I walk into the lion's den for your wolves."

And like with every other command he gave me, I obeyed.

FORTY-FIVE

I hated this. The stench of vampire was everywhere, infiltrating every-fucking-thing around me as Gavin led the way into the inner chamber of the Vampire Council.

He warned me before we'd left to let him do the talking, which was fine by me. With every step, my hatred of these creatures swelled until I was all but choking on it. It didn't help that we were underground. The scent of death and the trace of blood in the air, along with being in an enclosed space, had the night I lost everything rearing its head. It wasn't at all the same, but still entirely too similar.

Get it together, Bentley.

"You look like you're about to be sick. If you do, all I ask is that you don't get it on my shoes. These are Italian leather." Gavin looked me up and down while the two of us waited at the ostentatious French doors, polished ebony decorated with gilt carvings depicting humans being fed on, their faces contorted in pleasure and pain.

"Let's get this show on the road, shall we?" Then he took my hand, his voice echoing through my mind uninvited. *"Remember, they're as liable to kill you as help you. You have to convince them she's the true threat. Hold nothing back. This is your only chance."*

"W-what about R-Rosie? Th-they'll see."

Gavin's jaw set, a furrow deepening between his brows as he replied in my mind. *"I hadn't thought of that. You'll have to shield everything but the past from them. We can't let them know what she did, not yet. They'll punish her for her deception."*

Now I *was* about to be sick. What chance did I have against the vampires' leaders? I was just one wolf. They, the elite of their kind. If I was the reason they found out the truth, if I caused her to be in their sights . . .

Fuck, this was a bad idea. Even if we were desperate for their assistance.

"W-we should g-go b—"

"Don't you fucking dare. You and your brother are important to Roslyn. I've done many terrible things in my long life, some of them to her, and I intend to earn her love." The way his face paled as the words escaped him told me love wasn't something he'd planned on saying.

"H-how do I block them?"

He sighed, frustration leaking through his facade as he dropped my arm and raked his fingers through his hair. "You're not going to like what I'm about to tell you."

It couldn't be worse than letting them play around in my brain. "Try m-me."

"I can compel you to not think of her."

I was wrong.

It was a case of the lesser evil, and unfortunately Gavin was the devil I knew. But could he be trusted? What if I let him in and he made me lose her forever? What would keep him from erasing me from the board entirely?

"I . . ."

"If you aren't familiar with shielding, this is the only surefire way of protecting yourself. Do you really want to risk attempting a new skill on some of the eldest vampires in existence?"

No. I really fucking didn't.

"But the bigger question is, do you love her enough to let me do this? Or does your hatred of my kind run so deep you'd risk her safety?"

"F-fine. D-do it."

Gavin took my face between his palms and stared at me, his gaze instantly holding mine like a cobra mesmerizing its prey. *"Until we leave this place, Roslyn Blackthorne does not exist. You have no mate. You have nothing because Aisling stole everything from you. You will think of nothing unrelated to Aisling and what she's done."*

I was aware of his voice, but with each word my fear crystalized into white-hot fury. That vampire bitch had taken everything from Remi and me. Our parents. Our community. It was time for her to pay.

Without warning, the doors swung open, beckoning us in. Dread sat like a rock in my stomach, but Gavin simply strode in like he owned the place.

"Ah, my old friends, so good to see you. Thank you for granting us this audience." He was strangely friendly, at ease, and suspicion niggled at my mind.

"Your Grace, our condolences on the untimely passing of your father," the stuffy old Scot in the middle said, not rising to greet us.

"It was his time," Gavin replied, not seeming at all bothered by the mention of his dear old dad. "When one has as many enemies as he did, it's no surprise they came for him."

"Why are we entertaining a filthy shifter in our sacred chamber?" a female Council member snarled. I could barely see her face under the crimson hood of her robe, but her hair was as black as night and her skin bone-white.

"Because it concerns one of our problem children, Lydia. You know as well as I we're on borrowed time with that one. It was always a matter of when, not if, we'd need to intercede. She's grown too bold, which is why we've been keeping our finger on the pulse of Aisling's choices."

"So she turned that priest into a vampire. Sure he was one of the cogs in the wheel of the failed Apocalypse, but that doesn't mean she's any more of a risk than the rest. Cashel Blackthorne also created one of the harbinger's mates. He's not on the chopping block."

"Cashel is king in his own right. No one is calling him to task for anything without consequence. But this is not about that. This is a different sin, am I right, Your Grace?"

Gavin crossed his hands behind his back, standing tall. "Yes, High Chancellor. She is erratic, wild, and has been abusing two shifters with coercion and blackmail. Thus breaking terms of the centuries-long treaty between our kinds. We're lucky word hasn't gotten to the shifter council about this, or they'd have grounds to start another war."

"And why hasn't it? Why haven't you sought aid from your pack, wolf?" The High Chancellor asked, leveling his stare at me.

"Sh-sh-she killed th-them."

Of all the times for my stammer to clutch at my throat, this was not ideal.

"All of them?" the woman asked, intrigued.

"Y-yes." Technically that was a lie, so I amended. "All b-but m-my b-brother and m-me."

"The Mercers were the only two survivors of the

massacre. Any remaining in town scattered to the winds after the church was desecrated by her," Gavin offered. "His pack is dead."

I cut him a look. How did he know that?

"Look into his mind. He's already agreed to share his experiences with you unguarded."

My stomach churned as Gavin pushed me forward and the High Chancellor stood from his throne-like chair and descended the three steps that brought us face to face. He narrowed his red gaze on me, making my skin crawl as he inspected me like someone studying an insect. Then he was in my mind, memories of the worst night of my life flashing through my head one after another, replaying like a movie.

A scream was pulled from my throat, and my knees nearly buckled. I wasn't a man standing before them, but the same little boy who'd watched his parents be murdered right before his eyes. I could taste the blood in the air, hear their throats tear and the bodies thud on the planks of wood above my head. I saw the woman through the slats from my position under the floor, clear as day. Her red hair was the same color as the blood sprayed across the altar. But the worst part was her vicious grin.

My ears were filled with the sounds of terror echoing through the once sacred space. The last thing I saw before I lost consciousness had been the single red Christmas orna-ment she'd knocked off the tree in the narthex, the one my dad and I had cut down together. It rolled across the floor and stopped directly above the place Remi and I were hiding.

"Enough," Gavin growled. "He's lived through it once before. Don't break his mind."

The assault of images finally stopped, and this time I sank to my knees, bracing my hands on the cold marble floor as I fought the urge to vomit. That night was never far from my mind, but it had been a long time since I'd allowed myself to recall any of it in perfect detail. The truth was far worse than anything my fuzzy recollections painted.

I hated her with an intensity that bordered on insanity. Not just her. All vampires.

They'd ruthlessly slaughtered my kind. Innocent men and women, their defenseless children, and for what? Nothing more than sick pleasure.

I needed to get out of here. My wolf sat just under the surface, barely restrained and snapping at my control. If I shifted in front of them, they'd kill me without blinking an eye. On shaking legs, I stood, unable to get words out of my throat as the memories held me hostage.

"Have you seen enough to warrant bringing her to heel?" Gavin asked.

The High Chancellor nodded. "She will be dealt with."

I left then, without a backward glance. I didn't care if it was rude. They'd gotten all they were going to take from me. More, honestly, if you counted the people killed because of their negligence.

With purposeful strides, I walked until I found the edge of the surrounding woods, waiting until I was sure I no longer infringed on their territory; then I tore off my clothes and shifted, letting my wolf free. I started to run, only to be brought up short.

"Where do you think you're going? I'm your ride home!"

I cocked my head, assessing the vampire standing in broad daylight.

"Roslyn's blood is a gift in more ways than one, remember?" He stretched his face up, soaking in the sunlight.

Memories returned in a rush as soon as he said her

name, his compulsion vanishing now that we were out of the Council's grasp. Everything had changed because she'd come into my life. We were free of Aisling. We could breathe again. Because of Rosie.

I shifted back into my human form and stalked to Gavin. Leveling my stare on him, I said without a hint of stutter, "Take me home to her."

FORTY-SIX

PAN

I stared down at the black embossed card lying beneath my door as if it were a serpent about to strike.

Even if the red L.D. wasn't front and center, I'd know it was from Auntie Lilith. It reeked of *Iniquity*.

She was up to something.

Strictly speaking, demons weren't welcome in her den of sin. She didn't like competition, and she prided herself on being the only demon in residence.

Ever.

So you can imagine my surprise when I snatched up the card and flipped it over to find her feminine scrawl staring back at me.

You are cordially invited to indulge in a masked
night of sin.
Dress to impress. Or don't.
~ L

"WHEN THE BLOODY hell is this night of sin, Auntie? You should put the blasted date and time on the card. You know, the basic rules of etiquette. Emily Post, you are not."

My grumbled complaint trailed off as new script appeared under her initial.

Tonight, you twat.
Midnight
X

"And I suppose you just assume I don't already have another engagement. It's not like I'm helping end the world or anything."

I tapped the card against my teeth. I was free tonight, actually, and a chance to visit the infamous club was too tempting to ignore. It might be nice to cause a little mischief on the other side of the pond.

"All right, fine, I'll go. But I doubt I'll enjoy it."

Midnight was only half an hour away. I better shift it and get my outfit sorted. Perhaps I could find a delectable little morsel to take Roslyn off my mind. Someone who would appreciate exactly what I offered, who wouldn't abandon me the second my methods crossed from morally gray to pitch black.

I stalked to my closet, scoffing at the garments. What did one wear to a succubus's sex club? Leather? Silk? Both?

In the end, I selected a fitted black tux I'd had custom made when I'd attended the opening of the Royal Opera house. Some fashions never went out of style. Though the tails might be a bit much. I pictured myself striding in, tails swinging, my own actual tail long and flicking everyone I passed. What if Roslyn was there? Would she be jealous if I was the center of attention? If every single guest at this party wanted time with her demon?

She wouldn't be present, but that thought made me smile. She made me mad with jealousy, but I could do the same. I would, given the opportunity.

She needed *me*. I didn't need her. Tonight I'd prove it.

I halted in front of the mirror, inspecting myself and quite pleased with the picture I cut. I always had been a beautiful bastard. But the things meant to destroy us almost always were.

"Oh, right. A mask."

I didn't think she was speaking of the plague doctor variety. Pity. The smell of bergamot always was so soothing. It made me think of Rosie. Annnnd now I was hard. Bloody hell.

I palmed myself through my trousers, wondering if I should perhaps take care of my problem before leaving, but deciding against it. I'd save that privilege for a possible partner. This was a sex club, after all.

Without much in the way of options, I selected a simple black eye mask. It would have to do. I didn't need elaborate adornments. I was elaborate enough on my own.

As the clock struck midnight, I pressed my thumb to the Iniquity logo on the back of the card and closed my eyes as Lilith's magic took hold. I hated traveling via one of her portals. They were always gratuitously swirly and left my hair mussed and all over my face. Tonight's was no exception. As soon as the wind died down, I huffed because I could feel the thick, tangled strands across my nose, wrapped around my horns, stuck in my mask.

"Bollocks, why do I even keep this wretched mane? It's nothing but trouble. If it didn't draw the gaze directly to my best feature, I swear I'd chop it all off."

"And what a pity that would be," Lilith purred, running a hand down my long purple locks and giving them a teasing tug. "What would your little monster play with then?"

I slowly spun to face her. She'd pulled out all the stops for her special night. Not that I'd expected anything less. Her hair was swept to the side in a cascade of dark curls, leaving the slender column of her throat tantalizingly bare. Her dress was ruby red and glittered from its sweetheart top all the way to its flared bottom. It covered as much as it revealed, her bountiful breasts spilling out of the strapless top, the back nonexistent, and a thigh-high slit exposing every inch of her leg.

I'd find her attractive if she hadn't known me since I was a demonling. She wasn't my actual relation, of course. But when the mother of all demonkind takes a vested interest in you, you show her due reverence, or you learn a painful lesson.

Offering her my trademark smirk, I belatedly answered her question. "My dick, obviously. Or my tail."

A low hum escaped her before she flicked her gaze to said appendage. My tail. Not my dick, you perverts. I can't take you anywhere, can I?

"Why did you get rid of yours, Auntie?"

"Oh, I whip it out on occasion. It's simply no longer attached to me."

"And what occasions they are," a cultured voice drawled as a dark-haired man leaned in to press a kiss to her cheek.

"Pan, may I introduce you to my newest—"

"I do believe you mean favorite, Lilypad."

She glared at him. "You think highly of yourself, poppet."

He shrugged. "I'm the best you ever had, and you and I both know it. It's not arrogance when it's the truth, if your cries of pleasure indicate anything."

She blushed. My aunt actually blushed. Oh, this was intriguing.

"So, what's all this about?" I asked, waving a hand at the crowd.

"An orgy," her pet offered.

"A party, darling. Don't listen to him. The orgy will be later, with consenting guests only."

"We do enjoy an orgy," I murmured. It had been a while since I'd indulged, but who didn't love a good fuck fest to get the blood pumping?

That didn't ease my suspicion, though. "Why did you invite me? You never invite demons to your gatherings. Too much competition to take souls and essence, isn't that right?"

"Can't your favorite aunt simply want to spend time with you?"

"No."

She laughed. "You always were a smart one. Let's just say you keep popping up, and I was curious."

She threaded her arm through mine, and the two of us began walking the room, her pet trailing a step behind. "Now, darling, let us, as they said in Regency times, take a turn about the room whilst we catch up."

I knew trying to force an answer out of her before she was ready was a practice in futility, so I gave in. Every now and then, she'd stop to whisper in my ear or point out a guest of particular interest. Despite the dimly lit interior, it was easy enough to see.

The room was a study in decadence. All along the floor were nests of velvet pillows in rich jewel tones, soft blankets on the ebony hardwood, and heavy curtains hanging from the ceiling, which allowed for a sort of privacy pod should the guests desire. Already couples were making themselves at home, bodies writhing in ecstasy as they took advantage of the lush space their hostess provided.

We stopped in front of a curvaceous dark-haired beauty and two men. They sat with her, one murmuring in her ear, the other trailing his fingers up her inner thigh.

"Ah, Sunday, Thorne, Kingston, how nice to see you were able to get away this evening. Motherhood has been kind to you. You're looking . . . scrumptious."

The woman smiled, her cheeks flushed with arousal. "You as well, Lilith. But then you always do."

"Oh? This old thing." My aunt waved a hand. "But where are your other mates? Surely the good priest didn't want to miss out on such a perfect chance to watch."

"Caleb and Alek are at home with Eden. It was the only way these two could get me to leave her. It's our first night out since she arrived."

"Arrived. What a lovely euphemism for the harbinger."

My eyes widened, but I quickly schooled my features, thankful for this mask. She was practically my cousin. Daughter of War. The vampire next to her looked me up and down, his eyes instantly betraying his heritage. He was a Blackthorne. Roslyn's brother Noah. Oh, this was perfect. I could steal him and keep him hostage. That would bring my little monster back.

"I see you plotting," Lilith whispered in my ear, her hand tightening until her nails dug into my skin beneath my clothes. "Let this one go. He's under my protection, as are all my guests. Don't make me send you back."

Bugger. My tail flicked in pure irritation.

"Fine."

She booped me on the nose. "You're a bigger brat than my Crombie is. Careful, I might have to bring you to heel the same way I do him."

"The hell you will. We. Are. Exclusive, Lilypad."

She pouted, but I could tell it was a front. Whoever this fae was to her, he was special. I'd never seen her this way with anyone before. And there had been legions of them.

"I don't have to be the one to do the punishing, you know. I know people."

"Well, that's different. We could watch."

"Exactly, pet. I'm glad I keep you around."

"I keep you around. Don't forget, I gave my consent. I can take it back."

Her eyes narrowed as she stared at him. At first she didn't say anything, then murmured under her breath, "You're the one who came to me."

My brow rose, but it seemed the conversation was over for now. With a polite smile, my aunt tugged me away from War's game players and continued on with our tour.

We passed two women who were snuggled together, one pale with lime green locks that fell to her waist, the other with a rich darker hue to her skin and sleek black hair. They were witches, by the power they exuded. The smaller one with the wild hair offered Lilith a wave, then blanched as she took me in. I smirked. I had that effect on people.

"I know you recognized Noah Blackthorne, Pan. I'm well aware of your dealings with his little sister."

My stomach lurched. I'd done so well to keep it a secret. Only Mother knew.

"What are you on about, you crazy old bat? I wouldn't have dealings with a weak vampire hybrid." I spluttered the protest so vehemently I told on myself.

"You forget, dearest, I know your deepest desires. I

know what the hybrid means to you. How you crave her. I also know you marked her."

I couldn't breathe, nor could I find the words to deny her claims. If she'd seen my mark, there was no point in lying. But that begged another question. If she had seen it, had she also been the one to remove it? I wouldn't put it past her, Lilith was the most devious of us all, which would mean she'd only mentioned the mark to see how I'd react. Well, she wouldn't get a rise out of me.

"She's a means to an end."

"Silky liar. She's more than that."

"Stay out of this, Lilith. It will end badly for you if you don't."

Her eyes blazed with anger. "Do not think to threaten me in my own club. I am more powerful than you by leaps and bounds, child. I could raze your world to the ground if I so chose."

"Do you forget who and what my mother is, succubus?"

She snorted. "Please. Before there were horsemen or women, there was Lilith. I am as old as Adam and more powerful than Eve. Not even Lucifer was enough to defeat me."

Well, fuck. When she put it that way . . .

"Don't you understand what we're trying to do? The Apocalypse is nigh. You could help us end the world. You'd go down as a heroine for all demons."

She sighed and rolled her eyes. "No. Shan't. I quite like it here. And I do so enjoy watching you all fail. Why ever would I end the world I've grown to love? It keeps me fed and in comfort. Much more preferable to living in hellfire and smelling brimstone all hours of the bloody day."

I clenched my jaw, but she continued.

"Besides, you know the rules. No one is allowed to

interfere. Not the angels. Not the demons. If Armageddon is truly upon us, it must be the mortals' decisions to bring it on. It's their realm. Their choices to make."

"Oh please, don't act like you're Switzerland. You dabble."

"Dabble, sure. But I don't interfere. There's a line. We don't cross it. What you're asking of me wouldn't just be crossing. It would be obliterating."

"Bloody useless."

"Well, I've had about enough of this visit with your ungrateful nephew, Lilypad." Her captive lover sneered in my general direction. "He's proven once again how tedious family reunions are. Can we send him packing, please?"

Lilith leaned in until we were nose to nose, her gaze boring into mine. "Do not hurt her, Pan. Not if you want to keep her. I see your true desires, and they have nothing to do with ending the world and everything to do with making her yours."

Fear held me fast. All I could do was try to bluff my way out of it.

"Lies. She is a plaything. My toy, nothing more. I hate her as much as I want her."

"Hate wouldn't be the word I would use. No . . . not at all."

"What do you—"

She winked and lifted a finger, a portal opening as she did so. "Ta, darling. I'm sure we'll see each other soon."

I moved to close the distance between us, but the magic sucked me in, and seconds later, I was standing in my flat, hair a mess—again—heart racing, and cock still hard and aching.

"Bloody hell!" I growled. I'd spent all that time in her

sex club and hadn't even gotten around to the sex. "What a fucking travesty."

My balls were supposed to be a lovely shade of lavender, not blue.

Freeing my cock, I stared down at the impressive length. This was a blessing that shouldn't go ignored. "Don't worry. I'll take care of you."

I strode into my bathroom, conjuring an image of my favorite plaything, trussed up and waiting for me with an apology on her lips and tears in her eyes.

FORTY-SEVEN

The oven timer dinged as my latest culinary concoction was ready to come out. By all accounts, it should be perfect. It smelled divine in the kitchen, with not a hint of smoke. I even used the right pan. Ben was going to be so proud of me when he came through the door and had a perfect, beautiful lemon bundt cake waiting for him.

"Please don't be ugly, please don't be ugly," I chanted as I covered my hands in oven mitts and opened the door.

Heat washed over my face, and I held myself back, remembering Ben's lesson about singeing my eyelashes if I got too close.

I could feel Remi and Asher's eyes on me as I pulled the cake out as if I was holding some sort of nuclear device about to explode at any moment. I think we released a collective sigh of relief when I set it down with a flourish.

"Ta-da!"

"It smells amazing, baby girl. Great job. I can't wait to try it."

Remi ran one palm up my back before he squeezed the

nape of my neck gently. Then he let his fingertips circle his mark, sending shivers through me.

"I'll just need to flip it out of the pan now. That's the moment of truth."

Asher looked on, amusement in his gaze. "Don't you need to let it cool first?"

"No, then it will stick to the pan. I need to flip it while it's still moist."

He pressed his lips together but didn't say anything further. It almost felt like he was trying to hold in a laugh, but that didn't make sense. I'd checked the recipe at least a hundred times. I knew what I was doing.

Tipping the cake over onto the platter I'd bought from the cutest little store in town, Kitchen Witch, I held my breath and pulled the bundt pan off.

And I stared in horror as the center collapsed in on itself and became a puddle of liquid batter.

"But . . . I . . . how?" I sputtered.

"Oh, look, it's a lava cake," Remi said cheerfully, picking off a piece of the cooked side. He popped it into his mouth and immediately winced, though bless him, he tried to hide it. "Salted caramel?"

"Lemon."

He spit out his mouthful. "I think you mixed up the sugar."

"I'm hopeless. It's either food poisoning or a sodium overdose with me. You should run while you still can." I slumped against the counter, pouting and disappointed in myself.

Asher smirked as he sidled up next to me. "Too late. If your special Black Hat cocktail didn't make me run, nothing will."

I covered my face in my hands, thinking of the egg I'd

simply cracked over the cocktail that had sent him running for the loo. "We're doomed."

Asher crooked one finger under my chin to lift my gaze to his. "Hey, at least there weren't any eggshells in this one."

"Not so fast," Remi said, lifting the spoon he'd been using to stir the molten batter. Sure enough, a rather embarrassingly large bit of shell was present.

I THREW my hands in the air, on the verge of tears. "That's it, I quit! It's nothing but crisps and pre-packed pudding from here on out!"

"Or . . ." Remi started as he scraped the ruined cake into the bin. "You could just let us take care of you. We all know you get off on making other people happy, but remember, so do we. Let us feed you, okay? You take care of us in so many other ways."

"I mean, watching her 'Nailed It' moments make me happy. I don't have to eat her science experiments to enjoy them."

Remi shot Asher a warning glare. "Not helpful. But also not wrong. You are pretty cute, baby girl. Your nose gets all scrunched up when you're concentrating, and you stick your tongue out like the sweetest bunny."

"I do not," I grumbled, fighting a smile at the good-natured ribbing.

"You do. And when you're really proud of yourself, you shimmy your shoulders and wiggle your ass," Asher added.

"So fucking cute." Remi pulled me into his arms and nuzzled my neck. "You know what else bunnies are really good at?"

"This answer could go a few ways. One ends up in bed, the other . . ."

"In bed, *after* the chase."

He nipped at my earlobe, and I shivered, arousal replacing any lingering embarrassment.

"I do love—" Before I could finish the sentence, the front door swung open to reveal a haggard-looking Ben and polished as ever Gavin.

"Oh my God. What did you do to him, Gavin?"

"Why do you assume I did anything? He's alive, isn't he?" Gavin muttered as I rushed to Ben, reaching up his considerable height and taking his face between my palms.

"Are you all right?"

Conflict sat heavy on his brow. "I'm o-okay, sugar."

This was one of those instances where *okay* sounded like anything but. The masculine equivalent of 'it's fine.'

"You don't have to lie to me. I can see well enough that you're struggling."

"I-it w-was j-just a-a-a lot."

"Of course it was. Reliving all that . . ." I shuddered. "None of us would get through unscathed."

"I n-need s-some t-time t-to g-g-get m-my—"

The way he fought for each word broke my heart. He was frustrated. I could feel it coming off him, see it in the tension of his shoulders. This wasn't helping him. Ben had told me clearly he had to sit with his feelings before he could hash them out. He'd shown me that time and again. Pushing him on this would end up making it hurt more.

"Hey, let's get out of here for a little while, yeah? I really could use a run. My wolf has been barking at me for hours."

The way Remi swooped in to take care of his twin, the same way he'd tried to come to my rescue with the failed cake, had my heart inflating. He was such a good man. A caretaker, just like he'd said. It was then I realized Remi was the glue. Not in the sense that he was the one who'd brought us together—that was me—but he was the one who kept us together. I'd seen him do it for Asher, Ben, and me. Once they got over their differences, I was sure it was only a matter of time before he'd do the same for Gavin. It was simply in his nature.

With that little revelation in mind, I looked around and tried to place the rest of my mates into their roles. Most were obvious, like Remi. Asher was a fixer, and Ben the alpha who would ensure anyone he considered pack had what they needed. I thought perhaps I might be the heart, since I was the reason we were coexisting in the first place. But Gavin . . . I was less sure what he was in terms of the larger group, though I knew *exactly* what he was to me.

A furrow worked its way between my brows. I wasn't sure even he knew the answer to this particular riddle just yet. Maybe only time would tell.

Ben looked down at me, his beautiful blue eyes swimming with worry. "I d-don't w-w-want y-you t-t-to th-think . . ." he stopped, fighting with himself as he tried to tell me what he was thinking. I didn't interrupt him, waiting instead for him to find his words. "I'm n-not l-leaving y-you. I n-need to clear m-my head."

"I understand."

"Gavin had m-my b-back in th-there, sugar. He d-didn't have t-to, b-but he d-did."

My eyes shot to my husband's.

"Told you," he murmured.

Remi squeezed my shoulder. "We'll be back soon."

"Just keep him safe."

"Always do, baby girl."

Ben grabbed me by the nape, the tremors in his hand

betraying how on edge he was. Then he kissed my forehead and turned away. Remi followed him out, leaving me with Asher and Gavin.

Asher looked between the two of us, hands in his pockets. "I, uh, programmed the door at the end of the hall. It'll open with a thumbprint."

And with those cryptic words, he also took off.

"What the bloody hell was that?" Gavin asked. "Does he always speak in code?"

My belly fluttered as Asher's words registered. He was giving us a gift.

Everything was finally settling down. Ben and Remi were taken care of, their issues with Aisling resolved thanks to Gavin. Moira had healed Asher, at least for now. Lilith took care of my demon problem. I'd gotten to speak with my brother and repair the damage my absence had caused. But most of all, I had my four mates.

It was time to let myself enjoy them. Time to finally breathe easy.

"I think he just gave us the keys to the sexy dungeon," I whispered.

Gavin's grin was pure sex. "Well then, petal. Shall we play a game?"

CHAPTER

FORTY-EIGHT

GAVIN

Anticipation hummed in my blood as Roslyn pressed her thumb to the scanner next to the basement door. I honestly hadn't expected the hacker to be useful, and I'd yet to inspect this 'sexy dungeon,' as he called it. It probably comprised a bed with silk sheets and perhaps a paddle or two.

The door slid open like some sort of James Bond secret room. Lights flared to life along the stairwell as we exchanged a look and descended. When we reached the bottom, I barely suppressed rolling my eyes. It was more than I'd expected, but not by much.

Roslyn, however, let out a little gasp, her gaze bouncing from corner to corner, trying to take in everything at once. She radiated excitement and, most importantly, arousal.

There was a St. Andrew's cross set up on one wall. A couple of well-placed hard points for suspension play. A swing was already hanging from a track that would allow it to be moved and locked into place throughout the room. A mirror above the king-sized bed, and another full-length one on the wall opposite the bed. Shelves lined with various toys and items of interest sat nestled along the far end of the space. But I didn't see any of my favorite whips or floggers.

Amateur.

This was a starter kit, as far as I was concerned.

The only thing he got right was the atmosphere. It was dark, but not in an oppressive way. Rather it was welcoming, like a lover. Inviting you in, offering comfort with its warm lighting and lush fabrics. Helping you feel safe enough to lower your inhibitions and play.

"What is this?" Roslyn asked, trailing her fingers over the only piece of furniture I was keenly interested in.

"A spanking bench."

Her bright eyes found mine as she sat on the rich leather. "They make a bench for that?"

"They make all sorts of things for that. And this one looks brand new. In fact, everything in here is untouched."

"Really?" Her brow scrunched, and then her entire face softened. "He built it for me."

I was about to ask how she could tell, but the certainty in her voice told me I didn't want to know. I was the one who got to break it in with her. That's the part I was going to focus on. "Oh? In that case, tell him I have a list of additions I'd like. I'll put him in touch with my usual contractor."

"You have a contractor? For sexy dungeons?"

"Petal . . ."

She smiled, her hand running along the leather of the bench. "So, how do I use this?"

Oh, my depraved duchess wanted to play already. "You must first earn your spanking, and before we can do that, we need to have a discussion. A lesson in pain, if you will."

Biting her lower lip, she focused on me. "I'm ready for you to teach me anything you want."

Fuck, that made my cock throb. Everything about her did, from her wide-eyed innocence, to the submission in her voice, to the shine she was ready to let me tarnish.

"There are rules when we set foot down here, or anywhere we are when we enter a scene. It's important that you understand them."

She nodded eagerly, urging me to continue.

"The most important is that you tell me immediately through use of your safe word, or some other predeter-mined signal, if something gets to be too intense. The kind of play I have in mind is dangerous for a human. I'm trusting you not to let me go farther than you're comfort-able with. Just as you are trusting me. Do you understand?"

"Yes, my lord."

My cock gave another insistent twitch. But I couldn't rush this. I wanted to make sure she was prepared for what was to come.

"Rule number two: Just as we have a safe word, we will have one that initiates our scene. By scene, I do not mean the sorts of things we engage in already. I mean pain. Extreme pain. Blood and . . ." I almost couldn't say the words as anxiety crawled up my throat, but I forced away the memories as I continued, "Breath play. Bondage and impact play. Things best not dabbled with unless extensive care and training have been taken."

The hitch in her breath told me how much she liked the idea.

"Nothing can begin until that one word is said by you. It's your choice, and once you set it, I will always honor it. We will not play until you start the scene. The same goes for our safe word. Everything stops when that is uttered. No questions asked. Do you have a word or phrase in mind?"

She nodded.

"Tell it to me now, so I know it. Just this once, it will not start the scene, but the next time and every time after, it will. So choose it with care."

"Moonlight."

"And your safe word?"

"Blackthorne."

I stroked my thumb along the column of her neck, reading her pulse, pleased that she was as excited about what was to come as I was.

"Rule number three. When we enter a dungeon or begin a scene, I expect certain things from you. You will be naked. You will be on your knees. You will not speak unless I request an answer. You will keep your eyes down unless I ask you to look at me. You will be, in all things, my perfect little submissive slut. Do you understand?"

"Y-yes."

I cocked a brow, not even bothering to correct her with words.

"Yes, my lord."

"Good girl. Now, are you ready to begin?"

"Moonlight."

She was a quick study, and I almost mourned the fact that she hadn't tripped up and given me a reason to punish her for making a mistake.

"Clothes, petal. Ready yourself for me."

She stripped, only the tremor of her fingers betraying her excitement. She sank to her knees gracefully, like she'd been born for it, her eyes respectfully lowered, chest rising and falling as she tried to calm her breaths.

Her dark hair, so different from the woman I'd married

now that the ends were tipped with purple, hid her face as she bowed her head. That would not do. I craved the sight of her expressions as they changed with each burst of pain I caused. Reaching down, I fisted the thick length and yanked until she was staring up at me.

"Next time, your hair will be pulled back so I can watch your skin flush and experience every sensation as they play across your features."

She licked her lips and nodded.

"Now, petal. Tell me, what would you like me to introduce you to first?"

Her eyes darted around the room, lingering on the bench beside us and then trailing over the swing before settling on the cross.

"That."

"The St. Andrew's cross? A classic choice. Very well."

My God, but she was a vision as she began rising to her feet. But we couldn't have that. She'd fallen right into my trap. I hadn't released her hair yet, so I tugged downward until she whimpered slightly, the flood of her arousal scenting the room.

"I said you are to remain on your knees unless I tell you otherwise. If you want to use the cross, you will crawl for me."

A shiver raced down her back as I released her silky locks, and she dropped to her hands and arched her spine, pushing her sweet arse into the air. It was irresistible, and . . . she had broken a rule.

I let my hand crack over the pale perfection of the rounded globe, drawing a surprised cry from her. As she began to crawl, I had to suck in a sharp breath to stop myself from halting her progress. The plump lips of her cunt were visible between her thighs from this angle, glistening with the evidence of how much she needed me.

I could not let myself break this moment simply because of a pretty pussy. I'd have it eventually. I'd bury my face between her legs and eat her like a starving man once we were done. Then I'd drive my length deep and own her from the inside. But right now, I would make my duchess cry for me.

When she reached the black lacquered wood, she sat back on her heels, her legs parted at a slight angle, her palms resting on her thighs. It was a classic submission pose.

"You've been doing your research," I murmured.

My obedient girl didn't respond. So this time, I asked her a direct question.

"Were you hoping we'd end up here? Even after you ran from me, did you dream of giving me your submission?"

"Yes, my lord."

"Tell me, petal, did you touch yourself at night in your bed, thinking of me and the things I'd do to you when I found you?"

Her nipples were tight points, the piercing glinting in the warm light. I reached down and flicked the jewelry, her slight moan making my cock jerk.

"Where did you get this?"

She wouldn't meet my gaze, but even if she had, I could feel her hesitance through our bond. She was keeping something from me. That wouldn't do.

"Do not make me ask you again, wife."

"Pan," she whispered.

"The demon?"

"Yes, my lord."

Jealousy lit my veins on fire as I stared at the piercing. "Stand."

Scrambling to her feet, she stood before me, quivering as I traced her nipple with the tip of my finger. Then, without a second thought, I removed that bloody demon's jewelry. It was bad enough I had to share my wife with those other wankers. The only marks of ownership she'd wear were ours.

I flung the piece of metal across the room, a little sob escaping her as it bounced along the floor.

Taking her hair once more, I pulled, forcing her chin up. "You belong to *me*, petal. In here, there is no one else. Only us. That piece of jewelry was offensive and needed to go. If you enjoyed it so much, I will get you a new ring, but you will never again wear his. Do you understand?"

My voice was low and dark, thick with anger.

"Yes, my lord."

"Good. Now turn around and face the cross. Show me your perfect unmarked skin."

She did as I instructed, my toy ready to be posed exactly as I needed her. I began by kicking her legs apart, preparing her to be bound and at my mercy. Normally, I kept my distance from my partners in the past. I didn't need to feel their skin on mine; I only craved their pain. Roslyn was different. She always had been. With her, I wanted the caresses to mingle with the delicious agony. A cocktail of sensation creating its own kind of torture.

Starting at her ankles, I made quick work of the cuffs, trailing my hands up along her supple flesh so I could do the same with her wrists. Once she was restrained, I stood behind her, just close enough she could feel my body's reaction. Letting out a soft moan, she pressed back, rubbing against my cock like an impertinent brat.

My hand came down hard and swift, cracking against her arse with enough force to leave a crimson handprint.

"Behave."

She whimpered, body shaking with need.

My sweet petal, we'd barely even started. I slid my fingers over her skin, tracing the line of her spine until I reached her nape. The softness of her sighs washed over me before I returned us to the sharp sting of my blows. She shivered, her longing for me telegraphing through our connection.

Leaning close enough my lips brushed her ear, I whispered, "Just this once, my duchess, ask for what you want."

"I want you to do to me what you did to him."

There was only one *him* she could be referring to. Daniel.

"You want my whip, petal?" The thought of marking her back and thighs, painting them in my welts, had my cock weeping.

"Yes, my lord."

"Your hacker didn't see fit to stock one, so sadly, Duchess, that I cannot give you. Is there something else you'd like?"

She squirmed as I ran my lips over her shoulder, my palms skating around her ribs until I cupped the weight of her breasts and gave them a hard squeeze.

"Mark me. Use your teeth. I love it when you bite me."

"But I've already fed from you tonight."

"I didn't say feed, my lord. I said bite."

"Watch your tone, petal. Unless you want to earn yourself a real punishment." Nipping at her ear, I added, "Trust me. You will find no pleasure in it. I'll make certain."

"I'm sorry, my lord."

Taking pity on her, I backed away and let my thoughts

wander to all the places on her body I could use to make her writhe. My fangs ached in my gums with the thought of sinking into her flesh, but she'd given me a substantial amount of blood very recently. I couldn't take from her again. No, this was not about piercing her skin; it was about marking her.

That I could do.

This time I was the one that sank to my knees. Without warning, I bit the back of her waist, stopping just short of breaking her skin.

"Gavin!" she sobbed.

I slapped her arse, another brutal, punishing blow. "I did not say you could speak, petal. You asked for it. Now take it. Unless you need to use your safe word, do not talk."

She moaned and wiggled as she waited for me to do it again. Fuck, she was so wet her thighs glistened. I ran my nose along the velvet-soft flesh of her full arse as my fingers slipped between her legs, rubbing the slick lips of her cunt and teasing her before I cupped my palm over her heat. I knew she wanted me to give her needy little clit some attention, but she wasn't going to get off that easily.

My teeth found purchase, sinking into the firm cheek and making her cry out. Her pussy clenched. I could feel it even though I wasn't inside her.

Moving to the other cheek, I dropped a little lower, this time biting her just beneath the curve where her arse met her thigh. As I did, I moved my hand and sank two fingers inside her pulsing heat.

On edge, I used my free hand to palm my erection, needing some sort of pressure or friction. Something to ease the ache. Normally, I had no issue delaying my climax, but this was Roslyn, and everything about her tested my control. I would have to find release soon, or I'd go mad.

"Who owns you right now, Duchess? Who is marking you and fucking you with his fingers? Whose cock are you desperate for right now?"

I bit down once more, this time tasting blood and nearly coming apart from the burst of her flavor on my tongue and her howl of pain that mingled with pleasure.

"You, my lord. It's you."

"Say my fucking name."

"Gavin."

I tore myself away from her and freed my cock, needing to be inside her.

"I'm going to fuck you now, petal. From this moment on, speak freely. But I want you screaming my name when you come. I want everyone in this godforsaken town to know who owns your pleasure."

"God, yes, please."

It took all of a heartbeat for me to sink inside her to the hilt, my groan of relief echoing off the walls.

"Your cunt is so tight my cock barely fits inside you. The only thing tighter might be your arse. I love the way you squeeze me like you're trying to milk every last drop of my cum from me like the dirty slut you are."

She moaned, a flood of her arousal dripping down my balls and telling me just how much she loved the degradation. Fuck, but this woman was my undoing.

I ran my fangs down her neck and along the top of her shoulder. With one hand, I reached up and grabbed the wood of the cross; the other I wrapped around the front of her throat.

"I know your secrets, petal. I know what a filthy whore you are. How you want nothing more than to choke on my cock and bathe in my cum."

"Oh God."

"Don't you, petal?"

"Yes," she gasped, her breaths coming in shallow pants as I ruthlessly fucked her, my hand tightening as I began to cut off her air.

"Come, wife. I want you to come so hard your slick runs down my thighs."

My balls slapped her pussy, making her cry out and sending sparks shooting up my spine. I was going to find my own release in a matter of a few more thrusts, but she had to come with me.

"I need more," she panted.

Oh, I'd give her fucking more.

My hand tightened further around her slender throat, and her reaction was instantaneous. Her cunt spasmed around me, gripping me like a vise and pulling me over the edge with her as we shattered in unison.

I released my hold on her as we came with strangled cries, her body sagging into me as she gasped for breath. We may have found our releases together, but my work was far from over.

Unfastening her restraints, I scooped her limp body into my arms, not letting myself think too hard about how much I enjoyed the way she sighed as her cheek rested on my chest. Then I laid her on the bed with her back exposed so I could examine the evidence of our scene. Already the bite marks were a deep purple. She'd feel them for days, if not longer, unless I did something about them.

It wasn't just the physical effects I was interested in. Aftercare was arguably the most important part of this world, but not normally one I participated in. I'd never cared enough about my submissives to take on the role, leaving that to others better suited to ensuring the psychological and emotional well-being of my partners.

But for Roslyn, there was no one else I'd trust to care for her.

She needed a safe place to come down. Ensuring I was here when she returned from subspace and knew she was being looked after by the one who'd inflicted the pain mattered.

As she lay there, breathing slow and even, I gently massaged the marks left by the cuffs on her wrists and ankles first. Her dreamy smile and half-lidded eyes told me how suited we were as a pairing. She needed everything I gave her.

"You did so well, petal. My perfect duchess."

She let out a happy little hum as I brought my thumb to my mouth and pierced the pad with my fang. Then I slowly rubbed a drop of my blood into each impression of my teeth left on her skin, watching as the marks healed.

When I reached the final remaining bite mark, she stopped me.

"Leave one. I like wearing your marks."

I feathered my lips over it instead. "As you wish."

She gave me another sleepy smile. "When do we get to do that again?"

"You're insatiable." I handed her a bottle of water Asher had conveniently left on the bedside table. "Drink this."

She rolled over onto her side, accepting my offering. "Yes, my lord."

Something in my chest rolled over at her teasing use of the honorific, but before I could examine it too closely, a loud crash from upstairs had me tensing.

"What was that?" she asked, sitting up.

"Trouble."

FORTY-NINE

Something was seriously wrong in Aurora Springs. Everywhere Ben and I ran was coated in the stench of sickness and death. It curled up my nose, making my eyes water and my stomach churn. I skidded to a stop at the edge of the lake, where we both loved to spend our time during the summer. The once pristine glacial water was covered in a green film, dead fish floating on its surface.

Shifting back into human form, I stood, staring in horror. "What the fuck?"

"I-it's getting worse," Ben said, crouched beside me.

"Worse? How long has it been going on?"

"A f-few days, maybe?"

"Jesus. Let's get back, yeah? I don't feel good about being out here right now. Something's off."

Ben nodded, shifting into his wolf and bounding back toward the house. I gave chase, sticking as close to him as I could. No matter what I did, I couldn't get the foul odor out of my nose. It made me want to sneeze, like my body was trying to reject it. As if it could tell just the stench alone was enough to infect me too.

That's what it felt like. Infection.

Thank fuck shifters didn't get sick.

The farther we ran, the less potent the smell, but my skin still crawled with unease. There was more happening in these woods than our animals dying.

Ben and I changed at the edge of the trees as we approached Asher's compound, both of us breathing hard, fists clenched.

"It feels wrong out here," I murmured.

"S-smells wrong too."

"Well, well, look at that. I made a wish on a falling star and got two naked werewolves instead of the one I was hoping for." My stomach dropped as Aisling's sultry Irish lilt floated on the breeze.

"There's the stink. Evil just can't be washed away." I stepped out from the cover of trees and into the moonlight.

Ben followed, a silent threat vibrating through him. He'd already shifted, ready to let his wolf tear into her.

We couldn't see her and her trail led us everywhere. It was as though she'd cased the house while we were gone. Without warning, her lips were at my ear, a whispered, "Bad dog," making me flinch as I lashed out to grab her.

Fuck, she was fast.

All I saw was a blur of red until she stopped a few feet from us. "You think to undermine me? To use my own people to do your dirty work? I haven't lived this long by luck alone, wolf pups. It's like I told you the last time you came for me. You're going to have to try a hell of a lot harder than that."

So that's what this was about. She'd already learned of Ben's meeting with the Council. No wonder she'd gone she-bitch to the nth degree.

"Maybe you should blackmail people with fewer

connections," I called, my usual cocky snark taking hold. I wasn't afraid of her. Perhaps I should have been, but if she was already here having a hissy fit because her Council gave her a slap on the wrists, we'd gotten under her skin. We weren't just a threat, but an actual problem.

She snorted. "Connections? You call a deranged sadist with a title connections? When I'm through with you two, I plan to tear out Gavin Donoghue's heart and feed it to the bears. He's not even worth drinking from."

"Go ahead. You'd be doing us a favor."

She cackled. "Is that so? And what about when I get my hands on your delectable little mate?"

Ben growled beside me, my own wolf surging up at the taunt.

"Oh yes, that's right. I know all about your little secret. The Blackthorne bitch you've been hiding. I can smell her all over you. What do you think the Council will do to her when they find out?"

I went still, but my heart raced as I realized a horrific truth. When Lilith replaced Pan's mark, she'd ended whatever protection had hidden Rosie's scent.

Oh. Fuck.

"I think I'll make you watch as I flay her while she's still alive. Oh, perhaps I'll heal her and do it over and over until she's gone mad. Then I can turn her over to them. They'll likely give me more power than I'll know what to do with." She hummed and trailed a finger between her breasts. "I've heard pure sun blood is delicious."

Ben lunged, but Aisling was faster. She knocked him away with a laugh, sending him straight through the window of Asher's house. He landed with a broken whimper, jagged shards raining down on top of him.

"That's it, you cunt. You've tortured my family for too long."

"You think this is torture? I haven't even begun, you mangy mutt."

I leaped forward, transitioning to my wolf midair as I went for her throat. She blurred away, but didn't make it far.

Gavin stood in the doorway, likely roused by the broken window. He didn't need more than a second to take in what was happening, and he was able to snatch her before she could race away.

Fuck yes. We had her.

But Aisling snarled in his hold, baring deadly fangs and squirming as she tried to get free. She slashed at his face, drawing sharp fingernails down his cheek and leaving deep scratches in his skin.

Ben still hadn't gotten up, and instinct screamed at me to check on him, make sure he wasn't dead.

"Don't just stand there, wolf. Help me with this harpy."

Aisling let out a wicked laugh. "You haven't seen the half of it."

She grabbed him by the throat, digging her fingers into his flesh and drawing blood. Jesus, she was going to crush his windpipe if she kept going. Would that kill him? No. But it would slow him down for a while.

That wasn't what stopped my heart, though.

No, it was the sound of Rosie's shocked inhale and then her frantic, "Ben? Oh my God, Ben, what happened?"

Even held as he was, Gavin's attention turned toward the sound of our mate. Something a lot like fear flickered in his dark irises.

Rosie popped up, her gaze raking over the scene

outside, her face twisting in fury when she spotted Aisling and Gavin.

"I told you to stay put," he snarled, but Rosie had already darted away.

Fuck. This wasn't good.

Rosie was way too close to Aisling now, and if the vampire bitch's soft laugh was any indication, she knew she'd found our weakness. Hell, from her earlier taunts, she'd already known Rosie would be. But now our defenseless mate had practically jumped out of the frying pan and straight into the fire.

If Aisling got her hands on our mate, I would never forgive myself for failing as her protector. All I could hope was that Rosie had run for Asher's panic room. Surely he had one. Right?

Oh fuck, where was Asher? Maybe it was better he wasn't here, but I couldn't ignore the additional curl of anxiety in my stomach. I couldn't lose either of them, and they were both so much more vulnerable than the rest of us.

Wherever you are, Asher. Stay away. Don't come back. It's not safe.

"Scared little lamb, brought to the slaughter by the downfall of the very men sworn to protect her." Aisling winced as Gavin broke two of her fingers when he snapped them as he pried them off his throat.

"No one is slaughtering anyone but you," Gavin gripped her by the hair and began pulling back hard enough she couldn't keep her head straight.

Then he bared his fangs and brought them to the vampire's neck.

I shifted, my wolf taking control as I raced toward them to help. If I could pin her, he could do his worst. Who would have thought we'd be allies? Not even a week ago, we'd been fighting each other, but now we were working together, united by one thing—our mate.

Aisling screamed in fury when my jaws clamped down on her forearm, the bitter taste of her blood making me sick. But I wouldn't release her, not until I knew the job was done, or I died trying. Ben still hadn't moved a muscle. She'd hurt him bad enough he couldn't fight. She needed to pay.

Rosie rejoined us then, the soft click of a crossbow string heralding her return.

"Hold her steady. I don't want to miss."

Aisling took one look at my mate standing in the door-way, an avenging goddess with her weapon aimed straight at the vampire's heart, and laughed. My reaction was less gleeful. It was a strange combination of pride and horror. Pride, because she was so fucking brave. Horror because I didn't want her anywhere near this cunt.

Ben groaned and got to his feet, a panicked look on his face as he glanced down his body and pulled a large shard of glass from his side.

The rest happened in slow motion, the scene playing out like a disaster movie. Aisling ripped her arm out of my mouth, tearing her skin to ribbons in her effort to get free. Then with a vicious scream, she shoved Gavin hard enough he staggered back.

"Rosie, get a-away!" Ben lunged as Aisling blurred toward our mate and Rosie let loose the bolt, the shot going wide and embedding itself into the nearest tree instead of her target.

As if she was no more substantial than a paper doll, Aisling pulled Rosie to her, one hand on each side of her face as she twisted. The sickening snap of bones breaking was the only sound I could hear over the screams in my head. The crossbow clattered to the ground first, pulling me from my spiral.

Aisling grinned as she released my beautiful mate and let her fall, eyes still open but unseeing, lips parted in a shocked O.

Rosie was dead.

FIFTY

BEN

I knew before that evil cunt touched her that Rosie was in trouble. Fear was a heavy pit in my stomach. My eyes refused to believe what they could so clearly see. I felt frozen in place, my body unable to move fast enough to counteract the vampire's speed as she twisted Rosie's head.

Snap.

It wasn't until the hollow chasm in my chest split me wide open that I seemed to regain control of myself.

No.

This couldn't be happening.

But it was. The mate bond was gone. Rosie fell, and my world fucking ended.

I didn't go to her. Instead I pushed through the burning pain in my side and the soul-deep ache in my heart. Aisling had taken everyone I loved except for Remi, but that was a technicality at this point. Killing our mate was as effective as gutting us. And I knew, if given the chance, it was only a matter of time before she made it official.

Remi and I wouldn't survive either way. Most shifters

didn't make it more than a year after the death of their fated mate. They withered and slowly died, their hearts broken beyond repair. I'd rather meet my end getting vengeance.

The bitch shook out her hair and laughed, not seeing me coming from where I'd been standing inside the house.

I'm going to tear her fucking heart out, just like she did to me.

I didn't let myself change fully, opting for a quieter approach as my hands formed claws and I crept up behind her.

"Oops, it looks like your sad little mate had a bit of an accid—" her words cut off in a shocked gasp as I shoved my razor-sharp claws into her back until I met her ribs.

I gripped them on both sides and pulled wide, snapping bone and tearing flesh as she screamed and tried to get free.

"No," I growled. She would stay put. She would die in agony.

I continued pulling her apart until all that was left was a twitching mass of blood and bones, and I could see her cold heart. But it wasn't enough to sate my need for vengeance. It also wouldn't kill her.

Lifting my foot, I stomped down, ignoring the pain as shards of her splintered bones ground into my heel, focused only on destroying the muscle that would allow her to return. I didn't stop until it was a pile of gore-coated ash.

"Ben, enough. She's gone." Remi's voice pulled me out of the murderous rage I'd been lost to.

Logically I knew he referred to Aisling, but my soul only recognized the loss of its mate.

"Rosie."

A shudder ripped through me, and I pushed my twin

out of the way so I could get to her, now cradled in Gavin's arms on the porch.

"I told you to stay away, you little fool. Why did you choose this one moment to disobey?" The way Gavin's voice shook turned my pain to dread. Nothing fazed the arrogant prick. For him to be this upset . . .

"H-heal her. F-fix her." I dropped to my knees next to them, ready to give him anything if he would just bring her back. He'd fixed me after the Beast nearly tore me in two. Surely he could undo a couple of broken bones.

He was slow to look up at me, his pale complexion entirely leached of color as his dark eyes met mine. "I can't. I'm sorry, Bentley. She's gone."

FIFTY-ONE

PAN

"You useless fool. I never should have given you this kind of responsibility." My mother's voice bounced off the walls in my flat.

"What did I do this time?" I drawled, my temper frayed since the debacle with my ravens.

My mother froze, taking me in. "You haven't heard."

"That my hellions are gone? Yes. I'm aware. So what? I'll make more."

"No, you flaming twat. That the bitch is dead."

"You'll have to be more specific. I know quite a few bitches these days."

Her eyes narrowed. "I only ever come to discuss one person with you. Who in Lucifer's name—long may they reign—do you think I'm talking about? And to think, they labeled you as a gifted demonling."

My gut clenched as her words sank in. I didn't want to hear what she was saying, but I had to clarify.

"Mother, who is it? I need you to tell me plainly because I won't believe it otherwise."

"Roslyn Blackthorne is dead. You are a massive failure. My plan is hanging on by the barest of threads all because you just had to toy with her and make her your little pet."

Roslyn. No. She couldn't die. Not without my permission. I wasn't done with her yet.

"But . . . I don't understand. How? What happened?"

"It doesn't matter what happened. All that matters is we are failing."

I was numb. I wasn't sure why I felt like this. I'd lost her long before, but to know her soul was out of my reach now left a pit in my stomach. She was mine. Heaven couldn't have her. If I had to weasel my way up to those disgusting pearly gates and fuck an angel to get in, I'd take her back. She belonged to me. She sold me her soul.

My mother's palm cracked against my cheek, pain blossoming in white-hot sparks. "Focus, you sorry excuse for a son. You got us into this mess—"

"Me? I didn't kill her."

Unimpressed by my interruption, my mother continued, "—so it's up to you to fix it."

"How am I supposed to bring her back from the dead?" Hope sparked to life in my chest as I asked the question.

"I don't care about her fucking soul. I'm after her blood. Or have you forgotten that too?"

"Her blood? But you already had everything you needed."

"I did, until you got the brilliant idea to spread your silly little bird plague." She twisted the ring she'd taken from me off her finger, chucking it my way and then throwing her hands in the air. Letting out an exasperated growl, she continued her rant. "Did you think I wouldn't notice the missing drop? When have you ever been strong enough to take out an entire species? All you can do is spread the common cold and perhaps a few cases of polio."

"Well, if I'm so bloody useless, what do you want me to do about it? She's dead. Not like we can go and drain her dry."

"Actually, that's exactly what I need you to do. Now, before it's too late."

My stomach churned. "I beg your pardon."

"Go to the surface. March into that little nothing town. Take every last drop before she goes cold."

"But the vessel I've been using is nearly dead."

"For fuck's sake, must I do everything? Pan, you have a perfectly good vessel waiting there for this very thing."

"But . . . I thought he was too close to her. You told me to use him sparingly."

She squeezed the bridge of her nose. "Have children, they say. It will be fun, they say. Fucking useless."

"I've never taken his form. He's always been too much of a fighter for that." The vessel she assigned me served more as a conduit than anything else, a power source allowing me to walk in my demon form without draining my own energy by draining his instead.

"Listen to me very closely, you ungrateful, unmitigated mistake. He is your perfect vessel. I selected him for you. For this purpose. Use the gift I gave you and stop your pathetic whining."

A perfect vessel? That meant I could use him without fear of deterioration. No matter how long I borrowed his form, he'd remain hale and whole. Unaged. Practically immortal.

"There's just one problem."

She groaned. "Of course there is."

"I've been using my power to visit the surface. I'm not strong enough to manifest—"

She waved a hand, cutting me off. "I will open the hellmouth. It's why I chose that stupid town, after all."

A hellmouth? Hadn't Auntie War chosen that stupid school for the same reason? Hellmouths were known magnets for supernatural creatures. It drew them in without their knowledge, the power a paranormal flame and them the unwitting moths.

Aurora Springs didn't stand a chance once it was open. Glee bubbled up inside me. I'd be able to roam free in my perfect vessel, and the first thing I'd do after collecting my *petit monstre's* blood was kill each and every one of the fools who hadn't protected her.

Mother's eyes flashed with lightning as she raised her hands to the sky and began calling on her power. The ceiling cracked open, the fissure going all the way up until the bright light of the moon filtered down to us.

Already I could smell the fresh scent of pine and the promise of snow, even this late in the year.

"Go, Pan. Do not come back empty-handed. The fate of the Apocalypse once again rests on your shoulders. Do not fail me a second time, or Satan help me, I will unmake you."

With that little pep talk finished, I stepped through the opening between realms, my demon form dissipating as I assumed control of my vessel. There was always a moment of discomfort, like the stretching of an overused muscle, as I familiarized myself with a new body.

This time there was none of that. It truly was a perfect fit.

Glancing down, I flexed and unflexed my hands, watching as the cluster of stars on the back of the left one slowly started to fade.

"Like a fucking glove," I murmured, my voice not sounding like my own.

I could get used to this.

~

Don't worry, the games are just getting started. The Mate Games: Pestilence will continue with Captive of the Night.

THE MATE GAMES UNIVERSE
BY K. LORAINE & MEG ANNE

WAR

OBSESSION

REJECTION

POSSESSION

TEMPTATION

PESTILENCE

PROMISED TO THE NIGHT (PREQUEL NOVELLA)

DEAL WITH THE DEMON

CLAIMED BY THE SHIFTERS

CAPTIVE OF THE NIGHT

LOST TO THE MOON

ALSO BY MEG ANNE

BROTHERHOOD OF THE GUARDIANS/NOVASGARD VIKINGS

UNDERCOVER MAGIC *(NORD & LINA)*

A SEXY & SUSPENSEFUL FATED MATES PNR

HINT OF DANGER

FACE OF DANGER

WORLD OF DANGER

PROMISE OF DANGER

CALL OF DANGER

BOUND BY DANGER (QUINN & FINLEY)

THE CHOSEN UNIVERSE

THE CHOSEN

A FATED MATES HIGH FANTASY ROMANCE

MOTHER OF SHADOWS

REIGN OF ASH

CROWN OF EMBERS

QUEEN OF LIGHT

THE CHOSEN BOXSET #1

THE CHOSEN BOXSET #2

ALSO BY K. LORAINE

∾

STANDALONES

CURSED (MFM SLEEPING BEAUTY RETELLING)

∾

REVERSE HAREM STANDALONES

THEIR VAMPIRE PRINCESS (A REVERSE HAREM ROMANCE)

ALL THE QUEEN'S MEN (A FAE REVERSE HAREM ROMANCE)

ABOUT MEG ANNE

USA Today and international bestselling paranormal and fantasy romance author Meg Anne has always had stories running on a loop in her head. They started off as daydreams about how the evil queen (aka Mom) had her slaving away doing chores, and more recently shifted into creating backgrounds about the people stuck beside her during rush hour. The stories have always been there; they were just waiting for her to tell them.

Like any true SoCal native, Meg enjoys staying inside curled up with a good book and her fur babies . . . or maybe that's just her. You can convince Meg to buy just about anything if it's covered in glitter or rhinestones, or make her laugh by sharing your favorite bad joke. She also accepts bribes in the form of baked goods and Mexican food.

Meg is best known for her leading men #MenbyMeg, her inevitable cliffhangers, and making her readers laugh out loud, all of which started with the bestselling Chosen series.

ABOUT K. LORAINE

USA Today Bestselling author Kim Loraine writes steamy contemporary and sexy paranormal romance. **You'll find her paranormal romances written under the name K. Loraine and her contemporaries as Kim Loraine.** Don't worry, you'll get the same level of swoon-worthy heroes, sassy heroines, and an eventual HEA.

When not writing, she's busy herding cats (raising kids), trying to keep her house sort of clean, and dreaming up ways for fictional couples to meet.